“Okay, I am new at this. Where exactly does that leave me? My not having a pack, I mean.”

“Prey to any and all who want to take advantage of you. With no recourse and no one to protect you. Basically raw meat.” He was matter of fact, but still watching her closely.

“Ah, I thought as much. If it hadn’t gotten so bad, I would never have broken cover.” She looked down and was surprised to find that she was at the bottom of her glass.

“If what hadn’t gotten so bad?” His voice was distant, even though he was sitting across from her.

“If I hadn’t gone into heat again.” She shook her head to clear it. “The pounding in my blood is unbearable. My thighs are slick with my own juices, I want to touch myself, but it does no good, the fire only climbs higher.”

His head cocked to one side. “How often has this happened? It doesn’t seem like this is the first time you have gone into heat.”

She blushed scarlet. “May I have some more wine? Thank you.” She sipped again.” Naw, this is the fifth or sixth time it’s happened. The other times it started to go away after a few days, but this time, it just keeps getting stronger.”

“What did you do the other times?” His voice seemed to be coming from another room, but he was still there in front of her.

“Oh, I masturbated until it felt like my fingers were going to fall off. Burned out a few pairs of batteries, that kind of thing.” The wine was gone again. She giggled.

This book is a work of fiction. Names, characters, places and incidents either are products of the author's imagination or are used fictitiously. Any resemblance to actual events or locales or persons, living or dead, is entirely coincidental.

ISBN: 978-1-55487-023-3
Cover art and design by Martine Jardin

Library and Archives Canada Cataloguing in Publication

Grace, Viola, 1971-
The warders : collection 1 / Viola Grace.

Also available in electronic format.
ISBN 978-1-55487-023-3

I. Title.
PS8613.R333W37 2008 C813'.6 C2008-901506-1

The Warders

Collection 1

By

Viola Grace

To my brother, sister, Mom and her fella. They know what I write and still want to see me at Christmas and holidays. Supportive only begins to scratch the surface.

The Warder's Djinn

Chapter One

Albina Ophelia Warder Lakin was in the middle of restoring a canvas when she got the call. She carefully set aside her tools and wiped her hands on a nearby rag.

She sighed deeply. It was really hard to clean up after those particular curses. They tended to sink into the paint. She needed all of her concentration to pull the residue off the canvas. It was tiring work, but well worth the effort of restoring the masterpieces of centuries.

Her assistant Reginald brought her the phone. "Hello?"

"Am I speaking to Albina Lakin?"

"Yes." She blinked and slid her magnifying lenses out of the way. She put them aside as she waited. A shiver of dread snaked down her spine. This wasn't good.

It was a cold, impersonal voice that had made thousands of these calls before. "Miss Lakin, you need to come to the hospital. Right now. Your grandfather will not last the night. He is asking to see you."

A frozen wave began to course deep in her chest. "I'll be there within the hour. Thank you."

One week later...

Alby stood in the opulent office and looked around at the other three faces that had turned out for the reading of the will. Her stepmother and stepbrother were the only family there, and of course Gregg Maccario, her grandfather's oldest friend and lawyer.

He was the only one—aside from herself—that had shed a tear as they lowered her grandfather into the ground two days earlier. Rupert and Emily had seemed to gloat as the dirt was ceremoniously dropped onto the coffin.

"As we gather here today to discuss the last will and testament of Albion Lakin, I would like to take this moment to say that I will miss him, both as a friend and as his lawyer." Moisture pooled in Gregg's eyes. He stopped, clearing his throat, then went on. "He was a hell of a golf player, and one hell of a human being." He took a seat behind his desk and rolled up his sleeves. "Now, with all of the remaining family assembled, let's get down to brass tacks."

"This is the last will and testament of Albion Hector Lakin. Let's dispense with the boilerplate and get to the point. To my daughter-in-law, Emily Morris-Lakin, I leave the sum of two hundred and fifty thousand dollars, to be delivered to her upon my natural death, and not before.

"To Emily's son, Rupert Morris, I leave the sum of fifty thousand dollars, which he has no doubt spent already, upon the news of my death.

"And lastly, to my dear granddaughter Albina, who lightened my life and kept me from being an uneducated old man, I leave the remainder of my estate. She will know how I want certain items disposed of, and which of them are heirlooms. I trust her with the history and honour of the Lakin family. My house is hers, and a trust to pay the annual expenses has been arranged. Good luck, Albina, and say hello to Arov for me. He will continue to work for the Lakin family as long as you live."

Gregg concluded his recitation of the will and handed each of them a copy. Alby looked cautiously over at her erstwhile stepmother and brother, shuddering at the fury in their eyes. *They are not going to go quietly.*

Taking the coward's way out, Alby leaned forward to shake Gregg's hand, quickly saying her goodbyes.

She was out the door and down the hall before Rupert caught up with her. "Albina! Albina, wait a moment." He was not breathing heavily, but was slightly flushed at the effort he had put into catching her. As always, his clothing was impeccable.

"Rupert, how nice to see you again. How is your mother?" She kept things polite while she waited for the elevator. She fidgeted nervously, clutching the copy of the will tightly.

"Furious, but I am guessing that you figured that out already. Finding out that the old bastard had almost cut us out of the will was quite the blow." His handsome features took on a pleasant grin, but Alby wasn't fooled. He had stalked her the entire time that she had lived with him and his mother, while Emily had been married to her father. It was the threat of his unwanted attentions that had driven her to her grandfather's house for refuge.

He had assessed the situation at once and spoken to his son, who then made arrangements for his only daughter to be sent to school near some friends of his. He received updates on her studies on a regular basis and was pleased with her progress.

It was a tremendous shock when her father died in a car accident the summer after she had turned eighteen. She had gone home for the funeral, and when Rupert had made a move on her, she left town once again. Regular letters to her grandfather had become daily emails as the years wore on, until his sudden death shook her to the core.

She kept her composure only through an extreme effort of will. "That 'bastard' was my Grandfather. You will excuse me if I am not terribly upset at your mother's anger over money that was never hers to begin with."

"I am not trying to pick a fight with you, Albina. As you may remember, I have always been rather fond of you." He reached out and drew his fingers down one cheek.

She fought the violent nausea that claimed her at his touch and stepped back. The elevator pinged its arrival, and a wave of relief swept over her. "Please keep your hands to yourself, Rupert. I have nothing more to say to you. Goodbye." She slid into the elevator and hit the lobby button. Rupert's smirking face was left swimming in her mind as the doors slid shut and the box descended.

She winced in distaste at the expression that he had been wearing. He was not done with her, that much was certain. The sick lust that had burned in him when she was a teenager had not been banked by the years.

The doors slid open on her parking level. She walked quickly to her car and got in, shuddering with the effort to keep her composure.

She drove slowly out of the city to the expansive estate that her grandfather had called home. She swiped her key card through the lock, and the gates swung ponderously open. The state-of-the-art security system was just for looks. The real defence was the ward stones that her mother had placed around the perimeter fence. Renewing the charge had been one of her first chores when she had come to live with her grandfather.

It became a tie to the mother she had never known. One of the first. The acceptance of the Lakin clan, one of the premier warlock clans in Realm, had managed to give her the structure that she needed, as well as great-aunts to dote on her.

Albina lived twenty-eight years of memories as she drove through the park surrounding the house. Each memory had the strong touch of both magic, and her Grandfather. He had seen to her early training instead of sending her to weekend schools in Realm, teaching her to learn to control her gifts.

The warding came easily—it was the alchemy and scientific analysis of varying magical items that gave her some trouble. She eventually mastered enough to please Albion, but not to please herself. It was that early history of analyzing and dealing with badly treated magical objects that had led her into the field of restoration.

With her assistant's help, she 'un-cursed' cursed objects, repaired magical paintings and sketches as well as restoring family heirlooms that had faded in power during the centuries since they were created. All were skills that she had learned from her grandfather.

Gods, she was going to miss him.

She pulled up to the front doors, her tires crunching the gravel. This was it. He was really gone.

Alby drew herself up, squared her shoulders and left her car in the drive, passing calmly between the stone sentinels on either side of the steps. The gargoyles on duty made wonderful statues, but even more wonderful guardians. The instant that a person with malice in his heart passed the guardians, they would spring to life, defending the Lakin family.

The door swung open at her touch. The interior of the house was immaculate as always. Someone had drawn the curtains back to let the afternoon sun stream into the rooms. She knew who that was.

"Arov? Are you here?"

Of course he was here. It wasn't like he could travel without a member of the family with him.

"Arov?" Her voice broke.

"I am here, Miss Lakin. I am sorry for the circumstances that have brought you back." The deep, quiet voice emanated from a spot directly behind her. "I will miss him as well. He was a truly great man."

She turned to face him, and when she saw the genuine regret on his bluish-bronze face, she broke. Sobbing uncontrollably, she flung herself into his startled embrace. She let the magic that she had gathered spiral loose, filling the room and causing even the gargoyles outside to shift in discomfort. Her grief filled her and she let it find its way—sparks rocketing around the room, deflecting off the wards that had been set in place to confine magical energy.

Haltingly, she felt his arms come around her, stroking slowly up and down her back. She inhaled deeply, taking comfort from the familiar spice of his scent. It brought her back to the times when he had been assigned to keep her from harm while her grandfather worked. Falling out of trees, opening gateways into Realm in the front yard...all the things that a young witch could possibly get into. It had always been Arov that had been sent out to rescue her.

She needed rescuing now.

"It is the nature of life that it will end, Albina. Albion was old. He had lived his life to the fullest, there were no regrets." His hands continued their soothing motion, letting her come back to herself gradually. "At least you were there with him, at the end. It meant the world to him."

She drew back and tried to smile brightly up at the djinn. "He did seem happy to see me. Even after all this time."

His hands were still stroking slowly up and down her spine, comforting and offering support. "Shall we have something to eat? If I know you, you missed your breakfast." His smile warmed the cold knot that had bloomed when the hospital first called her. She withdrew her hands, noticing for the first time that she had clutched his shirt in her grief. Shaking with emotion, she stepped away.

Food. "Yeah. That sounds nice. Is everything where it was the last time?"

"Not quite. The library is now the kitchen, and the dining room is the lab." A hand on her back steered her to the new kitchen, her head shaking in amusement at her grandfather's penchant for having Arov move the rooms around.

"Your room, however, is still at the top of the stairs, overlooking the apple trees. It is the one room that he would never let me touch." With amusement dancing in his black eyes, he removed a tray from the refrigerator and set it on the sideboard. She peered over his shoulder and laughed.

Chapter Two

It was the first laugh that she had had in a week. Oh, it felt so good to release the tension with Arov smiling at her delight. She stopped when she felt it edging into hysterics.

All of her favourite foods were represented, and at a snap of his fingers, the hot items steamed gently.

Grabbing a plate, Albina filled it with some of the selections and wandered over to the table. She began to work her way through the hot wings and nachos, then moved on to the tea sandwiches. As the food disappeared, a cup of tea made its way to the setting in front of her.

The gesture made her blink. He never got her tea. Service was not precisely his forte. Arov had been a lot of things to the Lakin family, but a butler was not one of them.

With a hand slightly more steady than ten minutes earlier, she sipped at the cup. "Thank you, Arov."

"It is my pleasure. You seemed to need it."

The heady, aromatic steam soothed her. "I do. Thank you again."

"You are welcome. When you finish your meal, we have much to discuss."

"With a line like that, I think I *am* done." She got to her feet and took her plate to the sink. Under it, as always, sat the tiny gargoyle that acted as the garbage disposal. She put the plate down in front of him, and gave him a little pat on the head. "Nice to see you, Tiny. Have you inherited your name yet?"

The little creature sprang to life under her fingers, its tail wagging at her touch. It happily took the plate from her and began to munch quickly at the leftover sandwiches and pickles.

"No, he doesn't have a name yet. It will come soon, though, and you will have to get a new disposal." The voice right behind her caused her to jump, banging her head into the shelf under the sink.

"Ow. Could you not startle me for at least two days?" His arm pulled her upright and she rubbed at the sore spot on the back of her head.

"So you are going to stay?"

"For a few weeks at least, until I get his property straightened out."

His arms crossed over his chest, the serpentine tattoos visible through the soft white muslin of his shirt. "What are you going to do with the dagger?"

"Dagger?" It took her a moment to remember, "Oh, *your* dagger. I don't know."

She pondered his statement. "Oh, God. I just realized that I, you, the dagger..." She stood silent for a moment. "I thought that when my grandfather died...I mean, he was the last of the Lakin line."

"Not quite correct. You are the last of the Lakin line. Now it is you that I must serve." He didn't look too happy about it.

Frankly, neither was she.

Eight hundred years ago, Arov's father had invited the magus, Arthur Lakin, to rest in his home. Lakin was on the fourth crusade, days after the conquering of Constantinople. Arov's parents were djinn, and helped others with magic within them to flee the city. Lakin caught them opening a gateway to Realm and helped them to evacuate before the rest of the crusaders could reach them. His own powers kept the crusaders at bay until the families had made it through the gate.

His family offered Lakin hospitality, food and shelter. Arov tried to kill him in his sleep, his fury at the destruction of his city boundless. His own father bound him into Lakin's dagger until his family line ended by natural means. If Arov influenced the death of a family member in any way, he would be tied to that dagger for eternity.

The dagger could not be lost, stolen or destroyed, though many generations had tried. It was as much a punishment for the Lakins as for Arov.

Now he was hers.

Oh, hell.

"Uh, you don't have to serve me. You can just go and do...whatever you would normally do. Really." Albina was distinctly uncomfortable. She had no idea what to do with a djinn. Her teenage fantasies had long since worn off.

"Are you sure about that? Normally I sleep."

"In the dagger?"

"Sort of. In the general area of the dagger. More surrounding it, really." Now he was looking amused.

"Oh, um...would you like to help me, then? I mean, to catalogue the stuff that grandfather wanted to send to the Repository in Realm?"

"Certainly. When would you like to start?" His face was getting blurry, the room starting to spin.

She leaned heavily against the counter, shaking her head to clear it. "Uh, now, I guess. Is the room fuzzy or is it just me?"

Large spots of colour flew behind her eyes, growing larger. She felt bands of steel around her, then herself being lifted off the floor. Then everything went dark.

Chapter Three

Someone was standing on her head. There could be no other reason for the pounding pulse driving her into awareness. Her eyes cracked open to find a very smug Arov sitting at the end of her bed. He had drugged her.

"Arov, what?" Her voice was a hoarse croak. She tried to turn over and found that her limbs were quite securely fastened to the bed.

"Before your grandfather left for the hospital, he gave me one final order." He stood and began to remove his shirt. "I was to take care of you by whatever means I saw fit. You are to be my woman, and all that it implies."

The swirling tattoos were clearly visible now, black against the blue-bronze of his chest. Twisting and writhing against his muscled torso, alive with magic and the energy of the djinn. He sat back onto the bed, causing her to twist as the mattress dipped in response. One by one, his boots fell to the floor.

He unbuttoned and unzipped his trousers, and at that, Albina looked away. She had never seen a naked man up close before. Her inclinations had kept her in her studies for the last decade since she turned eighteen, and her grandfather had been relieved. Her gaze darted back and forth, glancing at the flesh that he revealed, then focusing on the open window behind him that let in the sweet breeze of apple blossoms.

When she felt his weight dip the bed again, her eyes widened in panic as her hands pulled at the restraints.

"Shh. I won't hurt you, but I need to make you mine." His voice tried to soothe her, but she was panicking now. He quieted her struggles by the simple expedience of dropping his full weight onto her.

At the full contact of his warm body against her, she stilled. She whimpered incoherently, and then met the warm black eyes above her. A lethargy flowed out of his gaze and into her limbs. She relaxed against him, inch by inch, her body soft against his.

The bindings held her legs apart, and his penis was nudging at the gate to her womb. One of his hands speared through the hair at the apex of her thighs and began to trail around the nerve centre to her pleasure. That was the only place that he touched her, his fingers moving faster and faster as her body began to respond.

With his thumb still circling her clit, he worked first one, then two fingers inside her. His eyes widened as he hit her maidenhead. "You are still a virgin?"

Her face flamed. "Yes. I never…"

"Ah, then I will have to take more care with you." With that, he took her mouth in a searing kiss, his tongue stroking hers strongly, and then tangling with it. He tasted wonderful, like chocolate and cinnamon. He had always had a sweet tooth. She relaxed under his ministrations and began to welcome the warmth that had started to burn in her belly.

He took his time, gentling her to his touch. Her arms were still trapped above her, arching her breasts into his chest. As her breathing became more rapid, her nipples rubbed against his skin, heating with the friction as her sensations increased.

Each drag of oxygen was both heaven and torture. His chest was smooth and hard—the muscle beneath the skin seemed to be on fire. Her legs began to shift restlessly, searching for the release that was only inches away.

"Do you want me now, Albina?" His voice was low, the question asked from his position at the sensitive portion of her neck as he worried it with his teeth.

Her breath came out on a sigh as her neck arched in response to his mouth. "Yes, Arov, I want you. I have always wanted you."

At her words, his eyes went hot, and he swiftly drew up to his knees between her thighs. Gripping her hips and splaying her thighs even farther apart, he dragged her body up to meet his.

He examined her sex eagerly, learning every fold and crevice with long, knowledgeable fingers. The slick moisture emanating from her opening assisted his exploration.

Two of his fingers returned to her cunt, opening her wide for him. He merely looked at her for a few minutes, heat beginning to build as she saw the approval and lust in his eyes. Obviously he was enjoying what he saw.

His grip shifted to once again cup her hips, and then he was dragging her onto him. Just a few inches of his phallus at first, but rapidly pain began to spiral through her as he pushed against her hymen.

Incoherent protests filled her as he continued to move within her slick passage, covering his erection in her yielding flesh. His grip shifted for an instant and he drove her onto him, breaking the barrier of the stubborn flesh.

Her scream rent the air, echoing in the chambers of the mansion, waking the gargoyles that were instantly on alert.

With her maidenhead sundered, he lowered himself on top of her once more and began a rhythm to soothe her devastated flesh. Forward and back, his phallus slid within her. The oceanic tide could not have been more soothing.

Her hands and ankles still bound, she could not grasp at him, nor shove him away. But gradually, with each careful thrust, he was rebuilding what the abrupt entrance had destroyed. She was once again feeling the tension low in her belly, growing with every stroke.

Each pass of his body on top of and inside hers pushed her closer to the edge. Sweat broke over both of them, coating them with a fine mist of slick dampness. His fingers slid once again between their bodies and across her clit. She flinched in response to the direct touch. With a few circles of his fingers, the coil of sensation snapped, and her back arched up off the bed as the orgasm overtook her.

Her eyes opened wide and her muscles locked, trying to hold onto the joy as long as they could. The side effect was that Arov's cock was both clamped and massaged by the muscles holding him in. He shuddered above her, and at the feeling of heat spurting into her—she guessed that he had reached his tolerance level as well.

His body collapsed against hers. "And so I fulfilled his last wish." It was only a whisper of sound, but it was enough.

So, her grandfather had ordered him. She had wondered. Tears slowly welled from her eyes and she cried for the death of a teenage dream, and the embarrassment of having Arov give her a 'mercy fuck'.

"Uh, could you untie me? This is not really comfortable." The lazy, satiated look in his eyes gave her heart another wrench. This would be the last time that she saw that expression on his face. Damn.

"Oh, of course." The bindings melted into nothing. "You may want to rest now, you have had quite a day."

She rubbed her hands and wrists, bringing them back to life. With him still lying on top of her, she stretched out her feet and rotated her ankles.

"Arov?"

"Yes, Albina?"

"I wish you back into your dagger. Now." Tears continuing to flow from her eyes, she barely saw the wild spiral of energy that he became as he went to reside in his home.

"So, I'll get up, have a shower and get this place sorted out." She rolled to the edge of her bed, wincing at the soreness between her thighs. Well, at least she wasn't a virgin anymore. That ought to cool Rupert down considerably.

It had always been her virginity that he coveted. Now that was a lost cause.

Slowly, carefully, she made her way into the bathroom. The shower started up without a murmur and she eased the sore muscles of her shoulders and thighs under the pounding jets.

Now what was she going to do? She watched the trickle of blood from between her thighs stain the clear water, and shook her head. She would leave him in the dagger for a few days, then, when she was emotionally no longer a wreck, she could deal with him as an adult.

The first thing she needed was to bring the unfinished commissions that she had been working on to the mansion. She fished her cell phone out of her bags. Wandering around the house naked and unconcerned, she began to make her calls.

"Reginald?" He hated being called Reggie. "Can you send all of the first quarter's commissions to me at the manor? Great. I have a lab to work in here, so I should be fine. Just use a courier. Okay, fine, bring them yourself, but call me when you get to the gate. I have to let you in. See you tomorrow."

She hung up with a rueful grin. The next call was to her best friend, her cousin. She sat in front of a mirror and drew her fingers across it. Anryn's face soon took the place of her reflection.

"Hey, cousin, I am sorry to hear of your loss. Albion Lakin was a great man and a better alchemist." Her olive-toned features were sombre, not a normal expression for her. She was usually obnoxiously cheerful.

"Thank you. I know that he thought well of you as well."

"That is extremely flattering." Anryn paused thoughtfully. "Okay, Alby. What do you need?"

"I'll let you know when you get here. You can come through the mirror in the great room. I'll be there in a minute."

"See you soon." The mirror winked out and once again Albina was looking at her own reflection, her white hair glowing slightly from the magic she had just been using.

It was the legacy of her early attempts at an illumination spell. She had gotten the spell to work, but it had bonded to her hair. Now, every time she was stressed, or used magic, she glowed.

She was glowing now. What was she going to do about Arov?

A peremptory knocking was coming from the great room, and she cursed and hurried down the hallway to touch the mirror over the couch. As soon as her hand came into contact with the silvered surface, a hand emerged from the glass, followed immediately by the rest of her cousin.

Anryn's skin was olive green in colour, with flowing black hair. She usually wore a glamour to make herself look more human, but did not bother with friends and family. Her exotic presence lit up the room, her amused gaze reminding Albina that she was still naked.

Anryn's mother had been a dryad—her father, a Warder with environmentalist tendencies. He had been warding old trees to preserve them from the lumber industry, when he met his match in a dryad from one of the trees. Mylawith had been enthralled at the thought of a human protecting the trees and was immediately smitten. Thus it was a perfect match, producing Anryn, the most powerful Warder in current history.

Anryn took one long look at Albina, then walked forward to give her a hug. She dwarfed her small cousin by almost a head, taking the willowy description to absurd heights. Most men were not as tall as Anryn, yet she carried the extra height with dignity and grace.

"So it isn't all about your grandfather. Something else is up as well." She got right to the heart of the matter, pulling away from Alby and examining her closely.

Her eyes flared green as she used one of her talents to *read* her cousin. "It's a man. Wait, not quite a man. You have known him a long time, and he has finally shown interest in you, and you don't know what to do. Am I right?"

"What was your first clue?"

The focus came back. "You're wandering around the dining room buck naked, and you have a hickey on your neck. Okay, Alby. Who is he?"

Albina sighed deeply and reached for the dagger. "He's the family djinn. His name is Arov, and my grandfather wished for him to look out for me, so he did. By taking me for himself."

Anryn stood, astonished, as she looked down at the antique metal. Then she began to laugh. "So your first time was with a djinn? Lucky. Mine was a goblin. I'm thinking you got a much better deal."

Alby made a face. "It isn't like I had a choice. He sedated me, then tied me to a bed."

"Ohh, kinky. So where is he now?"

"I locked him into the dagger. Do you think you can help me free him…permanently?" She would take any help she could, and if anyone could figure it out, Anryn could.

"Well, I don't know much about djinn personally, but today is your lucky day."

"How do you mean?"

"It's Djinn Market day in Realm. Get dressed and let's go shopping." She waited until Alby dragged on a blouse, skirt and sensible shoes. Then her hand grabbed Alby's shoulder, and she turned her to the mirror. "Bring the dagger and one of those tacky lamps that your grandfather was so fond of."

Chapter Four

THE STEP THROUGH THE MIRROR WAS ALWAYS FUN. QUICKSILVER WAS RUSHING AROUND them, and then a bright rainbow exploded in their faces. The first time, Alby had been terrified. After that, it was a great ride.

They stepped out into the perpetual clear sky of Realm. Various magical creatures were emerging from the other mirrors surrounding the main transport area. Anryn waved hello to a few of the other patrons of the bazaar, then led the way to the Djinn Market.

Djinns of various ages were shopping for and vending different items of exotic origin. They specialized in the rare and expensive. Contrary to popular belief, the genie in the bottle was a punishment that was only one step above a death sentence. Most djinn lived free as regular magical creatures, like elves, goblins and dwarves.

Albina trailed silently in Anryn's wake, letting her do all the talking. One after another, the djinn vendors shook their heads, amused, but unable to assist them. The bright glass lamp that she held in her hands was causing a great deal of amusement. It was so tacky as to be funny.

Finally one smiled at Anryn, nodded and gestured for her to follow him to the back of the shop. She in turn gestured to Alby, and soon they were both seated on cushions in the spicy, scented dimness of the tent in the back of the stall.

The djinn merely smiled at Alby, served her tea, and then sat back with his own cup in his hand. "So, you want to free a djinn from his binding, do you? There are only two ways."

Alby sat forward. "What are they, please?"

He seemed startled by the polite nature of the request. "Do you have the containment object with you?" He knew instantly that it was not the lamp. No glass lamp would be able to contain a djinn, but it was lack of knowledge that they did not spread about. Metal was the only way to contain one. Lead, gold, brass, or fine Damascus steel.

"Yes."

"Put it on the table."

With trembling fingers, she took the dagger out and put it on the table, carefully facing the blade east-to-west.

"How long has it been in your family?"

"Eight hundred years or so."

"The name of the djinn inside?"

"Arov."

The vendor blinked at her. "Did you say Arov?"

"Yes."

"What is his first name?" He seemed eager now, and he leaned forward to carefully examine the dagger. She did, however, note that he didn't touch it.

"What?"

"Arov is his family name. You can't free him until you have his true name."

"Oh. I just thought…"

"The first way to free him is to wish him to die. It is not pleasant, but it is a type of freedom."

She grimaced in distaste. "Not acceptable. What is the other?"

"Is he bound by a bloodline?"

"Yes."

"Then when the last member of that bloodline dies, they must wish him free, with their own blood used to break the bond. If they don't, he will remain bound to the dagger, but be able to be passed from owner to owner. One of those can just wish him free, but that almost never happens."

"So you mean to say that until the last member of the binding line dies, he can't be set free?"

"That's correct."

Alby sipped meditatively at her tea, absorbing the information she had gotten. Anryn sat quietly beside her, eyes alert and attentive, watching every move in the room.

"Well, I guess I'm stuck with him then." If she hadn't been watching closely, she would not have noticed the expression of complete relief that passed over his features. "So if I can't set him free, how do I control him? I owe him a bit of revenge." She heard her cousin let out a snort beside her. One sharp elbow to the ribs, however, and the dryad subsided.

"What do you need him to do?" One eyebrow rose in concern, again, an odd emotion from this stranger.

"I just want to hold him in one position for a while. I owe him something. Plus, I need to get his first name out of him." A blush rose in her cheeks, and thankfully the djinn seemed to get the hint.

"I believe that I have just the thing. Please wait here a moment." With a rustle of silks and brocade, he was gone.

"Are you planning what I think you're planning, cousin?" Anryn looked pleased and scandalized at the same time. Her voice was low, so as to not carry into the other chambers of the tent.

"Nothing of the sort." An evil grin fell over her features. "I just want him to know how uncomfortable being confined to a bed can be. Fair play."

"Is it revenge you're after, or something more?" With her usual deadly insight, Anryn had hit it right on the nose.

Alby took a long, deep breath. "For years, growing up in that house, I dreamed of something more with him. But now that I am an adult and can take any man I choose into my bed, I still only want him. Sad, huh?"

She didn't answer, but gently took Alby's hand in her own. "Not sad, but don't do anything to risk yourself. You deserve the best."

They were interrupted by the return of the merchant. "Here we are. Just call him out of the dagger and we can get these on him. You may not be able to do it on your own." The djinn came back in with a rustle of silk, holding a black velvet tray covered with writhing silver snakes.

"Wrap them up. We are not going to do this here." Anryn stood up and took the dagger with her, handing it to Alby carefully.

"But it would be so much easier to do it here, where I could help you." He seemed angry now, his bluish face purpling with agitation.

Anryn drew herself up to her full height, greened her body all over in agitation to match his discoloration and stated once more, setting the full blast of her glamour on him. "We are leaving. You have your payment, and we will have the binders."

"Yes, of course you will. Please, here they are. Take them with my blessing, and enjoy the use of them." The vendor bowed low. Anryn took the tray of silver snakes and with a jerk of her head, took Albina with her out of the room.

"C'mon, we had better be quick." Anryn strode off at a comfortable pace, dodging other customers at the bazaar with slick ease. "That ain't gonna hold him long."

"Why? Why did he want me to bring Arov up there?"

"I think that he wants your little friend. If he gets you to use the binders on him, then he can convince you to get the true name and take over the dagger, and Arov."

"Oh, my God. I can't believe that I didn't see that. But why are we hurrying?"

"Because as soon as he realizes that we left his tent with the binders he is going to come after us, so we had better get to the mirrors quickly." She looked back over her shoulder and says, "Very quickly."

They were coming. Two large bluish figures were weaving themselves through the crowd, approaching rapidly.

Albina took the lead, sprinting through the crowds, moving faster with every step. As a shout rang out behind them they both propelled their feet at full speed.

"Anryn, start the spell!" They were neck and neck as they hit the mirror station.

There were no spells or chants, only power flaring in bluish light as Anryn powered up the mirror that they had come through. "Already done! Jump!"

In a flash of rainbow light, a doorway appeared that would lead them into Alby's living room.

They jumped. Light exploded behind their eyes as the magic engulfed them and threw them through the dimension behind the mirror. Then they tumbled through onto the dining room floor and turned to look into the closing portal.

Laughing as the doorway closed on the djinn's angry face, they sat up from the floor where they had fallen.

"Ow, I think I have carpet burn." Albina checked her elbow, grimacing in mock dismay.

Anryn shook her head and laughed again. "Well, it's been fun. But it's past my dinner time, and we both know you don't have nearly enough food for me here."

"I honestly couldn't tell you. I haven't checked lately. Arov just makes it appear." She sighed heavily. "The longer he is in there, the worse I feel. My grandfather let him come and go as he pleased. It feels wrong to leave him in there."

"Well, you are just going to have to follow your heart. And have me over for lunch when you get it all sorted out." Anryn turned back to the mirror that they had just entered from. "See ya soon, Albina, don't be a stranger."

"Bye, Anryn. Thanks again."

Albina took the lamp and put it into the fireplace behind some logs. If she needed it again, it would be handy to have it where she could find it.

So, now she was left with a djinn in a dagger and a set of bindings in the form of snakes. She looked carefully at them. They seemed to have stilled. Maybe they had to be in proximity to a djinn to be active. That would make sense.

She carefully picked one up, holding it at eye level. The silver was bound in a clear film, and the feel of it was magic. That would make the silver a liquid. This might be why it drained the power of the djinn and made them helpless.

She picked up another, holding one in each hand. Then she took a deep breath and stated, “Arov, come out of the dagger.”

One second later, arms were around her and a determined mouth was on hers. His mouth was sweet and warm, and she wondered, not for the first time, if he ate while in the dagger.

“Ah, Albina, I have missed you. I have thought about when we were together and regret only that I could not take more time.” His lips drifted softly against hers and she felt her eyes flutter shut.

The snakes began to writhe in her grasp and she released one in surprise, then the other. Her arms went around his neck and her head fell back as she relaxed into his kiss.

“What the hell?” Suddenly she could not enjoy the warmth of his embrace. His hands flew from her as he tried to fight the binders writhing against his flesh.

The two that were on the floor were spinning into place around his ankles and as they closed a flash of energy came from them, locking his power within him.

Arov was looking at her in astonishment. “It’s only temporary, Arov. Until I get what I want.”

A sheen of sweat coated him, and he looked defeated. “And what is it that you want, Albina?”

“I want you on your back, held so that I can learn you. So that I can learn a man’s body, period.”

“When?”

“Now would be good. Shall we?” She led the way up the stairs and into her bedchamber.

He followed her in silence. She could feel his irritation at her back.

Chapter Five

THE DOOR TO HER ROOM SWUNG OPEN AS THEY APPROACHED. SHE WAITED UNTIL HE HAD entered the room and closed it behind him.

"On the bed, please, Arov. Legs about a foot apart, with arms wide. I trust that the restraints will hold you?"

"Yes, Miss Lakin." His subservient mode was on full. He assumed the position that she had described and laid there, sullen and not aroused. He was barefoot, but his trousers and shirt were still firmly in place.

She winced at his return to formality. Moments before she had been Albina, now she was Miss Lakin. Considering what she was about to do, this was not the mood she wanted him in. She sighed heavily. "Arov, this is my chance to give and take pleasure from you. Are you sure that you don't want to help me?"

"It is humiliating to be powerless and trapped in this manner." His voice was a sullen grumble.

"Now you know how I felt." She climbed onto the bed and sat back on her heels. Their gazes caught and held as she tried to explain her loss of control at his hands, and her need to reciprocate.

Finally, a grudging acceptance flickered through his eyes. An arched brow challenged her to take what she wanted.

"Yes?" Although this was her will and not his, she still wanted his agreement.

"Yes."

"Well, um. I guess I should undress then."

"It usually assists in the process, yes."

She blushed and fidgeted with her buttons nervously. "So you will offer no hindrance, but no help either?"

"Exactly."

"Okay." Quickly, before she could change her mind, she was off the bed and peeling off her blouse. The skirt that she wore pooled around her ankles as she release it. She kicked off her shoes, and Arov laughed as they hit alternate walls in her haste.

She blushed, trembling in confusion as she tried to think of what to do next. Then, closing her eyes in terror, she stripped off her bra and panties. She clambered back up onto the bed and blindly fumbled her way to Arov's shirt.

Her eyes opened a tiny bit so that she could make out his burnished skin in a wavy blur. She wrestled open first one, then the entire row of buttons, exposing his flesh to her eager hands.

She drew her trembling fingers down his chest, trailing over the tattoos. He inhaled sharply at her touch, and she jerked her hands back in surprise. Her eyes flew open and she met his surprised gaze as she tried to still the shaking.

He spoke quietly. "You really are frightened, aren't you? You won't get very far like that. Come up here."

Trembling, her breasts tightening up with the gooseflesh that rippled over her, she crawled up his body, keeping him between her knees. She straddled his hips.

Her hair was flaring violently with power and agitation, almost blinding them both as he whispered, "Kiss me."

Taking a deep breath and slowly letting it out, she lowered her lips to his in a gentle kiss that soon had soft warmth blooming within her. Between her thighs, she felt his body respond to her nearness and the gentle contact with her body.

It gave her the confidence to deepen the kiss. Slowly, her tongue crept out to duel with his, his lips opening beneath hers and welcoming her into his mouth. Suddenly he took over the kiss, turning it from a gentle exploration to a passionate ravaging in a matter of seconds.

She heard herself moaning and pulled away from him, blinking in confusion at the heat that was now beginning to beat a pulse in her belly.

He smiled at the look on her face and let the warmth in his own body transmit into his eyes. She smiled tremulously in return, and began the task that she had set herself.

She sat back and her eyes widened even more at the ridge of flesh that had sprung to life beneath her bottom. Alby rocked experimentally against him, feeling his flesh twitch in response. Her hands slowly began to caress his chest, circling, scratching and rubbing lightly. Each reaction that he had to her touch, she catalogued in her mind. Every twitch, shudder and flinch that emanated from him, as well as the increase in hardness beneath her, told her she was on the right track.

A little more confident now, she leaned forward to kiss him again. This time it was her mouth that ravaged his, and his chest heaving when they parted. Arov's lids were heavy with lust and he moved to take her mouth again, so she took his neck instead.

Licking and sucking at the cords that grew taut at her approach, she tasted as much of his skin as she could reach with his arms still bound by the shirt. His skin was smooth, with a hint of sweat and musk. Inhaling deeply, she learned the scent of his arousal. Her tongue traced the spiralling tattoos on his chest, snaking over his nipples and gnawing gently until a groaning shudder passed through him.

Her head drew back sharply. "Did I do something wrong?" Insecurity came flooding back in a rush, quelling the heat that had been rising to a fever pitch.

"No. Please, you are doing fine." He laughed, a harsh sound, as his eyes flashed open.

She watched him for a long moment, carefully studying the flush running under his skin.

Alby resumed her ministrations to his chest, licking a path to his navel. She smiled and paused as the muscles of his abdomen drew tight at her mouth's caress. She blew on the delicate, wet trail that she had left behind, and his skin shivered in reaction.

She scooted down onto his thighs, then hovered over his knees as she drew her fingers to the waistband of his trousers. Gently and carefully, she opened the snap and drew down the zipper. She placed her hands flat on his abdomen, spreading the trousers open wide and freeing his erection.

Her hands moved forward as if of their own accord, one on his shaft and one gently cupping his balls and rolling gently. Arov arched, his heels and shoulders pushing into the mattress.

Albina fell backwards and lost her grip, fortunately for him. She teetered for a moment on the edge of the bed, then fell to the floor with a thump.

"Albina. Are you all right?" Arov disobeyed her orders and sat up in concern.

She began to laugh. "I knew I wasn't cut out to seduce men. I'm far too clumsy."

"I beg to differ, you were doing fine." His voice was still husky as he viewed her naked form splayed out on the floor.

"Was I? I couldn't tell." She eyed the erection that beckoned her like a lodestone. "I guess I will just have to try harder." She stood, rubbed her sore backside gently, and once again mounted the bed. "As you were, Arov. Please," she added in a husky tone, and he slowly lowered himself back onto the bed. This time, she kept one hand bracing herself on the linens, wrapping the other around the shaft of his cock.

Slowly she worked her hand down, then up. She moved to take him in her mouth, flicking her tongue over the flaring head, licking at the pearly drop that had formed. He groaned in response, and she kept her balance as he shifted and shuddered.

She sucked on him slowly, then shifted to balance on her knees as he held still for her ministrations. She took her time as she began to rub at her clit with two fingers, stroking his shaft with the other. Slowly she built her own orgasm, her folds growing slicker with every moment. Each groan from him drove the flames in her body higher as she approached her release.

She could feel her own heat, and drove her mouth around his cock with worshipful devotion. He was leaking precum almost constantly now, her tongue nipping and removing every drop. He tasted strange, but she found the flavour rather appealing. At least coming from him.

His balls tightened beneath her and she drew her head back. A shout erupted from his throat as his cock spurted in her mouth. She drew back after the first load hit her mouth, so the next few caught her on the chin and throat.

She sat back on her heels, still frantically fingering her clit until a shivering wave of tremors locked her own gasps in her throat. She crawled off him and lay down, using his arm as a pillow. She sighed deeply, "That was nice."

"Yes, it was. Do you have what you need of me?" His voice was flat.

"Oh, the links, of course." She reached over him, her breasts rubbing against his chest as she flicked off the first binder. She gripped the snake in her hand, crawled backward to his other arm and pulled off the other.

She tossed them out into the hall, and they slid into the room across from hers. The bands on his ankles were removed when she climbed over him and snapped them off, then launched them in the same manner. "There, all gone."

"I see. Thank you." His voice was rather amused. It suddenly dawned on her that she was straddling his abdomen, he was aroused again and she was still completely naked.

"Uh, yeah. I'm done. I'll just get out of your way now."

His hands caressing her buttocks belied her last statement. She shifted and tried to move off him, but his fingers dug in and held her in place. "Where will you go?"

"Oh, I'm expecting a call. My assistant is dropping off some projects, and needs me to get him through the safety gate."

His fingers were now running up and down her backside, making circles on her buttocks and lower thighs. She realized with shock that she had given him full access to her body, and had no way to rescind it. One of his hands wrapped around her thigh as his deft fingers worked their way inside her. He began to pump them gently.

She moaned and arched her back like a cat, trying to drive them into her and keep them there. He pulled his slick fingers out, and she mewled in protest. Her hips shifted toward him to try and recapture him in her heat.

"Arov, please." It was a whimper—her body had flared out of control at his touch. She could almost smell the magic coming from him now.

Suddenly he pulled back by her hips, and his thick cock made its way within her. Air rushed through her lips as she closed her eyes to savour the sensation. Oh, gods, it felt so good to have him within her again.

He slowly began to move, using his grip on her hips to pull her down onto his cock, and then to raise her to the point that he almost slipped from within her. Her eyes closed. The only thing that she knew—that she could feel—was him sliding in her cunt and the power flaring around them.

Faster and harder he drove, his hips arching up to bury himself to the hilt. She could feel the impact of his balls on her clit as she came slamming down onto him. With a buck, a moan and a shudder she came, her body trying to slow his pace and enjoy its own rhythm.

He kept plunging within her until the last spasm eased, then turned her to face him. He moved out of her and she mourned the loss of his heat, until she heard his announcement. Then he had her complete attention.

"Albina Lakin, I would like to fully introduce myself." Arov drew her down to him and kissed her gently. "My name is Imaran Arov, of the House of Nayan Tarak."

"Imaran? But I thought…I mean…you just…" She stopped and shook her head. Her hair fell around them in a glowing cloud of silk. "Did you just willingly give me the power of your true name?"

"I did."

"Why?" She was truly appalled, and she knew it showed on her expressive face. He began to laugh and pulled her onto the bed next to him, then loomed over her in a playful manner. He began to drop tiny licks and kisses on her face and neck. "Because you freed me when you didn't have to, and kept me restrained only to learn to please me. Those are not the acts of a woman that I cannot trust."

"But how do you know that you can trust me?" She wove her fingers through his hair, tugging his head up so that she could look him in the eye.

"Look down." He directed her gaze to her own breasts, which now bore an echo of the tattoos on his chest.

She tried to sit up and examine them further, but he merely leaned some of his weight on her to keep her in place. She frowned. "How did those marks get there? I didn't feel anything!" She was slightly indignant.

Then it was his turn. "Did not feel anything? I know it has been a while since I took a woman, but I never recalled one as referring to my manhood as nothing. Most of them did feel it when it was giving them pleasure." He was scowling at her now, but she could see the humour lurking behind the stern mask. Funny, she had never thought of him as having a sense of humour.

"That isn't what I meant! Of course I felt you…I mean…Damn it, how did those tattoos get there?" She tried to cross her arms over her breasts, but was thwarted in that as well.

"They are the marks of my house, my family. I may be bound to you, but now you are bound to me as well." His head dipped and his tongue slid out to trace the marks on her breasts. She felt the shock of having magic wrapped around her sensitive mounds and gasped as his tongue made the designs come alive.

Magic snaked around her breasts, wrapping and tugging with a will of its own. She shivered as her nipples contracted in reaction and Imaran's mouth engulfed them, one at a time. He exhaled heavily over the wet peaks and smiled at her clutching at his shoulders in response.

He bit gently on one straining nipple and was rewarded with her shriek, wetness flooding her thighs. She had not felt this aroused the other times that he had touched her. He repeated his bite and her hips rocked in response, thighs rubbing together as her clit came to straining attention.

He pried her thighs apart with one knee, sliding his hips between them. Imaran's head remained between her breasts as he began to ease into her seeping pussy. The head of his erection stretched her wide open and she smiled through the sweat that was beginning to coat her as he started to move. She would bet that he had used his magic to prove his point.

But who cared? Alby suspended her sense of time and just enjoyed the sensations of him thrusting slowly within her. All too soon, he was driving harder and faster, moving toward his own orgasm. As he groaned her name and shuddered inside her, she felt the sting of magic in her breasts, running in a burning line to her clit and causing her to join him over the precipice.

She could feel the jets of seed inside her, each causing a new spasm of her own contractions in response.

Her eyes fluttered closed and she lay back, satiated. She flinched as he withdrew. Their joined fluids began to seep from her channel, across her anus and onto the sheets beneath. Suddenly the whole wet-spot problem that her cousins mentioned made a lot of sense. He moved off her body and lay next to her, his head pillowed on her breast, one arm draped over her hips to hold her in place.

Despite her aches and the mild discomfort that she felt, she drifted off to sleep.

Chapter Six

ALBY WOKE UP IN ROSE-SCENTED DARKNESS. WELL, NOT TOTAL DARKNESS. THERE WERE candles hovering around her room, casting a golden glow around her, but not disturbing her sleep.

The rose scent was due to the thousands of petals that were strewn across the bed, dusted with gold powder. She raised her hand, and giggled at the shower of flower petals and gold that cascaded to the bed. She sat up and they tumbled from her torso, pooling at her hips. A few tenacious petals stuck to her breasts and belly. She smiled and looked around for her lover.

He appeared in a shimmer of energy with a tray of food in his hands. "Your dinner, Albina. You haven't eaten all day."

"Well, I wouldn't say that." She grinned impishly and left him to figure out her meaning.

It didn't take long. His slow smile caused her stomach to flip. "You are correct. But you still need sustenance."

"I agree. What do you have for me?"

"Hmm…I didn't want to leave you too long, so it is mostly a selection of fruits, breads, meats and cheeses. The wine is on the floor behind you."

Alby leaned over the edge of the bed and sure enough, there was the wine and two goblets. It was her favourite vintage. Her own.

"Where did you get this? I thought that Grandfather said that he had consumed the last of it at New Year's."

"He did. This is from the cellar in your house."

"What? How did it get here then?"

"*Silhar,* I am a djinn." He shook his head. Shooing her to one side, he sat next to her on the bed. He was surrounded by rose petals, but looked not the least bit effeminate. The red of the petals drew the blue out of his skin and caused him to glow in the candlelight.

"*Silhar?* What does that mean?" She watched his hands work at the wine bottle and open the strawberry wine that she had made two years before.

He deftly poured the wine into the two goblets. "It's djinn for beloved."

"Am I?" She sipped delicately at the wine, laughing at her own giddiness.

She felt different, somehow, as if a weight had been lifted off her shoulders.

His hand reached out to grasp her chin. Firmly he tipped her head back until their eyes met. Not an easy task. She wouldn't look at him.

"Albina!"

Her gaze flicked to his, and locked.

"You are my *silbar*, or the magic would not have taken you like it did." His fingers caressed her cheek, and her eyelids fluttered shut.

She opened her eyes once again and touched his own jaw with her fingers, shivering with delight as he turned his head to kiss her palm. "This is a little sudden for me. I don't have a lot of experience with this sort of thing."

He grinned again, "I know."

She sighed deeply and reached for the food. "Yeah, I guess you would."

She ate in silence, noting absently that he did not join her. "Don't you eat?"

Come to think of it, she had never seen him eat.

"I eat when I am alone. It is not appropriate for me to eat with the guardians of the dagger."

"You might have to adapt your reasoning. If, as you say, I belong to you and you belong to me, then there is no reason for you not to have some fruit now?" She bit into a ripe strawberry, catching the juice on her tongue as it tried to run down her chin.

"You are absolutely correct." He had an intent look on his face as he watched the trail of juice she missed run over her chin to drip onto her breast.

Her hand came up to wipe it away and was caught by his. He drew her forward by her wrist and applied his mouth to the strawberry juice on her nipple, licking and sucking with fervent attention.

She moaned, almost choking on the rest of the berry then braced her hand on his shoulder. "That's not what I meant." But she was enjoying his caress too much to put much force behind her protest.

"Perhaps I have been short-sighted in my habits. I think you need to reacquaint me with the social mores of eating with a companion." His eyes danced with mirth again. He moved past her to situate himself against the pillows. Dragging the tray within his reach, he lay with his body exposed to her and his arms crossed over his chest. "Feed me."

With good humour, she scooted up next to his torso and reached for a slice of cheese. She broke it into pieces with her fingers, moving one piece to his mouth. As he parted his lips, she popped it in and drew her hand back.

"I don't bite," was his grumbled response.

She looked down to her breasts and the obvious marks around her nipples, then back to his face, raising one eyebrow in challenge. “I beg to differ.”

Next, she selected a piece of apple. It was too large to for him to eat in one bite, so she held it as his strong white teeth bit through the flesh and peel. Juice leaked from the corner of his mouth and without thinking about it, she darted forward to lick it up.

This simple instinct gave birth to one of the most sensual kisses that Alby had ever experienced. Magic flared between them, circling all points of contact, flowing from flesh to flesh at every point that they touched. The djinn magic flowing from him had a wild, musky taste, like a desert spice. She knew that her warder magic had an almost pine fresh scent. It was an odd combination that left her light headed.

Shaking, she broke the kiss, her body screaming in protest. “Wow.” She leaned back on her heels and turned back to the tray with studious focus. Unthinkingly, she took the rest of the apple slice and popped it into her own mouth, looking for the next tidbit to feed to her djinn. At his groan she realized what she had done, and glancing over, she saw the pearly drop at the head of his cock that eloquently spoke of his interest.

A tiny piece of bread was paired with a morsel of sliced meat, and as she placed the offering in his mouth, she let her thumb graze the wet fullness of his lower lip. She knew that her own lips were probably just as swollen.

She ruthlessly reined in her lust and began to feed him in earnest. Light caresses ensued, and by the time the tray was depleted by one quarter, she was lounging on his chest and feeding him with one hand. The other was bracing her against him, her breasts crushed to his chest as she fed both of them, one tiny morsel at a time.

They were both laughing as she tried to manage the food with one hand while keeping her balance against him. He kept one arm around her to keep her from taking another trip to the floor. She licked the juices and crumbs from him, and he did the same for her. Of course, she occasionally missed and had to chase a drop across his chest, but he didn’t seem to mind.

She giggled as he lifted her to return the favour for her when she let a morsel slip as well.

As their bodies heated, the smell of the roses grew sweeter. The petals clung to every moist portion of her body, and as the perfume of her body reached her own nostrils, it blended seamlessly into a heady musk that caused Imaran’s eyes to heat.

“Enough.” He lifted her above him and settled her thighs astride his hips.

Teasing the petals of her sex apart, his fingers stroked deeply, his thumb rubbing against her clit. Her eyes closed and her hips began to move in time to capture his fingers as they moved inside her. The wet sounds of their union caused even more of a flush to rise beneath her cheeks and down her breasts.

Then in a move that caused her to jump in surprise, his fingers left her moist depths and circled her tightly puckered hole in a slow caress, then pushed inside with gentle insistence. "What are you…?"

With his fingers still buried inside her ass, moving softly, he flipped her onto her back and came down on top of her. She squealed as he pushed insistently into her and as his cock filled her, her body remained clenched around his invading fingers. She went over the edge before he even got fully seated inside her. She screamed and arched, forcing his cock deep and his fingers deeper. Her throat locked as she struggled for air, and she lost consciousness.

Chapter Seven

The morning was creeping through the window as Alby woke. She had been bathed, her hair combed and braided, and a loose pair of trousers and a tunic made of gauze covered her. She was also not in her bedroom. She was in Imaran's.

The mahogany four-poster bed was hung with blue silk, complimenting his colouring. A wardrobe was against one wall, again in rich, dark wood. A large mirror took up the other solid wall. She wandered over to it, stroking the inlaid wood of the frame. It tingled as she touched it, and an image appeared. It was her house. Her fingers brushed against it again, but were unable to improve the focus.

She went into the bathroom down the hall, the gauzy clothing flowing around her, and attended the call of nature. Oh, gods, she was sore. Everything ached. But nothing was more than sore. All of her tiny bites and scratches had been healed to prevent infection. Only the muscles that were unused to such activities were protesting her movement.

She checked her hair and was amazed by the precision of the braid. It was far beyond her capabilities to tidy her hair in such an efficient manner. Alby wandered downstairs and looked around for her purse. She eventually found it behind the couch and dug out her cell phone.

She had seven calls recorded. Six from Reginald, and one from an unknown number. That one sent a shiver down her spine. She had had the phone for over three years and never gotten a wrong number—it was warded against them. In fact, only Reggie and her grandfather had the number, and her grandfather was dead. That meant that whomever had dialled it knew that it was hers. That was the condition of the ward. They had to know the number, and that she was the owner.

She called Reggie back. "Hey, Reg. Sorry that I missed your calls."

"Where the hell were you? I was forced to take a hotel room in town."

"I was occupied with some details of the estate. I left my cell phone here."

"Can I come now?"

She looked down at herself. She would definitely have to get dressed in regular clothes first. "Sure. Call me when you get to the gate."

"Will do, boss." Reg hung up.

She disconnected her phone and ran back up the stairs. She went to her closet and stood amazed at the array of clothing that was hanging there. Beautiful laces, delicate silks and bright velvets and gauzes filled it to overflowing. Her dowdy little suits and blouses were gone.

The town was only a fifteen-minute drive away, and she had no time to lose. She grabbed a loose set of trousers and a matching buttoned sleeveless tunic, flinging them onto the bed. She paused. There was no trace of the debauchery of the day and night before. The rose petals were gone, the sheets changed and a new comforter was in place with bolster pillows.

She opened her drawers and found new bras and panties where her staid white silk and cotton had lain before. She shook her head and remembered the djinn's primary power. Transformation. He could not create matter, but he could change one thing into something else. You would never starve if you had a loyal djinn at your side.

Apparently, Imaran had a fascination with seeing colour against her pale skin and hair. She chose an azure blue set to compliment the buttoned vest and trousers that she had chosen. She dressed quickly and checked her reflection in the mirror. Only a hint of the bra showed through the top, and the vague outline of her new tattoos were only visible if you knew to look for them. Alby breathed a sigh of relief.

A pair of sandals that matched her outfit appeared next to the mirror and she jumped, looking around her.

In a contrasting vest of gold and loose trousers of black, Imaran lounged in the chair in the corner. He looked extremely satisfied to see her in his creations. "You look well this morning."

She curtsied with a grimace. "As do you. I see that you have been frolicking in my clothing."

He spread his hands helplessly, "I don't sleep much. It pleases me to see you wear colour."

"Where were you when I woke up? In your room, I might add."

"I was arranging the items that Albion wanted sent to the Repository."

"Well, Reg is on his way to the gate, and I need to meet with him to collect some of my work." She sounded apologetic, and she realized that she was. She wanted to be alone with him, and do some more experimenting.

He looked pleased at her expression and began to approach her. It was not her will that stopped him. It was her cell phone that gave him pause.

"Damn, he's here." She rushed to him and gave him a quick, teasing kiss. Before he could grab her, she had slipped from his arms and out of the room, answering the phone as she went.

She ran over to the door and entered the code that would open the gate. She watched the monitor to made sure that the gate closed behind his car as he drove up the driveway.

She stepped between the gargoyles at their posts. Her powers could keep them passive if it came to that. She didn't worry about Imaran. Reg had met those of her non-human association before. He was warded against being able to tell anyone about them, though. It was a vow that he had agreed to before taking on his position in her employ.

His car glided smoothly into the cul-de-sac next to the front steps and he reached into the backseat of his car to fish out the canvas and a small bag that he had stored there. Reg was not very intimidating, and flamboyantly gay. He had met his current boyfriend while on a job for her, and they would be heading for Hawaii in a few months. It was true love, and she applauded them for it.

She escorted him past the gargoyles, though they still shifted nervously, which got her attention. They had tea, as a tray had been set on the table before they arrived. She chatted about any new clients who may have contacted them, and he gave her a number of a woman who needed to have an opal necklace un-cursed. It was an act of will that kept her from rolling her eyes. Opals were always trouble, and the most common item to carry a tiny curse. Unfortunately, the largest curse was the clumsiness of the owners who didn't understand the delicate composition of the gem.

"Quote her the standard," was her only reply.

The rest of the conversation revolved around his boyfriend Michael and their plans to marry. She offered to pay for the cost of transporting friends and relatives for them, and Reg began to weep. That was to be her gift to them, and he was so grateful he hugged her.

"Get your hands off her." Imaran Arov had been lurking in the shadows. Now he walked into the light.

"Dear God, is he real?" Reg was practically drooling at the impressive display of threat and muscle. She knew what he was seeing and couldn't blame him for his admiration. She still didn't believe it herself.

"Yep, a real pain in the ass." She crossed her own arms across her chest and looked over at her lover. Imaran's eyes promised revenge, and she winced as she imagined what was going through his mind. Her mouth had just bitten off more than she could chew.

"I am sorry to have stepped into your territory, but she just gave me the best news I have had all week. My boyfriend and I want to get married, but need to do it out of state or it won't be legal. Alby has just offered to help us bring our friends with us to share our day."

Imaran looked bewildered. Albina decided to explain it to him later, and she saw a dawning light in his eyes. She assumed that he figured it out.

"Reginald, this is Arov, our family djinn."

"Ah, that explains your new wardrobe. It suits you, you should wear colour more often."

"Oh, God. Don't encourage him."

Imaran was looking smug. He eyed her carefully, and she could feel him making alterations as he went. When she looked down, a lot more cleavage was exposed, embroidery bordered the garment in a subtly darker shade and the weave had thinned, her tattoos blue swirls beneath the lighter blue of the fabric.

"Stop that!" she hissed at him, and he grinned back unrepentantly.

A few more pleasantries and details of the work that he had left for her were exchanged, but she regretfully had to end the visit. Reginald could talk for hours if allowed.

"Well, I hate to rush you when you have been here only an hour, but you really need to go now, Reg. Just so that I can finish those projects and have you pick them up in a few days." She tried to seem apologetic, but her crossed arms over her breasts and her impatience as Arov kept fooling with her clothes was obvious.

Reg grinned and shook his head. "All right, I'm going. But thank you so much for the offer earlier. I'll try to keep the invites small." With a limp wave and a whisper of expensive cologne, he left.

Albina sighed and flopped back on the couch, a tea sandwich still clutched in her fingers. Deprived of his audience, he left her clothes semi-sheer. "I know he enjoys playing the gay stereotype to the hilt, but I wish he would relax it when we are alone."

"He prefers men?" He seemed a little puzzled. It was not unheard of across his eight hundred years, but lately he had stayed at home with Albion and not been exposed to modern culture. Well, he had gotten the hang of email, but that was it.

"Yep." She shrugged and finished her sandwich. It had never even entered her mind. It was just the way Reg was. Plus, she knew that he secretly watched football, so it made his affected gestures amusing to watch.

Imaran suddenly looked alert. “Is he coming back?” His body bristled with menace.

She stood and viewed the display of Reg’s car leaving the gate and it closing behind him. “No. He’s gone. The gate just closed behind him.”

“Well, someone is here.” He moved to put his body between her and the door, and that was when it exploded into black flame.

Chapter Eight

Arov's body struck hers and knocked her to the ground as the burst that came through the door shattered the magic protecting the house.

Albina struggled to make her way out from under the unconscious djinn, and that's when she saw her worst nightmare.

Rupert. Surrounded by hellish flame, with madness burning in his eyes.

She could feel the evil pulsing off him. An evil that had not been there the last time that they had met, unless he had better protection than she could have imagined.

It was the unwholesome power of an Az demon. He was being propelled by the greed inherent in a bargain with one of their kind. As she struggled out from under Arov, she fought to pull her magic into a protective shielding around him. She warded his clothing, turning the fabric into a cloak of invisibility. It was all she had time for.

"Albina. So happy to see you." Rupert knelt at her side, completely oblivious to the djinn lying only three feet away. It was working. Thank the powers.

He pulled out a gun and pointed it at her, making it obvious that his burst of power had been only to make his way into the house without challenge. She wondered how the gargoyles were doing.

"Rupert. You could have knocked." She pushed herself off the floor, avoiding his 'helping' hand.

He simply grabbed her arm and hauled her with him as he stood. "I thought that the element of surprise would come in handy." He began to drag her through the house, his gun held before him.

"How did you manage that magical display? You don't have any talents."

He took her to the room that used to be the den. It was currently the pantry. She was not about to assist him in navigating around the new arrangement.

"I made a deal with a demon. If I hand over one of your grandfather's old artefacts, I get a full compliment of powers." His grip on her arm tightened as he hauled her into yet another room that was not where he remembered it.

"Which artefact? There are a few hundred here."

"A lamp. An enamelled glass lamp. It is of vital importance to the demon." He was getting frustrated at his inability to find the room that he was looking for.

"Why that lamp?" As if she didn't know. She and Anryn had indeed been spotted when they went to the market. Someone had reported it back to a demon that had an interest in possessing the djinn that was obviously inside.

"There is a genie or something inside. Haven't you wondered why your family has always been wealthy? Why they have always been successful?" Blood began to seep from her arm where his nails were digging into her skin.

"I thought that it was just because we don't gamble and we pay our bills on time. You and your mom should try it." That was the last quip that she got out. He struck her with his fist in his rage. She woke on the floor, dazed and confused, as he'd left her where she'd fallen. She heard him find the lab and begin to ransack it.

Moving slowly, she crept over to the fireplace and retrieved the lamp and the dagger. She swiftly ran to the kitchen, put the dagger in the oven, then moved to the cupboard and slammed it hard.

She didn't have to wait long. She half-heartedly tried to hide the lamp behind her, shoving it toward the sink.

"Give me that damned lamp, or I swear I will shoot, Albina." Rupert was completely mad, his eyes wild, showing the cracks in his composure.

"What will you do after you shoot me, Rupert? I am the last one of the family able to use the lamp's secrets." She whirled and clutched the lamp, holding it in front of her like a shield. "I am useless to you dead."

"Then I will keep you alive and make you do as I will. I will fuck you when I please and chain you to a wall when I don't." He seemed pleased at his line of thinking, the hard on he suddenly sprouted in his chinos evidence of his less than brotherly feelings for her. Creepy.

"What if I refuse to give up the lamp?" Her heart was pounding in her chest. She was backed up against the kitchen counter. There was nowhere else to go.

"Then I will just call the demon and let him take it. He promised you to me after he gets the lamp anyway. But he might enjoy taking his time with you as well." A smarmy smirk passed over his face, and the sick lust spurred her panic as nothing else had yet done.

"Never! You are not getting anywhere near me!" She threw the lamp at him, and he clutched at it blindly. It tipped from hand to hand, then connected with the gun and shattered.

"Bitch! You vindictive bitch!" The gun swung toward her, and since she had nowhere to go, she was standing when the first bullet hit her.

She felt as if someone had struck her shoulder, slamming her back into the cupboards. A second pop, and a burning filled her left side. She slumped to the floor, meeting Rupert's eyes as it dawned on him what he had done.

She heard the gun clatter to the floor, then his frantic footsteps out the door with a slam to tell her that he had left.

She began the arduous task of crawling to the stove. It took all of her concentration just to remember why she was crawling on the floor, leaving a trail of blood behind her. *Oh, yeah, the dagger.*

After only a few moments that seemed like hours to her, she reached the oven. Her hands gripped the handle, and she let her weight pull the door open. She dragged herself out of the way and reached inside, sighing in relief as the familiar metal shape appeared beneath her fingers. With arms shaking and eyesight going dim, she stroked the steel gently, trailing her blood across the surface.

"Arov, how nice to see you again. I have one more wish for you." Her head fell back and she smiled as a shimmering materialization happened before her. Smokeless fire.

He appeared before her, bruised and battered by the explosion, and knelt in her blood. "Oh, Albina, what happened to you?" One large hand caressed her hair, and he kissed her gently.

"Hey, mister, no distractions." She struggled to clear her head, and as her vision began to fade she whispered her last wish. "Imaran Arov, Djinn of the dagger, I wish you free."

His expression was the last thing that she saw as darkness claimed her, and she smiled. She had never seen him that surprised before.

Chapter Nine

SHE AWOKE WITH LIGHT ALL AROUND HER.

It wasn't heaven.

In heaven, someone was not next to you snoring.

Albina's eyes blinked and widened slowly, taking in the sterile accoutrements of the private hospital room. The snoring was coming from the cot that was next to the bed.

Imaran was lying with his long limbs dangling off the edge of the bed. His skin was now an even bronze, the bluish tint no longer in evidence.

She tried to reach down to wake him and only then felt the searing tug of the bullet wounds and stitches. She groaned, fell back into the embrace of the pillows and tried to be as still as possible.

The sound she made woke him. "Albina! How do you feel?" His black hair was tousled, and she wanted nothing more than to run her fingers through the silky locks.

"Sore. What the hell happened? How did I get here?" Her voice was hoarse. He quickly got her a glass of water with a straw in it and held it for her while she sipped.

His face grim, he stated, "Rupert shot you."

"Oh, right." She sat up a little, aided by the electronic lift of the bed.

"You wouldn't happen to know why, would you?" His arms crossed over his chest and he scowled down at her.

"He wanted the lamp."

"Yes, that is what he said. In fact, that is why he broke into Reginald's car and stowed away in the trunk. That is why he broke in, and that is why he shot you when it shattered."

"Well, then you know as much as I do."

"No. You know one other thing that I do not."

"What would that be?"

"Why did he think that there was a djinn in the lamp?" His eyebrow rose and he kept his gaze steady on her, waiting for her to lie about it.

So she didn't. "My cousin Anryn and I took your dagger and the lamp to the

Djinn Market in Realm. That is where I got those binders. We carried the lamp to make an obvious target for anyone seeing us. I hid the dagger under my clothes."

She watched in fascination as he almost breathed fire for a moment. His eyes flared red and his skin blued, his hands moved to his sides, clenching repetitively in agitation. He was angry. "You went to the Djinn Market without a djinn escort? You risked your life and safety to bind me for a few hours?" He took deep breath. "You are never to risk yourself in that manner again. You could have been killed, enslaved or worse."

"What would have been worse?"

"You could have been given to Rupert."

"Oh, right. That would have been worse."

They lapsed into silence. He sat next to her bed, taking one of her cold hands in his.

Medical personnel came into the room and checked on her, a few of the nurses smiling at Imaran's grip on her hand. A doctor came in to check on her stitches, notified her that the bullets had been removed and set her mind at ease that Rupert was being held without bail.

When she looked over at her djinn, she was astonished at the harshness of his features. He obviously wanted to engage a more final solution to the Rupert problem, but something had stopped him.

A detective came in to get her statement. She told him that Rupert had broken in somehow, the door had blown in and injured her. She didn't know what he had used. The detective told her that they were looking into it.

She told him about being dragged through the house as he looked for her grandfather's lamp. Being struck and taking the lamp to the kitchen to hide it. The slight noise that let Rupert know where she was, and the shattering of the lamp that broke his control.

The detective stopped her at certain points to gain details. Having the truth behind all of her statements made it so much easier. She hid nothing, except any mention of the dagger.

If Rupert had not been looking for it, it didn't matter to anyone else.

An hour of questions and answers ensued. She answered everything truthfully, detailing what she knew of Rupert's character and his menacing moves on her on the day of the will reading.

"I believe that Albina needs her rest now. You have enough information, Detective." Imaran met the eyes of the detective, and he suddenly agreed.

"Yes, I can imagine that you are quite exhausted, Miss Lakin. You were lucky that your fiancé was on his way over and was able to call 911 for you, as well as subduing Mr. Morris before he could get away."

"Ah, yes. My fiancé is a special man indeed. I am a lucky woman." She maintained her light grip on his hand, and squeezed gently.

"And I am lucky that I got there in time, *silbar*. You were almost dead." He leaned down and laid a kiss on her forehead.

"According to the ambulance crew, you did die for a few minutes, Miss Lakin. But they were able to revive you." The detective stood and left the room. "You are one lucky woman."

"I was dead?" She looked deeply into the eyes of the djinn that she loved. She had realized that at the last moment as she lay dying. Freeing him was the most important thing that she could do for him, so free him she did.

"Yes. And in that moment of your death, I was freed." He stood over her and tears welled in his black eyes. "And more terrified than I had ever been."

"I called the ambulance and slowed time at the manor. Rupert had not made it out of the house yet and I restrained myself from killing him, but instead rendered him unconscious and tied him. I opened the gate and waited with you bleeding slowly to death in my arms.

"As the medics entered the manor, time resumed and I gave you over to them. They restarted your heart and stopped the bleeding. The police arrived and arrested Rupert, and I got the car and followed the ambulance."

"So you are completely free now? There are no more restraints on you?" She was wistful. He would leave, and return to his home.

"Only one." He was grim.

"What? Was there another binding on you? The djinn that I spoke to didn't mention that."

"You. You and I are bound together. Until death. You are bound to my life, and I to yours." He kissed her, a slow and thorough meeting of the lips that shared breath and life.

"You kept me alive, didn't you?" She was amazed. At the point at which she died, all ties with him had been severed.

Now he looked impatient, he sighed deeply and explained things to her. "Yes. The magic freed me, but my heart kept me bound to you. I could not let you go."

"Do you really mean that?" She winced at the desperate nature of her plea.

He just sighed and shook his head. "Yes, I mean it. And eventually you will come to believe it. Now rest, you are exhausted."

Her lids felt heavy and she felt fatigue come over her in a wave. She suspected that he cheated, but couldn't figure out how he had caused it. As she drifted off, she felt his lips against hers, once more breathing life and magic into her as she gave herself over to the warm security of his presence.

HER RECOVERY ASTONISHED her doctors. In only three days she was able to make her way down the halls, and one week later she was on her way out of the hospital.

The nurse pushed her wheelchair down the hall and out into the bright sun of the courtyard. Imaran was waiting for her with an SUV that she did not recognize. He carefully tucked her into the seat, easing the seatbelt into place. With a final wave at the staff that had gathered to wave her goodbye, she sat back and watched the novelty of a djinn driving down the highway.

"How long have you been driving?" She tried to make polite conversation. She didn't want to startle him.

"Six years or so. Albion had trouble on long journeys. He asked me if I would be willing to learn and paid for driving lessons for me." He laughed and shook his head. "He could have just wished for me to have the knowledge, but felt that it was better that I learn."

"That was Grandpa. Knowing was one thing, but learning was better." She sighed, then smiled. "Did you know that he made me take weaving lessons? Spinning, sewing, cooking and even car repair. He wanted me to know how everything worked, so that whatever happened I could start over."

"Yes, he told me of your accomplishments."

"He did?"

"Yes, he even kept every single trophy that you won, every award, and every piece of artwork that you created. He was always very proud of you."

She was astonished, and not a little embarrassed. "He told me that he was, but I thought that when I started to restore artwork and cursed objects that he was a little disappointed."

Imaran took his eyes off the road for an instant to meet her watery gaze. "He was always proud of you, no matter what you chose to do. Simply because you chose to do it."

She smiled weakly, ignoring the tears that slowly tracked down her cheeks. She turned her head to look at the trees and livestock that they passed. In her life, it had never crossed her mind that what she did was not as important as whether or not she made the choice on her own.

She spent the one-hour drive in quiet reverie, mulling over her place in the universe and in her djinn's life.

When they reached the gate, she sighed in relief. It opened smoothly and she felt the wards close around her as they made their way to the main house.

"Someone reset the wards."

"Yes, your cousin Anryn called your phone and asked if she could help."

"She did it all?" There were several hundred acres involved.

"No. She called in some of your other cousins and threw a warding party. The gargoyles were hiding for days."

A single giggle escaped her lips, then another. Seconds later she was guffawing in earnest, only the pull of her stitches keeping her from venturing into hysterics.

"You haven't met many of my mother's relatives before, have you?"

He still looked a little haunted. "No. I had no idea that the Warders were so, enthusiastic."

"Yeah, they love a party." Albina remembered some of the 'family events' that she had attended in Realm. The Warders preferred to hold their festivities there, as there was less of a chance of noise complaints and police being called.

"Then we will have to invite them to the wedding." The truck stopped in the drive and he got out then came around to assist her.

"Who's wedding?"

He was careful to avoid her wounds, but had to grip her suddenly when he answered, "Ours."

"Our wedding? You, and me?" Her head tilted up and she tried to read his face, but it was difficult as he struggled not to injure her. He finally simply swung her off her feet and walked with her into the house, the gargoyles looking sheepish as their mistress was carried past them.

"Yes, you and me. Today we will travel to Realm and get you the healing you need, and then we will see if I can find my parents."

"You want me to meet your parents?"

"It's traditional. They have to approve my bride before we can marry. After that, you are all mine."

"Your parents have to approve me?" Suddenly she felt more light-headed than she did when she was bleeding to death.

"It is only a technicality. If we can't find them in two hours, we will return home." He carried her effortlessly through the house. She noticed that all traces of the explosion were gone.

"Couldn't we look for them another day?"

He sighed deeply and laughed at the fear in her face. "Today is the day of the Djinn Market. We will have the best luck of finding them today. It will be fine, I promise you."

He walked with her to the mirror, and the magic swirled through it and opened into a doorway. He stepped through, coming out in the bright sunlight of Realm.

Chapter Ten

If he had not been holding her, she would have run. The instant that they stepped into Realm, they both took on their natural appearances. His skin blued in hue, his eyes slanted and ears pointed. She felt her own skin glow and started as the marks that the magic had burned into her flesh began to pulse insistently.

"This is such a bad idea, Arov." She crossed her arms over her chest and hugged herself, using the pain of her injuries to keep herself alert.

"Hush, it will be fine." He started off toward the healer's tent, crossing the field with ground eating strides. "Just relax. And when the healer starts to work, hold still!" He gave her a slight squeeze to drive home his sentence and smiled at her as she nodded in grudging acceptance.

Being healed would improve her disposition. He was right to insist on it. She had refused to enjoy painkillers in the hospital and was using the endorphins to keep herself mobile. The side effect was that she was in an extremely foul temper most of the time, and the littlest thing would send her into tears.

The healer was professional and direct, if you thought that a nagging blue grandmother was professional. Her hands skimmed over Albina's torso, 'reading' the energy that she crossed. "Oh, those humans did make a mess when they tried to repair you. Don't worry, we'll have you fixed up in no time." Her name was Tovah. She was definitely a blooded djinn. Her skin had the same smoky blue tinge as all of the vendors in the marketplace.

She bustled off into the next room and came back with a pot of tea. It was always tea with the djinn. She served Arov, and then settled down next to Albina. "All right, let's see the damage."

Albina moved her fingers to the buttons of her shirt and slowly undid them. "Arov, would you mind leaving the room?" She arched one brow and looked over the shoulder of the healer as she waited for the reaction of the djinn across the room.

"Yes, I would mind. I am not leaving you alone with anyone. Not even a bound healer." At the word 'bound', Albina's eyes searched Tovah's neck and wrists. There it was—a brilliant silver band circling her left wrist. She had been bound to do no harm to any under her care.

"Oh, gods. I am so sorry." Her eyes reached those of the healer, and she saw humour in them.

"Don't be sorry. It was a choice that I made, and the only reason my husband has survived all of these centuries." She smiled for a moment, then was back to business. "All right, now let's see those wounds."

Blushing furiously, Albina opened her shirt. This was the first time in over a week that Imaran had seen her without her clothing. Her skin still bore the violent marks of her trips to the floor as well as from the initial blast that had knocked Arov out. None of those marks could cancel out the swirling pattern that crossed her breasts. The staff at the hospital had thought that they were a strange tribal tattoo, and she had tried to keep her gown on as much as possible, not an easy task when she had two bullet wounds in her upper body.

Tovah smiled. "Your magic has marked her, and she still blushes. You must not have been together very long."

"Not nearly long enough." Imaran looked over at Albina's exposed breasts and his mouth tightened. Suddenly Albina realized why she was being healed within an hour of arriving at her home. He wanted her back in his bed. Now.

Tovah laughed and began to run her hands lightly over the bruised tissue. The warm air of the room should have kept her goose bumps at bay, but Alby shivered anyway. It was the fixed gaze of her erstwhile lover on her while the purple tissue faded into yellow and her body flushed the damage away that was causing her discomfort.

Tovah started on her sutured wounds, pulling the stitches free of her flesh. Alby winced as they came out, then sighed as the warmth of the healing took over. The throbbing pain receded, and she fell asleep.

OVER AN HOUR later the healer finished and gestured for Arov to join her in the other room. He rose from his chair and joined Tovah in the anteroom. He kept his voice down and spoke to the healer. "How is she?"

"She will be fine. But I think that you need some healing as well. There is the stink of demon near you."

"It was a demon's power that broke the wards and caused her injury. Can you heal it?"

"Yes. Sit."

"Thank you." He sat, but kept the curtain to the other room pushed back so that he could see Alby. He had a thought, "Do you by any chance know the Arov family?"

"Yes, of course. They have a vendor tent near the Great Hall. I noticed that your lady has the markings of one of the Arov clan." Tovah quietly pulled an amulet out of a drawer and placed it against Imaran's chest.

"Yes, she does."

"Then you would be a member of that clan."

"Yes, I am." The amulet was held against his skin while she ran power through it. The energy of the djinn flowed through her hand and into his flesh, scraping the demonic residue from his flesh, then pushing it into the amulet. She finished the healing and sealed the amulet, binding it with her own energy.

He thanked her and gave her a pouch full of coins. Albina was still, her breasts moving gently in the rhythm of sleep. Quietly, he crept into the room and sat next to her, one hand gently smoothing the hair off her forehead. He left her shirt open, admiring the view. Her skin had gone from pale to grey after the wounding, and he was glad to see the bluish veins beneath the cream of her flesh.

She had been so still after she had freed him. Her skin had been chalky white, marred with the brutal red of the blood that was coursing from her. With every heartbeat, more blood had poured out, bringing her closer to death until she slipped away from him.

He had wanted nothing more than to destroy Rupert Morris in that moment. That was when he knew that he loved her, not when he wanted to kill her attacker, but when he didn't slaughter him. Instead, he paralysed Rupert and restarted Albina's heart, applying pressure on her shoulder and side with his hands. His magic had kept her breathing and her heart beating while he waited for the ambulance to arrive.

Albina loved that house. Her grandfather's house. She would not be happy leaving the mundane world and living in Realm. He had to do things the human way. That meant making sure that Rupert was taken away by the human authorities, and leaving him alive.

The demon that had sent him was another matter. It had wanted Albina to die, whether she knew it or not. His prison could not be used by anyone who was not a Lakin, unless all of the Lakins were dead. He needed his family to help him find that demon.

Albina stirred, her lashes fluttering. Her clear blue eyes met his, and she smiled. "Hi. I feel better." She reached up with both hands and tugged his head down to hers, scorching his body with a single kiss. “I feel much better.” Her hands threaded into his hair and she sifted them through the strands. She arched her breasts against his chest and froze with their noses inches apart. “Is my shirt open?”

“Yes.”

“Did you know that there is a very upset looking djinn right behind you?” She let him go and her hands flew to her shirt, closing the centre button and working her way up, then down.

Chapter Eleven

THE OLDER DJINN STARED AT THE YOUNGER, WHICH LEAPT TO HIS FEET TO FACE HIM AND protect his woman.

"Imaran?" It was a whisper, the black eyes tearing up and flowing freely.

"Father." Imaran executed a formal bow and was caught up in a hug that should have broken bones. Tears flowed from both men's faces as they reunited for the first time in eight hundred years.

Tovah slipped in behind them, crossing over to the pallet where Albina was sitting, tears in her own eyes. "While he was waiting for you, I found his father for him. It is common knowledge that he was imprisoned in servitude to the Lakin clan. But you have Warder blood, which means that you are the last Lakin. I also felt your death, and knew that he was free. He needed to be with his own family."

The implication that she did not belong was palpable. Albina squared her shoulders. She knew that Tovah was wrong. She could feel it in the way that he touched her, looked at her, and watched her when she slept. She could feel that he loved her. And she loved him, damn it.

"Father, I would like to introduce you to someone." Imaran pulled away from his father's embrace and gestured toward Albina. "Albina Warder Lakin, this is my father, Artan Arov." He drew her forward.

Albina met Artan's black eyes with her own, keeping her gaze steady. His first look was insulting, lingering on her breasts and hips. "You are the last of the Lakin family?"

"Yes, I was."

"Was?"

"Yes, I died. That ended the family line. And freed your son." She stood firm.

"I thank you for bringing him back to us. It ends our obligation to your family. I am sure that you want to get back to the Warders, then." He nodded toward the curtain where he had entered the room.

"Father, she is my *silhar*. We have bonded and are hoping to get the family's blessing on our union." Imaran moved to put himself between his father and Albina. She stopped him.

"Imaran, it is obvious that something else is going on here." She glared at his father. "How long have you know about the demon hunting him?"

"*What?* How could you know about that?" He looked vaguely ill.

"An Az demon paid someone to kill me with magic as the coin. Someone else would have hired the Az demon. They don't work for free." She turned to Imaran. "Were you betrothed to anyone before you were bound?"

"Yes, to Keyah Gal. The betrothal was broken by her father when I fell into disgrace." He looked puzzled. Then the light dawned. "Father, has Zhian Gal been in touch with you?"

"You couldn't just have gone home, could you? You arrogant warlock's brat!" Artan began to build his power, preparing to strike her down.

"Father! Step away!" Imaran began to flare with his own power, tinged with Warder magic. A bubble of energy swelled around him, pushing everyone out of his radius, with the exception of Albina.

"Imaran! Stop it. He's your father, damn it! Calm down." She stepped between them. Not the safest place to be. Her hair flared a brilliant white as she began to pull power from the fabric of Realm itself.

She bound Imaran, then Artan. Tovah was next, and the energy spread outward. The djinn magic that Imaran had blended with hers was heady, and it was the first time she had been able to free it.

She bound everyone to the spot that they were standing. Ripples on a pond of magic. Then, just as quickly as it had grown out of control, it flared back into her.

Albina staggered as the magic pulsed back into her. Imaran caught her.

"Father, since I am not welcome, Albina and I will be leaving. You will receive an invitation to our wedding. Please let us know if you will attend."

Artan was blinking in astonishment. No Warder woman had chosen a djinn in over nine hundred years. The talents of the Warders were specific, but powerful. Only when a female Warder truly loved a male of the djinn did their powers blend together like that.

"Son, I am sorry. I didn't mean to lose my temper like that."

"It is not I that you owe an apology to, Father."

Artan faced her and bowed low, raising her hand to his heart. "Albina, I beg your pardon for the insult that I dealt you."

"Why did you?"

"Keyah Gal never married. When her father heard that the last Lakin was a female, he approached me in an effort to get me to reinstate the betrothal."

"And what did you say?"

"That when Imaran returned, I would talk to him about it. Zhian pressed for a date. His daughter was not getting any younger, and he wanted grandchildren."

"Zhian, of course, told Keyah, and she wanted a specific timeline. He could not give her one, and he took matters into his own hands."

"They have a connection with the Az, do they?"

"Yes, one of Zhian's other daughters married an Az."

Albina kept her face straight. She knew a lot of women who had married an ass...uh, Az. "So, why didn't you warn your son?"

"The wards around your home prevented any of our kind from entering unannounced."

"Why didn't you ask one of my clan? They would have been happy to do it."

"The djinn don't have contact with any other clans."

"What about Market Day?"

"Well…"

"In fact, it was one of your clan that told me how to free Imaran, giving me all the options and keeping me from making any mistakes."

Imaran was behind her, wrapping his arms around her. "Was that the one who gave you the binders?" It was a hot murmur in her ear.

"It was." She smiled and snuggled back against him. The power that they shared was resonating between them.

"It was Kassim." Artan was looking a little flustered. This was not going the way that he had planned it. Imaran was supposed to return to him, marry Keyah and move back to Realm. Now, he was attached to a Warder, living in the mundane world and rejecting his family obligations. Moreover, he seemed to be in love with the Warder, and she was sharing his magic. That meant… "Albina? Are you pregnant?"

Tovah gasped at this breach of protocol. She had not checked for a pregnancy, and with the damage that Albina had taken, there was no way to have sensed it.

"No, not yet. But soon." Her eyes closed and she could see the child that she would bear. It would have its father's eyes, and family markings. The rest was covered by a cartooned diaper.

Imaran asked in a husky voice, "How soon?" His hand moved down over her abdomen and his erection prodded against her from behind. Apparently the idea of getting her pregnant was working for him.

"It could start today if we're quick." She turned her head and kissed him.

He held her mouth to his, refusing to end the kiss when she tried to pull back. She felt the building of magical energy and in a thunderclap, she and Imaran were making out in front of the mirror station.

He picked her up and tucked her under one arm, carrying her through the mirror to the manor and charging all of the wards to full. Then he took her to bed. Not his room, not her room, but the master suite. All of her grandfather's things had been moved to one of the other rooms long before he had died. He didn't want to take up all the space in the house, being an old man.

Their new chambers were huge. Brightly coloured silks, mahogany furniture and great silken pillows. He simply flipped her through the air and she slid across the sheets to the headboard, laughing all the way.

She watched him disrobe with rapt fascination. His body was displayed for her in the bright light of day, and it was a wonderful sight. Each inch of rippling muscle made her heart beat a little faster, and the pulse in her thighs was growing insistent as he bent to remove his trousers. At last she was watching him from a distance, and she had seconds to admire his body.

He stood for a moment and she warded him in place, with a smile on her lips. He was held, standing at the foot of the bed, his erection beckoning her with a tantalizing musk.

She rose up on her knees and took the minute that she had before he broke free of her hold and ran her hands down his arms, his shoulders, massaged his fingers and sucked on one or two of them, then ran her hands down his chest to the centre of his arousal and wrapped both hands around it.

She stroked his hot flesh, smiling at the moisture building at the tip. Every stroke seemed to get a reaction. She sat next to him, fully clothed, and stroked at his hardness. One hand reached below to tickle at his balls, rolling them and squeezing gently. Then, as a wicked thought broke through her, she snuck one fingertip to his ass, trailing gently around his anus. She brought that evil finger to her mouth, wet it in saliva and returned it to his ass.

Teasing him while he was immobile was a lot of fun. She should have tried it a while ago. Her finger worked into his ass delicately, feeling the soft heat and the grip of the muscle that tried to push her out and take her in at the same time.

She was grinning with evil triumph, stroking his shaft while her finger explored his ass in a persistent way. So wrapped up was she in her tormenting of his conscious body while he couldn't move that she forgot to monitor the ward. It wore off.

"Albina, get your finger out of my ass and let me between those pale, smooth thighs." His voice made her jump and she scooted backward on the bed, hopefully out of his reach.

He stood still for a few moments. The amount of precum dripping off his cock indicated that he was close to orgasm. She just wanted to be with him when it happened.

He crawled onto the bed, moving like a giant feline. She tried to stay out of his way, but suddenly he pounced, and his reward was her shirt. He grinned, a feral smile, and came back for her skirt, flipping her to her belly and unzipping the clothing that he had helped her don hours before. Her skirt flew off to the side of the bed. She was wearing nothing beneath it. He hadn't brought underwear to the hospital.

With a snarl of triumph, he turned her and rubbed his body slowly against her. She groaned in relief at the contact of his warm, hard flesh. Her thighs parted in welcome, and he slid between them.

With a few thrusts to coat himself in her slick juices, he slid home. She cried out at the feeling of fullness that she had been craving since Realm. As he drew back to thrust within again, she cried out and raised her legs to bring him deeper.

He draped her legs over his shoulders and began to thrust in a slow, heavy rhythm. She relaxed and let him make love to her, purring as his mouth reached her breasts, mewling as he inserted one finger between their heaving bodies, rubbing her clit. She cried out in surprise as his caresses sent her over the edge, and she felt his body wrapped tight in the grip of hers.

She revelled in the reacting pulse within her body to every thrust of his, screaming and laughing at the same time as he poured both himself and his magic into her in one furious burst.

Sparks and pulses flew around the room and caught in the glass balls that decorated every surface.

Imaran rolled to his back. "I want to stay like this all night, inside you all night. Our baby starting within you."

She gave him a passionate kiss, duelling tongues with him for several minutes until she came up for air. "Okay. So, at our wedding. Your family is invited, but the Warders will plan it. Deal?"

"Deal. Now stop wiggling, unless you want to start something, and I believe that you called me a pain in the ass?" He made a move to pull her off him, and she batted at his hands.

"I'll be good, I'll be good. I just want to lie here with you inside me, love, and wake up like this tomorrow."

"Did you just call me love?" He tugged her hair so she'd look him in the eye.

"I did."

"Why?"

"Because, as I was dying, I realized that freeing you was the only thing that mattered, that had to be love. And because you look at me like I'm naked. All the time."

"You *are* naked." He smiled.

"And because seeing your face calms me, makes me feel warm and when you smile, it makes me feel hot." She felt the reaction of his flesh within her and knew that the sleeping plans would have to be altered to include at least one more interlude.

"Ah, I love you as well." His kiss explained a thousand things, and none, and she was all right with that. She had a few hundred years to figure him out. She could wait.

The Warder's Dragon

Chapter One

THE ANCIENT HOUSE ROCKED WITH LIGHT, LAUGHTER, AND THE OCCASIONAL BURST OF magical energies. The sombre stones were decked out with brightly coloured balloons and the fairies in the garden reeled in drunken circles around the windows and doors. They wanted to join the fun.

Anryn Warder looked around the room and smiled at the guests that had gathered to celebrate the engagement of her cousin Albina and her fiancé Imaran. The mix was a bizarre blend of human and magical creatures. The wards that were set around the estate would wipe the memories of the humans as they left, transforming the faces of the djinn women and the elves into normal, if beautiful, humans.

Which was a handy thing, as some of the more inebriated guests were comparing species-specific physiques. A 'how many breasts do you have?' contest was underway in the foyer under the watchful eye of the Lakin portraits. The old gents in the paintings had never had such a show.

"I can't thank you enough for this shower Anni! I was never expecting anything like this." Albina wandered over with a glass of wine in her hand. She was glowing. Literally.

"Alby, you're quite welcome. What have you been up to? You are lit up like a Christmas tree." The snicker was unmistakable.

"Oh, I was just having a conversation with Imaran's mother, Delileh. She wanted to look at my markings in front of other djinn witnesses." Not only was Alby's face flaming, her hair was glowing in the afternoon sun. The nearby paintings sparkled in the luminescence cast by her braided tresses.

When Anryn and Albina were first learning to cast wards, Albina made a mistake in her focus. Her spell blew up in her face and she had to spend the rest of her life with glowing, magic-sensitive hair. It was Anni's favourite point to tease her cousin with.

"So basically, a group of djinn women cornered you and said 'Show us your boobs'. What did you do?" The giggles were coming fast and furious. She fought desperately to keep her face straight.

"I flashed them." She took a hefty slug of the wine that one giggling dryad was serving to the crowd. She watched the dryad and asked her cousin, "So, how is your mom enjoying the party?"

"She's having the time of her life. And since she is a couple of hundred years old, that really means something." Anryn was driving, so she stuck to soda.

Smiling, she watched her mother flit among the other women. Mylawith looked not a day over twenty-four. Her delicate green skin had been bequeathed to her daughter, as well as her bright green eyes. Hair that was a strange combination of green, gold and brown rippled down her back. She preferred the solitude of the forest, but the company of other magical creatures always warmed her.

Anryn's black hair had come from her father, a warder who worked to keep the old-growth forests from predation by logging companies. Her mother had taken one look at the handsome mage and jumped out of a tree and onto his startled form.

Dominick had been astonished to have the warm womanly body drop on him, and as she began to grind herself against him, he had decided to accede to the lady's wishes. He visited her every chance he got until she announced she was pregnant. For one month he had stayed away, frantically making phone calls. Laying claim to a portion of old-growth forest was not a task for the bureaucratically challenged.

Then, one day, a building crew arrived in a nearby meadow. They excavated with extreme care and using sprayed concrete and a frame of metal, they created an underground warren. They back-filled the site and the meadow grew again.

Dominick Warder made a place in his lady's world, and that is where his daughter was born one winter night. They couldn't get married right away, as Mylawith did not exist to the human world, but a binding ceremony with Dominick holding his daughter brought a wild Warder party to the deep forest in the dead of winter.

"So, how many have RSVP'd already?" She dragged her mind back from her father's favourite bedtime story and focused on Albina again.

"Around six hundred." This was about right for a Warder wedding. It was a favourite place for them to shop for men.

"All races are being represented?"

"Through our family alone." She rolled her eyes to the ceiling. The Warders were bound by law, to mate outside their own clan. This kept their most desirable talent from being used for evil, as it had at one time in the past.

The Warders had made a bid to take over Realm by starving out the population and only allowing access to those who supported them. The Dragon Council had collected an army and broke the wards, killing all males of the clan, and imprisoning the women. The women were tried, put to the Question and those who were guilty of planning the attacks were put to death. Only seven women survived. Seven Warders.

They were given to the clans they had wronged, and their bloodlines were forbidden from inter-marrying. Warders had successfully married and produced offspring with twenty races, humans being one of them. They moved from Realm to earth, and used mirrors to go back and report to the Dragon Council every five years.

Their family crossed over twenty races, but no one could stop the ties that bound the Warders together.

Anryn started to set her cousin's mind at ease about the wedding preparations. "Music wise, I have the Goblin Rulz playing at the reception."

Albina's blue eyes danced in delight. "I love them!" She was practically hopping in her chair. "How did you get them? I thought they were booked."

"Never underestimate sleeping around in your youth." Anryn winked slowly and watched the light dawn in her cousin's eyes.

"You mean that you…?"

"Six years ago. But he and I are still friends." All of Anryn's lovers became her friends after the relationship was over. No one could hold a grudge against her perpetual cheer.

"Wow, if I had friends like that…well, Imaran wouldn't be marrying me."

They both laughed. It was a well-known fact that djinn preferred virgins. That she was no longer in that condition was strictly due to her fiancés actions.

"Delileh seems happy enough with her son's choice." The djinn women were mingling a little, occasionally making forays to the snack table. The stern matron in question was holding court in her daughter-to-be's home.

"That's what she said once she saw the family's markings. It isn't like she could deny they are Imaran's. Each djinn has his own pattern and this is definitely his." She peered down into her shirt and shrugged. "I haven't learned to read them yet. I can't get beyond the ABC's of the djinn script yet. Goblin was much easier."

"You're drunk." The happy bride-to-be was listing gently to the right. Anryn held out a steadying hand and held her.

"Yes, I am." A blinding smile broke free. "I really do love him, you know. He makes me feel…happy."

"Yes, Alby. I know." She stood and scooped her cousin up in her arms. Albina was as light as a feather. Anryn quickly walked into the dining room and through the mirror, taking her cousin to Realm.

The Djinn village was over three hundred miles away. She stomped her foot on the ground and sent a wave of power through Albina. Moments later, a djinn appeared in front of her. "Albina, what is wrong? Anryn, is she alright?"

His face was concerned, the black eyes searching her burden for any sign of injury. Once in his lifetime was enough. He took her gently from her cousin.

"She's fine, but my mom got her drunk." He grinned in relief, chuckling as Alby burped and began to snore against his chest.

The twinkling in his black eyes let her know that he had figured out what happened. "She had to deal with my mother, did she?"

"Yep, and the rest of her attendants. She had to show them the djinn marks, and promptly got loaded after that. Can you keep her with you here for a while? I want to kick out the party goers and clean up a bit."

"I can do that when we get home."

She blinked and smiled ruefully. *Oh, right. Magic. He used to be Albina's housekeeper. Lords, if only she could find a guy who did housework.*

"Yeah, okay. Give me six hours to get rid of the stragglers." She turned to leave, "Oh, and Alby came out of the bridal shower with quite a haul. Thirty pounds of gold jewellery and seventeen pieces of edible underwear. Hope you're hungry." She winked at him in the mirror and passed through to the bright tune of his laughter.

Her cousin was a lucky woman.

Chapter Two

"So how was the shower on Saturday?" Bethany was as chipper as always. The perfect secretary. She would dump hot coffee in your lap if you called her an executive assistant.

"It was a blast. Any messages for me?" She moved past the reception desk and nodded as she took the sheaf of pink papers with one hand and balanced her coffee with the other. "Yeesh, serves me right for taking a Friday off."

She dipped and levered the door to her office open with her elbow. Sitting at her pressboard desk she flipped through the notes and sorted them by urgency. Several were queries about her schedule over the next few weeks. Anryn worked into the stack and found the note that she was looking for.

It was the call from the dressmaker for Albina's wedding. The woman was a miracle worker. The lesser-known fact that she was a spider goblin was the only thing that kept her from being a top international designer. Well, that and the extra sets of arms that she had. She swiftly dialled the number.

"Morcalla? Hey. How's it going?"

"Great, Anryn. Business is booming."

"So, you called? A status report perhaps?" Anryn dug out her day planner and started to write in her appointments for the next few weeks.

"You know it. The dresses are coming along well. They should be done in plenty of time."

"You know that I am going to check up on you."

"Yeah, yeah. But I tell you, those seven layers of Warder formal wear are hell to embroider."

"Yes, but you are being compensated handsomely."

"Indeed, I can't argue with that. When are you running the next wards?"

"Later this week. Do you have a date for the concrete?"

"Next Tuesday. The crew is roughing out the foundation this week."

"Fine, then I'll call you on Thursday and set them before Sunday."

"You don't know how much this means to me."

Tears pricked Anryn's eyes. "Yes I do. Just remember to recommend me to your friends and family. I don't work cheap." She forced a laugh and heard an echo on the other end of the call.

"I don't either, take care."

"Take care. Bye, Morcalla."

As she hung up Anryn took a deep breath. All that Morcalla wanted was a set of wards that would let her have human guests in her house without freaking them out. She enjoyed the company of men and didn't enjoy it as they ran screaming from her bed when she left the glamour off. The wards would keep the glamour in place until they left her presence.

She also was afraid of paparazzi, afraid that her glamour wouldn't hold. The wards that Anryn had planned would keep any lens from focusing into any window. It would give her privacy and security.

She drummed her fingers on the desk. *All right, back to work.* She took out her day planner and began to schedule appointments. Being a massage therapist was not a nine to five job. Each client had a set time that they preferred to be treated and would not deviate from it.

She called up her normal Monday client list and had several happy people that she would be seeing, starting in less than one hour. She had a new client on the list for today- a businessman. His appointment was in his offices.

Decklyn Ringler was a CEO of some company or other. His executive assistant had called on Friday for an appointment, and had been disappointed to find that it was her day off. So she asked for her employer to be worked into Anryn's schedule late in the day. No one else would do.

She picked up her folding table, her bag with her essentials and left for her first appointment for the day. She worked on any number of people, some old, some young, and some who had medical conditions that made her wince in sympathy. But she did her job. All day, every day.

It was a relief to see her schedule and note that only one name was not crossed off. She hauled the table to the elevator and pressed the top floor button. It was thirty flights in the air when she came out and saw that the entire upper floor was glass. Not one exterior wall marred the beauty of the skyline. The interior walls were arranged like spokes on a wheel, with the receptionist holding court in the centre.

She walked up to the reception desk and waited for the receptionist to notice her. "Anryn Warder to see Decklyn Ringler. We have a five o'clock appointment."

"Please, have a seat over there. He'll be with you in a few minutes." She dismissed the visitor and went back to typing a document with no particular urgency, to prove that she was far too busy to be answering questions.

"I didn't notice you announcing that I was here. Perhaps it slipped your mind." She waited and kept her even gaze on the little secretary trying to throw her weight around.

She gave Anryn a hate filled glance and put one hand to her headset. "Mr. Ringler, there is a Miss Warder here to see you." Her eyes widened with surprise as she was given her instructions.

"Please come with me, Miss Warder." She led the way down the hall to a conference room. It had the same panoramic view as the reception area.

"Please get comfortable, can I get you anything?"

"Where is the nearest restroom?"

"There is one behind this panel." She walked to the wall, and a panel slid back at the touch of her hand. It was well hidden, and Anryn wondered how many other doors were attached to this room. The receptionist stood and waited for her dismissal.

"A soda would be great, and everything I need."

"I'll only be a moment."

"Fine."

She flipped the massage table upright and secured the legs into place. One client on the floor in her lifetime had been enough.

The receptionist returned with a can and a glass, and she left them on the conference room table and quit the room. Anryn looked around for any chance item to give her a clue as to Mr. Ringler's occupation. There was nothing.

No magazines, no documents, and no workstations of any kind marred the glass and steel of the room. She shivered and looked around once more. She hated waiting.

She tried to occupy herself. She wandered over to the bathroom that had been pointed out and ran warm water in the sink. She sat the bottle of oil that she used on her clients into the sink. She opened the 'client' pack that she retrieved from her car, after dropping the sheets and towels that she used on her previous client in the laundry bag that she kept in her vehicle for such a purpose.

The laundry found her fastidiousness in packaging of the sheets, towels and pillows excessive, but since she was prepared to pay for the extra work, they had stopped commenting after her first payment.

Just as she was snapping the sheet over the table, her new client arrived. Decklyn Ringler. It was no wonder that he had called Relaxed Realms Massage Therapy. He was a dragon.

Relaxed Realms specialized in non-human clients. It took a certain amount of strength to work on supernatural creatures.

"You are the massage therapist?" His brow rose in astonishment. She was tall, slender and looked incapable of applying the necessary force to engage in therapeutic massage. Her olive skin made her look Mediterranean at first glance, the dryad was only there if you knew to look for it.

"Yep. You would be Mr. Ringler?"

"Yes."

"Please remove your clothing and lie face down on the table. If you like, I can leave the room for a few minutes." She turned to prepare the second sheet, then saw him unbuttoning his shirt with a lack of concern.

"I am fine with it if you are." The challenge was obvious. He was quite an impressive specimen, and as he removed his clothing, she found that he was older than he looked.

With a dragon, you could tell the age by their bodies. He bore a series of scars that she acknowledged as territory dispute markings. The claws of another dragon had ploughed through his golden skin. His hair was quite long, hanging below his shoulders within the confines of a strip of leather. It was a rich chestnut, which contrasted starkly with his golden eyes. When he undid his pants, she watched with interest.

From what she had heard, dragon scales remained on the phallus, no matter the form he took. Huh. Nope. His cock was a slightly darker shade of gold than his skin, but was snug in a nest of silky chestnut curls, just like a normal male. The lack of hair on his chest had made her wonder, but now her curiosity was satisfied.

"Are you enjoying the view?"

She jumped. She had been lost in her own thoughts, and most of them x-rated. "Oh, yes. Quite nice. Now if you would lie face down on the table please?"

He looked startled, but moved to do as she asked. His cock had begun to rise under the attention that it was getting. When she had him settled to her satisfaction, she flipped the second sheet over him and moved to get the warmed oil.

Apparently he was not used to being referred to as 'quite nice'.

She placed it on the table and coated her hands, then applied herself to her work. "Wind and wards you are tense, Mr. Ringler." She worked at the taut muscles and smiled when he grunted at the force she was required to apply.

"Oh, I should have warned you, therapeutic massage can lightly bruise tissues. You will be more relaxed, but the first day you'll feel like you have been hit by a truck." An evil grin spread across her face as he made a harsh sound as she bent to her work.

It was well over half an hour of hard work later that she asked him to flip over. As he turned, not without some difficulty, she flexed her hands and wiped the sweat off of her brow. "Just lie back, Mr. Ringler. Do you have any other spots of tension beside your back and neck?"

"You can call me Decklyn." He shifted around and draped the sheet across his hips. It tented in a most obvious way. "My neck and hands are the only residual bits of tension. Unless you would be willing to address my erection."

"That is not a muscular problem, that's a hydraulic one." She smiled and moved behind his head. Rubbing her slicked hands up his neck and pulling gently on his skull. Being this close to an attractive aroused man was having an effect on her. But she had to put her job first.

"Ah, but would you be willing to address it? You didn't answer that." His upside-down smile was engaging, and she smiled back when she saw his hunter's gaze on her breasts. It wasn't like he could miss them, but she did bind them down when she worked or they got in the way.

"Not while I'm working. But contact me another time, and we'll see what we can do. Now let your head relax." She continued the stroking her hands from his shoulders, up his neck, and to the back of his skull, flipping his hair out of the way each time.

The smile this time exposed his pointed white teeth. Dragons could not hide their eyes, or their teeth. It was a flaw of the magic that let them change shape. Or a warning to their prey.

In silence, she continued down his arms, kneading the tight skin and digging into the muscle underneath. Each arm was treated thusly, and then she came to his hands. She loved a man's hands.

She sighed heavily and kneaded the tension out of his fingers. Tugging at each finger until they were totally relaxed and his eyes closed in bliss. Her fingers slid through his and she felt a tugging at her womb. It was not unexpected. She had been attracted to him from the start.

The liquid heat that she began generating caught her by surprise, though. His arousal had not diminished as she worked, and having that pillar beckoning her was shaking her self-control. She caught her own scent and flinched.

If she could smell her own heat, then he surely could. The satisfied smirk on his face stated as much. His eyes had flared open at the first rush of wetness that delivered her interest to him, and he was watching her massage his hands with a hunter's attention. A hunter being stroked by his prey.

The hour was up. With a relieved sigh and shaking hands, she stood and removed the oil from her skin with one of her towels. "There, all done." Over her shoulder she quipped, "Was it good for you?"

His voice was husky and far too close as he responded, "Not yet, but it will be."

"What?" She began to turn and felt a sudden rush of magic flow over her. She had no chance to defend herself and buckled under the wave of lust that followed in its wake. Her eyes searched Decklyn's and she realized that she had been caught in his glamour. She fainted into his arms.

Chapter Three

Heat, everything was hot. Damn. He had given her a full dose of his glamour and left her sensitive to the slightest thing. Right now it was heat, and it was coming from her clit. Perhaps it had something to do with the dark head between her thighs working his tongue into the folds and petals of her sex, flicking her clit with his tongue on the upstroke, sipping at her nectar as she flowed freely.

She refused to moan, her throat was aching and air was whistling in and out of her lungs with a vengeance. She was normally vocal when she had sex, but she was damned if she would give the dragon the satisfaction.

Her fingers dug into the sheets she was lying on and her thighs flexed in reaction to his ministrations. She began to shiver and recognized that her orgasm was an instant away, so did he. He pulled away, and replaced his mouth with the erection that she had admired earlier.

Her lip was bloody where she had bit through it. And with her eyes closed, she never saw his face approaching hers, but she did feel the delicate flick of his tongue in harsh contrast to the heavy thrusts of his hips. He carefully licked the blood off her mouth.

She opened her eyes in statement and that is when it hit her. Her orgasm roared through her, and her eyes were on his when the pleasure storm hit. Her mouth opened, but she still refused to make a sound. Her body shook and spasmed around him, then slowly relaxed, one muscle at a time.

He frantically thrust into her quiescent body and shook in his own release, his head resting on her shoulder, his teeth digging lightly into her.

"You taste like the forest." It was the first sentence she had heard since she came too.

"You taste like a dragon." It was heat, musk and magic.

"But you are human as well, it is in your blood."

That irritated her. "Why are you tasting my blood?"

"Because, I have you in my power and I want to know more about you."

"You have me in your power? How?"

"Check your ankle."

The conversation had been held while his head was on her shoulder, his cock softening within her. His weight kept her from moving.

She slowly lifted her left ankle and saw a manacle there. She tugged at it and it was attached to a chain, probably bolted to the floor.

She took a deep breath, absorbing the scents of sex, dragon, musk and the room, then sent a bolt of power through her leg to blast off the manacle. It didn't budge, but the power did fly around the room, as if seeking a home. Eventually zapping her in the right buttock.

"Ow! What the hell was that?" Her hand belatedly went to the damaged spot.

"You tried to open the lock?" His head was still in the joint between her neck and shoulder. She felt his tongue snake out to lick at the little wound he had left behind. She shivered and felt her nipples rise in response against his chest. Her skin healed as his tongue lapped at her wound, closing under the effect of his saliva. He began to swell inside her, as he tasted her blood.

"Of course I did!" What did he think? That she jumped and slapped herself in the ass all the time?

"Why don't you just enjoy yourself for now?"

"Because you have me shackled to the bed?!"

A wave of lust went through her—that damned magic again. He had no qualms about throwing her into a frenzy of lust. "Is it really so bad?"

"It isn't that. I just like to be on top." She pouted prettily and he raised his head to look her in the eye. After a long moment staring into his golden eyes, she found herself flipped through the air and she landed astride him. His hard shaft still buried to the hilt within her.

All of the air huffed out of her lungs and she shivered and gasped as another wave of magic ran through her. "That's cheating!" Her hands braced against his abdomen to keep her torso from collapsing against him.

An innocent smile was her answer. "What is?" Considering that his hands had reached up to fondle her breasts, and were devilishly working her nipples, the innocent act was taking it a little far.

"Running magic through me like that!"

His hips rose against her and she felt the deep stroke to her soul. "Oh? What ever could be wrong with it?"

"It's giving you an unfair advantage." She began to raise and lower her hips, riding him with slow, luxurious strokes.

"Ah, well, against women, I'll take any advantage that I can." As she lowered her hips with a twist and a rocking motion, he thrust upward. Hard.

She shrieked and went over the edge again, forgetting her vow not to let him hear her scream.

Her body arched against his and he held her hips to him, letting her have the full measure of her release as he rocked her against him. As she subsided, and her dazed eyes met his, he grinned again and flipped her so that she was now beneath him, on her knees.

She mewled as he pulled out of her to reposition them, and gasped as he thrust deep once more. This time, driving for his own pleasure. She heard the harsh breathing and the sharp slapping sounds as they came together. Her body pushed back to meet his oncoming thrusts as her gasping took on a more urgent tone.

She had always had a 'hair trigger' and it didn't take her long to dance on the edge of her orgasm once again. This time he was with her, and as he began to pulse and shudder inside her, she felt his teeth digging into her shoulder once again.

The combination of pleasure and pain was too much and she screamed, trying to buck him off as her own body shivered and convulsed in a welter of confused sensations.

His weight bore her to the bed and she floated through her own mind absently. Thinking about how warm he was, and how heavy. She dozed off, only vaguely noting that he slipped out of her body and curled her against him before he nodded off as well. One hand held her hips against him, and the other cupped a breast. Wow, he was warm.

A phone was ringing. It was a cell phone. No other ring could be that annoying. The warmth went away and she looked up, frowning.

"Hello?" Decklyn was standing beside the bed, his back to her. Man, he had a great ass.

"Yes, Dominick. She's fine."

"The Az demon never showed up." He nodded to the voice on the other end of the line. "She's going to stay with me until we get this settled."

He turned and found her watching his backside. "Sure, she's right here."

He extended his hand to her, and she took the phone, winking at his smirking face.

"Hi, Dad." She rolled her eyes and glared at the dragon as he started to flex for her benefit. A series of muscleman poses almost had her laughing at him, she threw a pillow at him instead.

"Hey, Walnut. How are you?"

"I'm fine. What's going on?"

"Well, you know that trouble that Alby and Imaran had with the Az demon that his ex sent after her?" He had ducked out of the way and was now weighing the pillow in his palm. He shrugged, dropped it and went into an adjoining room.

"Yeah." She was wary now. That had almost cost her cousin her life.

"It's after you."

"WHAT?!"

She heard a deep sigh, and knew that her father was trying not to hide anything from her. "Apparently the demon decided that since Alby wasn't killed, and you helped with the lamp misdirection, you had to be to blame."

"Oh, crap."

"Cathal is coming after you. He has put a hit out on you."

"Oh, crap."

"That is why I contacted Decklyn. He's willing to protect you, for a price."

"What price?"

Now her father got quiet, which was not like him. He was normally very forthright with her.

"What price, Dad?"

"He wants a child. That means a woman who isn't sensitive to dragon venom. In this case, that means you."

"So this was an elaborate charade? My going to his office and his appointment with RR? Is Bethany in on this?" Okay, she was a bit shrill—a demon was after her—she felt entitled.

"No. No, Walnut. Decklyn had his choice of ways to get to you. We just left it up to him. He thought that it might be the best way to get you alone."

She put her forehead in one hand and began to rub at the tension that was rising. "Fine, so did you take care of my equipment and my car?"

"Yes, they are both at your house. Safe and sound."

"How is Mom taking this?"

"Not well. She has every plant in a six hundred mile radius from your location, watching for any disturbances. The second Cathal moves, the Warders will be there."

"If I'm not dead by then."

"Walnut! Don't say things like that. Decklyn is going to keep you safe. No matter what."

"Sorry, I love you, Dad. Take care of yourself."

"You too, Walnut. Be safe." The line went dead and she disconnected the phone.

Stunned, she sat still against the pillows. She shifted her left leg and heard the clink of the manacle against the chain. This was not how she had planned her week to go.

Chapter Four

DECKLYN HAD LEFT THE ROOM DURING HER PHONE CONVERSATION. SHE LOOKED around and found an open door. The flushing noise gave her a good idea as to the nature of his departure.

He wandered back into the room, completely unconcerned with his nudity. Fine with her, she was never one for clothes if she could help it. She sat back against the headboard with one leg bent, the other straight in front of her.

"So, you have gallantly offered your services to assist me in avoiding the hit on me?" Her thighs were sticky with cum. The scent was thick in the room. He sat facing her on the edge of the bed.

"Well, it isn't like I wasn't offered something in return." His hand caressed the bite that he had left on her neck, a blue trace appearing under her skin. It was the venom that he had injected her with, beginning its journey through her system.

It used to be thought that a dragon's lust would kill a woman, but later it was found that it was the venom they exuded when they tried to reproduce that did the job. To breed a dragon, the egg needed to be fortified to support the offspring. The venom acted in this manner. It ran through the mother's bloodstream and toughened the DNA in the egg, infusing it with the magic needed to support a dragon.

For a normal woman, this process had the effect of draining her, leaving her womb unable to support life after the dragonet had been born. She would only have the one child.

Magical creatures were better able to tolerate the venom and the effect on their eggs. Decklyn had probably jumped at the chance to have a magical female handed to him.

"You know that he had no right to offer me to you?" She had all the power of the modern woman's fury at her disposal. No one had the right to hand her off.

"Not by dragon standards. The father has the right to arrange the mating of any of his female offspring."

"I am not a dragon."

He was stroking her hair now, untangling it absently. "No, but your great-great-grandfather was. Livonath was the one who gave me the rights to you. Your father only gave me the information that I needed to keep you safe."

"Livonath gave his blessing? When?"

"Thirty years ago, when you were born."

That impressed her, a little. "And you waited this long? Wow, I hate to wait for microwave popcorn."

"Arranged matings are the dragon way. You are worth every second that I waited." His golden eyes were glowing violently again. She knew what that meant.

"Oh, no, mister. Not until I clean up." She put one hand out and slapped it over his mouth as he started to bring his head to hers. She felt his lips twitch against her palm and smiled. "I am sticking to myself, and everything else here."

"Did you know that your cum tastes like maple syrup?" His eyes were dancing as he mumbled that observation against her hand.

"Yes, I did." She stood on wobbly legs. "Now you can change the sheets, so that I am no longer the victim of the wet spot, and I am taking a shower."

She walked and noted the long coil of chain under the bed. "Will it reach?"

"It should, but I've never actually tested it." That made her feel better for some reason. Jealousy? Nah.

She couldn't close the door with the chain there, but it did reach into the shower. First, she used the rest of the facilities, and in the time-honoured tradition, he had left the seat up. *Men. Lots of fun, but hard to housebreak.*

The shower felt fantastic, the hot water pounding on her stiff muscles. She stretched as best she could in the shower stall, soaping everything and wincing at the soreness between her thighs. It had been a while since her muscles had had a workout like that. She had to leave the shower door open a crack as well, damn that chain.

So, Livonath had offered his granddaughter to Decklyn. She wondered absently what he must have paid for the privilege of getting her pregnant. Dragon compatible females didn't come cheap. Especially ones who had the bloodlines to start with.

She used his shampoo, noting that he had conditioner as well, a rarity in a guy. Her hair hung to well below her shoulders, and she normally kept it bound in a braid. The damned stuff was so thin that the slightest wind would wrap it around and throw it into the air. She hoped that he had a brush.

As she rinsed off her hair, she moved to the edge of the shower, blinking water out of her eyes and groping for a towel. A strong warm hand brought it to her, and she laughed in surprise at the greedy look that Decklyn was giving her wet, slick form.

She wrapped the towel around her, tucking it in over her breasts and reached for another to dry her hair with. "Hands off, mister. Unless you're planning on doing my hair."

She clanked past him with her head held high. The rustle of the chain on the floor setting a weird beat as she moved.

Anryn smiled at the freshly made bed, and the tray of crackers and cheese that he prepared. Or that she thought he prepared. A second tray of fruits floated in on ghostly hands and she realized that he had a spirit servant.

"So, did you make the bed? Or did your flying buddy here do it?" She took a seat in one of the comfy chairs in the corner near the window, and began to dry her hair with brisk movements.

"Jeeves is a great butler, but he got the food. I made the bed." And he was lounging on it with an invitation in his eyes. She ignored him. His golden skin and mouth-watering erection were difficult to ignore, but she wanted some answers.

"What did you give to Livonath for his descendant?"

"Mining rights to a small mine in Arizona." His knee was waving as he watched her struggle with her hair. "The brush is in that drawer." Decklyn jerked his head over to the dressing table near the window.

"Thanks. Did you approach him? Or did he approach you?" After opening two other drawers, she found the brush.

"I approached him. I had known your father for some time, and figured that any daughter of his would be exceptional. Livonath was not known to treat his women folk well, so I thought it best that I step in as soon as possible."

"Here is the other question, why did you wait thirty years to come get me? And why the elaborate charade?" She struggled with the brush. It was a little too large for her hand.

"This modern world is a little more complicated. I wanted to make sure that I was ready to support a family in the appropriate, modern manner."

She was wrestling the brush through the tangled tresses and at his sentence, she froze. Laughter bubbled out of her in waves. She put the brush down, and hooted with mirth. That was too funny.

In an era where a growing percentage of children did not even know their fathers, he was worried about spending time and money on children who did not even exist yet. Dragons were obsessive parents for the most part, Livonath being the exception. He had spread his seed in as many women as he could, leaving his bastards to starve or survive on their own. Like her great-grandmother, Eisha.

As the tears of laughter faded, she looked over at the serious and protective dragon that was laying claim to all of her offspring. He would probably make a great father, but a tyrant of a husband.

Whoa. Where the hell did that come from? She peered over at him through squinted eyes. He was wearing that same innocent look as he had when he had pumped enough magic through her to light up a small city. He was using his damned talents on her again. Either that, or they had started bonding. She shuddered slightly, that would be bad.

"Stop that." Anryn was scowling now. Her earlier laughter forgotten. "Stop using glamour on me. It's tacky."

"Glamour? What glamour?" The innocence was in full bloom now. He could have posed for the Renaissance painting of an angel.

She scowled harder. "The one that is telling me what a wonderful father you would make."

"But it's true. And you missed part of it."

"I don't doubt it, and what part exactly?" Now it was her turn to be all innocence. She glanced into the dressing table mirror and winced. She looked like a wind-blown whore. Her eyes were wide, lips bruised and her hair was still half-tangled. The towel only covered the lower half of her breasts—the upper cleavage was a little inviting.

"The part about me being a good husband. I will be, you know." He stood and began to approach her. Lifting her from her chair, he held her and sat back down with her in his lap. "Give me the brush."

Mutely, she did so. He continued his explanation. "I have been working these thirty years to establish myself in the human community as a venture capitalist. It has been my every effort to create a human persona with a steady income and a sterling reputation in the business community."

"First, I had to get birth records, then set up an imaginary family that would be able to inherit my fortune as I aged. The transfer from my original persona to Decklyn Ringler occurred five years ago. Then all I had to do was wait for you."

She was astonished. There was more to being a magical creature leaving Realm than she had thought. "Me? Why did you wait?"

"You seemed to be having so much fun with your friends and family that I didn't want to intrude." His hands kept brushing in long slow strokes, he had made short work of the tangles and was now only dragging the brush through to sooth her. Like an upset cat.

"You do know that whatever we do end up as, I am not leaving my family, or friends."

At this he scowled, "Dragons are solitary by nature."

She crossed her arms over her chest, "Tough. I'm not." Something moved out of the corner of her eye. She turned her head just in time to catch a glimpse of something in the mirror.

"Uh, Decklyn? Are you sure that you are up to taking on Cathal?"

"Who?" He was a little distracted by the silk of her hair. Even with his shampoo, it smelled distinctly like her.

"The Az demon."

"Yes, why?"

"Because, it's watching us from the mirror right now!" She darted out of his grasp and jumped for the door, only to be brought up short by the shackle on her leg. She had made it into the hall outside the master suite and fallen flat on her face. Twenty feet was her maximum distance it seemed.

"Calm down, Anryn. It can't get through the wards." He had moved to put himself between her and the mirror.

"It did at the Lakin Estate. Blasted right through them!" She began to fire magic at the shackle in her panic, waves of prickling pain spread through her as she found herself unable to stop. The hysteric fear of being chained like bait filled her and she screamed as the pain flowed over her, taking her into darkness.

Chapter Five

"Walnut. Walnut, wake up." Her mother's voice was calling her. Its gentle cadence pouring over her in a soothing wave.

She was in her own bed, in her own home. "I don't want to go to school!" She rolled over and buried her face in the pillows. Laughter erupted in the room around her. Two men and her mother.

"Walnut, you don't have to go to school, but you do have to get up. Decklyn is worried about you."

"Decklyn who?" She pouted and pulled herself upright, noting the white nightgown that her father must have insisted on. She looked into the dragon's stricken face and sighed. "Come here Deck."

He sat next to her, apologies in his eyes, and she quickly drew his head down to kiss him. "It's okay. I am assuming that the demon didn't get me?"

"No, but you were right. Cathal did break through the wards. It will take him a while to rebuild his energy, so your parents thought that you would be more comfortable in your own home."

She looked closely at him, he was wearing a buttoned shirt and trousers again, and she thought she could smell… "Did he hurt you?" It was blood. Decklyn's blood. Tiny pinpricks had seeped through the shirt.

"Nothing that I haven't had done to me before. I'm far more worried about you. You almost drained yourself while fighting the shackle." He caressed her hair, sifting the black silk through his fingers.

"I panicked." She blushed.

He smiled, "I noticed."

"I wasn't expecting the attack, and then I couldn't defend myself, or get away. I freaked."

"It's alright, under the circumstances I should never have confined you. Even if it is dragon tradition. At least until this matter was finished."

They locked eyes and reached an understanding. She read a question in his eyes. "What? What do you want to know?"

He leaned in and whispered in her ear, "Why do your parents call you Walnut?"

"Because she fell out of trees and never broke." Dominick's voice was right beside them and their heads turned as one to look at him. "If you two are finished, we need to make a plan for the next attack by the Az."

"I always thought it was because my head was shaped funny, huh. Who knew?" Anryn shrugged and looked back to Decklyn. "Shall we?"

"Indeed." He scooped her up and took her out of the bedroom and through her hallways to the living room.

"Why did you decide on my house?" He set himself down on the couch with her in his lap, the white nightgown flowing virginally around her.

She couldn't be sure if he was blushing or not, but he looked embarrassed. "Yours is the best warded house in the state. Nothing is getting in here."

Oh, right. She had put all of her weekends alone into wards on her property. "Ah, well. Everybody needs a hobby."

"Walnut, how many layers do you have on this house?" Her mother settled in next to them, her scent like flowers in the rain. Anryn breathed deeply and was instantly calm. It was amazing what the familiar scent of your mother could do for you.

"Around forty-seven. Maybe a few more. Why?" She looked absently around her home. All was in order. The flowers in the window were blooming, the plants were lush. Her backyard was wild and untamed, the tree house visible from where they sat.

"Do you see what I mean?" Dominick looked from his daughter to her lover. A lifetime of living with a driven female in his eyes.

Decklyn started to move underneath her, and she felt his laughter, "Yes, I am beginning to see."

"Okay, enough. Lets talk strategy." She crossed her arms across her chest and glared at both of the men, quite sure that she knew what they were talking about. So she was a tad obsessive, so what?

"Fine. Let me get the tea." Mylawith rose gracefully and ran around the kitchen for a few moments. She returned with a full tea service, cups and saucers on a tray.

Mylawith loved tea, and as she served them, it showed in her graceful and economical movements. The heady scent of the wild berry blend filled the room, and Anryn smiled at the memories of childhood that it evoked. As the tart sweetness rolled across her tongue, she was suddenly five again and talking about her first day of school.

When everyone had a cup of tea in their hands, she sat back. "Alright. I think that after this one attempt at a frontal assault, Cathal is going to try a new strategy."

"Or an old one." Anryn sipped delicately at the tea, then took the rest of the cup in one heated gulp. She had never achieved her mother's grace and style. She had dropped more cups than she could count.

"What do you mean?" Decklyn was just as serious as her parents. Everyone was now looking at her.

"When he attacked Albina's he made a deal with a human. I think he might try it again." She gave her mother the empty tea cup, and she suffered Mylawith's reproachful glance. A lady was supposed to sip her tea. That is what the books had said.

When Mylawith married Dominick, she studied human etiquette and society so that she would fit in. The glamour that she used in public made her appear to be Mediterranean. She was expected to behave like a lady.

She had tried to raise her daughter the same way, but her little Walnut would never do anything with delicacy and grace. It was always full steam ahead.

"Deck, do you have any humans that he may use?"

"Do I have any humans? No." He did look puzzled.

Anryn decided to let him in on something. "Your house is warded right?"

"Yes."

"Then how did he find me? No one knew where I was except you and Dad." A dawning sense of horror was crossing Decklyn's face.

"Your receptionist, right? You told her that you would be at home for a few days. And she connected my appearance with your disappearance." She patted his shoulder to comfort him. "I thought I smelled demon on her, but I thought I was imagining things."

"Ariane couldn't be the one. She is totally professional." He was sputtering now. Anryn got stiffly to her feet and faced him.

"If it wasn't her, then come up with someone else who knows where you were. My father was behind his own set of wards and couldn't have been the one. And my mother is a dryad, she is immune to demonic influence." She began to stretch, her body rolling from one pose to another.

"I'm going to go climb. I need to think." She walked to the back door and went out into the afternoon sun.

Decklyn was stunned. He had never thought that *he* could have brought the danger to her. As she crossed the backyard, she stripped off the nightgown and he noted that her parents were sitting quietly, their eyes fixed and looking within. Telepathy. Damn. He wondered if he and Anryn would develop the same ability. There were some signs already. He'd felt her panic back at his home, and her gentle acceptance of him when she woke. That had to be something.

He followed Anryn to the yard and watched her climb the tree. She wasn't a creature of the woods, but she was at home there. Her muscles stretched and grew taut as she pulled her body up the tree. She was fifty feet in the air when she reached her tree house. She dangled her legs off the porch and stared into the sunset. He wanted to leave her to her reverie, but more than that, he wanted to join her.

There was no way that he was climbing that tree. So that left one option. Shedding his shirt, exposing the burn marks to the fading light, he shifted into his winged human form. The warrior shape. In this form, he could speak, fight, fly, and mate.

Bending his knees, he pushed off and shoved down with his wings and a burst of magic. He circled the tree slowly, climbing ever higher, until he was engaged in a shaky hover near Anryn.

She had watched his ascent with bemusement. This was new. Although she had seen several dragons in her lifetime, this was the first time she had seen one in flight. He was gorgeous. His skin was now a rich, navy blue. His eyes a startling contrast, yellow against the blue. His wings were enormous, the heavy strokes needed to keep him in flight blasting her with gusts of wind.

"For winds sake, sit down!" She moved aside and he landed next to her. She could see the marks that the demon had left, and winced at the healing scabs on his dark skin.

"This is quite the tree house."

"It has three bedrooms, I used to invite Ruana and Albina to camp out. When I moved from my parents' place, they said I could take it with me."

That puzzled him. "But the tree is grown through it. How did you move just the house?"

"We didn't. This is my tree. It has seven hundred wards on it. My father started on them the day I was born. It walked here." She leaned back and the leaves rustled in contentment.

"What will it do when you come to live with me?"

"If you have a safe place for it, it will walk to us."

"Us?"

"Yeah, us." She stroked her hand up his thigh, kneading at the muscles as she went.

White pointed teeth gleamed in the dark face and his eyes danced with glee. "That reminds me. I owe you a massage."

Faster than she could move, he had her up in his arms and was walking into the tree house. He looked around the comfortable living room, and walked into the first open doorway. A bedroom. Score!

"Do you have any oil around here?"

"None that you are getting your hands on, mister." He had dropped her onto her belly on the small double bed. It was only a mattress on a frame on the floor, but it would do. She craned her head around and tried to keep him in her sights. No use. He found her stash.

"Well, well. What have we here?" He lifted a box out of the chest at the end of the bed.

She buried her face in the covers and tried not to hear Decklyn rummaging through her collection of sex toys.

Chapter Six

Judging by the sound of bees behind her, he had found her vibrator. He was humming softly to himself as he planned his attack. He switched the toy off and continued to sort through her dildos, clips, gels and lubes.

"Before I start with your massage, are you sure that this place is completely warded against attack? Not that it will stop me, but it might keep me from getting lost in the moment."

"I would love to lie, but I will know if anything even comes on the property."

Delight was heavy in his tone, "Oh, someone will definitely cum on this property, but not until I say so."

"Oh, hells." Her head was under a pillow now. She was trying to pretend that he wasn't blocking her exit from the room in her tree house. Despite her trepidation, she had a throbbing in her clit. Her body would love whatever he chose to do, and the moisture that she was producing was ample proof. He hadn't even touched her yet and she was almost ready to cum.

She heard the click of a bottle, and the snorting noise that always accompanied the lube leaving the container. She didn't feel anything.

With two strong hands moving as one, he started a kneading motion on her shoulders without any warning. She almost jumped out of the bed in surprise. His thumbs ran a strong line down her spine and she arched and purred in reaction. Based on the smell, it was one of her 'heat on contact' oils.

"You are a vocal thing aren't you? Funny. I hadn't realized. You were so quiet the first time, I hardly knew your were breathing." He was enjoying this. Her body throbbed where he touched her and the oil kept the sensation repeating.

"Mff..." Anryn squirmed under his hands, the feel of the oil on his hands building her arousal until she couldn't stand it anymore. Then he was gone.

"Hey! What the hell? Yikes!" She had begun to rise from the bed in protest to his absence and suddenly she felt something cold and thick on her ass. She only had one toy designed for that and she had bought it on a self-dare. She had used it once and then promptly tried to forget that she bought it.

Sure enough, with delicate and deliberate insistence, the butt plug was slowly creeping into her ass. "Shh, just relax and push against it. It won't hurt a bit."

She took a deep breath and forced herself to relax. The plug slid home and she whimpered in discomfort. Her ass clenched and relaxed against the toy, trying to both pull it deeper and expel it.

Decklyn flipped her onto her back and looked at her discomfited face. "Aw, doesn't it feel good?"

"Not particularly. No."

"Then why do you have it?"

"It was an experiment. It failed."

"Maybe you just didn't do it right." He spread her thighs wide and carefully inspected the arrangement between them. Her pubic hair was trimmed neatly in a triangle that left her inner and outer labia bare. He could clearly see the anal plug base where it was resting and noted the sign of juice that was leaking from within her channel and following gravity's trail.

A light touch from his finger and her inner lips fell open, exposing deep green petals around a pink bud. Her clit was standing at attention and as he watched another tiny trickle of her juices leaked out and trickled down to her ass. So, she didn't like the plug. But it seemed her body did. Hmm.

He continued her massage by oiling his hands and massaging her breasts. The steady motion of his hands had her arching and purring again. He moved his hands across her belly and to her thighs, then changed his focus.

He picked up one of the smaller vibrators and played it gently along the open slit. His composure buckled and he reached out with two fingers to taste her. Sweetness. Just like maple syrup.

"Taste yourself."

"What?"

He took her hand and used his to glide it down her body. To her flowering sex. She took over, dipping one, then two fingers into her channel and bringing them out to circle around her clit. Her fingers stayed hard and flat as they circled it, then she drew her fingers to her mouth and licked delicately at the slick juice that they were coated with.

His cock nearly exploded. His skin flushed from blue to black with lust. He took a calming breath and started again.

Two of his fingers slid into her, gently moving in and out of her, curling them upward, searching for the g-spot. When her hips arched and her eyes fluttered, he knew he was on the right track. He stroked against the spot with a rapid motion, his fingers using her lubrication to ease the strokes.

She started to shake and make that mewling noise that he loved to hear, and then she squeaked and came. It was a shivering orgasm, not a bucking one. Her whole body shivered for a few long seconds, then relaxed.

He started again. Leaving the plug in place in her pert little ass, he began to suck on her nipples. First the left, then the right, and as soon as both mounds of olive flesh were tight with arousal, he brought out the clamps.

She winced as the first one clipped onto her nipple, then again as the second one arrived in place. She had them set for a comfortable pain. Light compression without loss of blood flow. Her favourite setting. However, since he had kneaded, chewed and sucked on them, they were a little more swollen than normal, which increased the sensations.

He could immediately tell that she liked the clips. Her clit shivered again to attention and her pussy began to weep with excitement. “Mmm. Progress.”

His head dipped and his tongue found its way into her navel, then trailed lower licking his way down her right thigh, to the knee, then making his way up to her vagina. She was moaning and sighing in a relaxed arousal that he had generated. She bit at her lip in her distraction and tangled her hands in hair.

She simply drew her fingers through the thick strands of his hair as he teased her flesh with his tongue lapping up the juices as they flowed from her. Sweet, so sweet. She could feed a hummingbird out of her pussy if she wanted to.

He withdrew his ministrations for a moment, and just watched. Her hips were shifting in their own rhythm. Her breasts heaving and shoulders shaking at the pressure of the nipple clamps. She may not prefer the anal plug, but it did work for her.

He slowly crawled up her body, kissing his way as he went, finding a spot below her navel that made her moan, and almost made her cum. Sweat was coating her body, she was sighing and moaning almost constantly now. He continued up to her neck, and the head of his desperate cock was nudging for entrance between her slick petals. He slid in to the hilt in one long motion as he reached her neck and jaw.

She began to shake the instant he started to thrust, his cock pressing against the anal plug through her delicate skin, her body completely sensitized to his touch. He picked up the thrusts and lifted her hips to drive deeply into her to get his own release in her sweet womb. Her orgasmic shocks burst through her with every pulse of his cock past her g-spot. She screamed and then stopped, her eyes fluttering shut.

He was amazed at her sudden silence, only to realize that his sex companion was asleep.

Unable to stop, he pushed his hips into hers and felt his cock spurt its payload inside her. Even asleep, she grunted as he came inside her.

She awoke to silence. Then she heard him breathing. The chirping of birds alerted her to the dawn that had started without them. *Damn, I slept all night!*

She sat up and checked. Oh, thank gods, he had removed the plug and the clips. She was so going to trash that plug. Although, she did go off like a rocket with it inside her. Maybe she wouldn't destroy it quite yet.

She stretched and looked at her companion. He was in full human now. She shook him awake, and said, "We have to finish meeting with my parents. I have an idea."

He shrugged "Okay, how do we get down."

"Oh that's easy. There is a lift on the other side of the tree. You must have missed it last night." Her smile was angelic. She thought about the way that the light came in through the window and danced across his skin.

He smiled. *Thank you. You look amazing this morning as well.*

She looked at him with her mouth hanging open. *You heard that? Oh, crap.* She looked at him in dawning horror. She could distinctly hear him in her mind.

Yep. I think we are bonding. He looked terribly smug, as if this had been part of his plan all along.

Oh, crap. She buried her head in her hands and shook herself. This was so not the way she had thought her week would go. Developing a mental bond with Decklyn was not on her list.

She showed him the lift, and let him do the muscle work to haul the basket up the tree. They wandered across the yard and she stopped and put the nightgown back on, for her father's comfort. Decklyn took her hand and led her into the house, then started the coffee.

Her parents were asleep in her bed, so she bounded in and jumped on the end of it. "Wake up. I've figured it out."

They sat up blinking sleep from their eyes. Even after over thirty years together, her mother and father still held each other as they slept. She only hoped that she and Deck would be as happy.

Whoa. Where did that thought come from? With a final bounce on the bed, she left them to their waking.

She got breakfast ready. Fruit for her mom, and eggs, sausage and bacon for the guys and herself. Mom had always despaired of her lack of vegetarianism. She had given birth to an omnivore, and there were no two ways about it.

As they all gathered for the meal, Anryn dropped her little bombshell. "We'll need to use me as bait. I'll go into Deck's office after work and make sure that she calls the demon to come and kill me. It's the only way to get it over with quickly." She gnawed on a sausage and kept her eyes on the dragon. He seemed as upset with the solution as her parents were, but he gave in.

"It's stupid, risky and idiotic. But it will work. Az demons don't have the longest attention span. They don't have any patience. He'll jump at the first chance to kill her."

"Will you promise me, that you will not let anything happen to my little girl?" Dominick was sombre.

Mylawith's green eyes were flashing. "Yes, if anything happens to her, only the wastes will be hospitable to you. Nowhere that has anything green and growing will accept you."

"I hereby swear, that I will allow no harm to come to Anryn Warder. Your daughter and my mate." He bit his finger and bled on the table. A burst of magic and the blood exploded. "That will be my fate should I fail to protect her."

"Wow, folks. That is kind of serious isn't it? I mean, he didn't need to make a blood oath for it."

"This is a serious matter." Her father merely looked at Decklyn in satisfaction.

She shuddered and hoped for Decklyn's sake that she came out of this in one piece. "Fine, now for phase one. Calling Ariane and telling her you will come to work late, then when you get in, you will be expecting a guest to pick you up at seven."

"What's phase two?"

"I find a slutty outfit that will tick her off, and make her summon the demon while I am there."

"Oh, I'll help with that." Dominick rolled his eyes at his wife's outburst, but she was good at fashion, even the slutty kind.

Six hours later Decklyn had gone to work, scowling the whole way. Five hours after that, she was ready to enact phase three. Set off the secretary. Easy. She took a deep breath as the door to the elevator opened and she saw her nemesis at her post.

Chapter Seven

"What's the matter, Ariane? Didn't expect to see me again?" She sauntered forward, hips swinging, breasts barely bound by a delicate wisp of a bra that only supported her by a stretching of the term support. She had left her hair loose, the better to confound her enemy. The black silk hung heavily down her back and almost reached her butt. She knew she looked good.

Ariane looked appalled.

She plastered her best sex-kitten grin on her face and parked her breasts on the top of Ariane's computer. "Please let Decks know that I'm here, okay?"

"Decks?"

"Oh, sorry." She let out a cutesy giggle. "I mean Decklyn Ringler. Could you let him know that Anryn Warder is here?"

Ariane looked like she wanted to punch someone. Namely Anryn. "Just have a seat. Please."

She smiled brightly at the receptionist and took a seat, crossing her legs and exposing her thighs to all and sundry. Her skirt rode up and she opened her purse to touch up her makeup.

"Mr. Ringler, there is a *person* here to see you." Her voice could have frozen steel. The scent of demon was rising hard. The faster that she got irritated, the faster she would summon Cathal.

"He'll be with you in a moment. Please excuse me."

She's left me alone, you had better get out here.

On my way. Try and keep a low profile.

She looked aimlessly around the room, and only then noticed that the damned doors to the elevator were mirrored. "Oh, crap."

She backed against the solid wall in the centre of the hub and watched the flame and smoke eyes of the demon come through the mirror, attached to a very large and scary body. Twelve feet of fang and scale of a blood red hue were approaching her with a deadly leer in his eyes.

"Cathal, I presume?"

His claws were flexing in a preliminary practice of rending her flesh. "You cost me my reputation, bitch."

"Nope. You screwed up, Cathal. Everybody knows that you can't hold a djinn in a glass vessel." She rolled her eyes in exacerbation. "How dumb can you be?"

"Die bitch!" Saliva flew from his mouth and he charged.

She cowered against the wall and pulled her magic into a column of protection. It wouldn't last long, but it might buy her some time. She had no time to pull up a full ward.

She ducked under his claws and rolled out from under his reach. She flipped off her shoes and ducked his second charge as well. His third scored her skin and she shrieked as he cut through the upper portion of her thigh. It continued to burn after he had been pulled from her cringing body by a roaring dragon.

"Holy winds!" It was a breath of amazement. In the room before her was a fully formed dragon. Navy blue scales were glowing in the lights thrown by the office fixtures. He was crouched tightly with his wings folded against his back and was munching the demon in his jaws.

Cathal was screaming. But soon his screams died as his limbs and body parted company. Anryn watched in horrified amazement. It took a while for him to consume the demon, apparently they were really chewy.

The dragon finished eating the traces of Cathal and looked over at his mate.

"Decklyn? Wow. You look great." The enormous head nuzzled her, leaving demon blood on her blouse and skirt. "Eww." His tongue flicked out and trailed over the claw marks that the demon had left behind. They began to close immediately.

"Thanks. How are you going to get out of here? I don't think you'll fit in the elevator."

Don't worry, I have a special exit for just such an occasion. He shook his head in amusement. It almost bowled her over.

Care for a ride? He dropped his head and licked his muzzle in anticipation. He knew something that she didn't. *"Hop on."*

Shrugging in resignation, she hopped up onto his foreleg, then had to hike her skirt up to her hips to put one thigh on either side of his neck. The ridge of his neck rubbed her between her thighs and she felt her panties growing damp as he began to walk to one of the transparent walls.

Oh, you are so evil. You knew about this. He refused to comment and let out a snort as he tripped a switch with one claw, and the wall swung open, letting in the evening air. His steady motion through the hallways was beginning to have the effect that he had anticipated.

Hang on, Anryn, don't let go! With that he launched himself out of the window and opened his wings to glide across the cityscape. She was too busy hanging on for dear life as the ground dipped and swayed as he began to pump his wings in powerful strokes. The heavy beats lifted them away from the earth and into the stars as she tried to keep her balance.

Having achieved his preferred altitude, Decklyn began to glide forward, only beating his wings to keep them high above the city below. *Open your eyes, Anryn. See what I see.*

She opened them and peeked. It was amazing.

The city below was spotted with lights, fireflies on a black sea. The landscape tumbled below them in a cloak of darkness and the stars glittered and gleamed, lighting their way home. She was seeing the night through his eyes, and it was beautiful.

The air smelled of forests and honey, a fresh scent. Under it all, she could smell herself as he breathed her in. She let him see himself as she did for a moment, and he almost fell out of flight.

She shrieked and clutched at the neck ridge as he dropped while trying to look at her. *Watch where you're flying!*

How can I, when I know that you find me beautiful.

I'll find you more beautiful if we land! I promise. In her mind, she heard him laugh and he wheeled into a turn, then began the trip home in earnest.

She eventually relaxed enough to unclench her thighs and the pleasurable sensations began all over again. The constant rubbing against her clit with every stroke of his wings was driving her nuts, and her breath came harder with every wing beat. Sparks began to fly behind her eyes and she came, shuddering and moaning with the burst of sensation.

As she fought to regain her breath, she could have sworn that she heard him chuckle. *There is nothing more unattractive than a smug dragon you know.*

Me? Smug? That was a cough.

Liar.

His eyes narrowed in laughter and she clutched him again as he began to descend. A slow spiral started and she could make out his house and yard in the dimness of the night. *Your house, huh?*

The danger is over, and I have Jeeves to wait on you hand and foot.

Hmm, you have a point. Let's go home.

Your wish is my command. His wings beat hard as he lowered his legs to land, keeping his neck up as he touched down.

Now that the wind wasn't rushing past her ears she could speak out loud again. "Hey, that is Imaran's line."

If he ever offers to grant your wishes, I'll eat him. He was serious. His head swivelled around to look at her in a solemn manner.

"Do you eat all your enemies? Or do you save that for special occasions."

I used to hunt werewolves. They were good. Taste like chicken.

She looked at him in horror. One of her cousins was a werewolf. Sure she couldn't change shape, but where would Decklyn draw the line.

Relax, Anryn. I don't eat family or friends. I have standards.

She skipped talking out loud. It was too tiring trying to meet his eyes as she spoke to him. Her neck wasn't up to it. She leaned her head against his scales. *Well, that's comforting. You had me worried.*

She thought of something that had slipped her mind. *What happened to Ariane? She didn't appear after she summoned Cathal.*

She's keeping him company.

Anryn felt ill, *You mean you ate her?*

When she came in to distract me, she spilled her little plot. She hated you and was making plans for the next demon. She was going to conjure a Druj next. I couldn't let her live.

Will you get in trouble?

No, of course not. The dragon council will do a memory wipe as soon as I contact them. Ariane will become a traffic accident, with no body.

Have they had to do this type of thing for you before?

Only since the 'information age'. What a pain in the ass.

So when are you going to change back to bipedal form so I can jump you?

In the morning. It takes a while to digest a demon. They are kind of chewy.

Ew.

Go in to bed. I'll be out here all night. His muzzle nudged at her gently, shoving her toward the house.

No. I am staying out here with you. Curl up, and I'll snuggle in. You are warm enough to keep me snug for days.

Alright. He shifted and wrapped his tail around and tucked his head on his rear leg. *C'mon in, sweetness.*

She climbed in over his limbs and snuggled down as he draped one wing across her to keep her warm. His heartbeat was so soothing that she was sleeping only a few minutes later. His muzzle touched her gently, and his tongue flicked out to taste her skin.

It would be worth a thousand battles to have her curled against him in this trusting manner again. Even knowing that he had eaten his receptionist, she still stayed the night with him. Whether or not she knew it, she was his forever, and he had just the way to keep tabs on her.

Chapter Eight

The next day dawned bright and clear. Decklyn woke before Anryn and slowly changed his shape to human. She blinked the sleep away as she found herself lying in the back yard and on top of his naked, human form. Her clothing was gone. Weird. She looked over and saw them in a pile of fabric and demon blood, next to her high-heeled shoes. She sighed as she came to grips with the fact that the clothes were ruined. The next time that Decklyn ate someone, she wasn't getting near him until he cleaned up.

She moved slowly, sliding her knees to either side of his hips, cradling his erection against her pussy. She rocked her hips against him—a lazy shifting that soon had his body surging for penetration. Because of her angle, he couldn't make the thrust into her channel and was being tortured by the slow writhing of her body against him.

His mouth tightened and he flipped their positions, her thighs spread wide, and the head of his cock pushing against her. He reached to trace her moist slit with one finger as his mouth moved to suckle her breast with savage ferocity.

He slid one finger into her, then two. She shuddered and shivered against him, all traces of sleep erased.

"Oh, winds! Just fuck me already Deck!"

He froze. That was not something that he had had on his list of possible happenings. "What exactly do you want?" His tone was sly.

She grabbed his chestnut hair and hauled him up to meet her eyes and told him graphically and concisely. "I want you to take your hard, throbbing cock and put it in my empty, aching cunt and fuck me senseless."

"I want you to pound into me as hard as you can and give me all that I can take. And when you cum inside me, I want you to start all over again." She smiled and took his mouth in a voracious kiss that almost made him cream right there. When she relaxed her grip and let him go she smiled with her lips swollen and moist. "Tag, you're it."

Shaking with lust, he pushed into her. Her head fell back as his lips found her neck and he bit down as his hips began to thrust his cock deeper and deeper into her with every stroke. She moaned as he pumped into her, sighing with every deep stroke and groaning as he pulled out. The pain from his teeth was rapidly turning into pleasure as the venom triggered a euphoric rush that raised her pleasure threshold until she thought she would fly apart before she came.

His thumb grazed across her clit with relentless pressure and she mewled and caught her breath as the coil tightened even more. "Deck, please."

His cock seemed to swell inside her, filling her as never before. He was huge, and the pressure made her feel fuller then ever before. With one more savage thrust, she came. The sparks flew behind her eyes and she squealed in her release.

The next thing she felt was a warm washcloth being stroked over her well-used flesh. She was in Decklyn's bed, but this time there was no shackle on her leg. Smart dragon.

Her thighs were being held apart by his knees as he cleaned the last traces of his seed from her skin. "Did I faint?"

His smile said it all. "Yep. Shrieked like a banshee too."

"Didn't I say that no one likes a smug dragon?"

"Yeah, but you still love one."

She froze. Her eyes searched his face, looking for any traces of mockery. "Yes, I do."

"You admit it. Good. I have something for you." He reached over her to the drawer beside the bed.

"If it's a condom, you're a little late."

He drew back a jewellery box and gave it to her, while on his knees between her thighs.

"This is for the mate that I choose for life. I had it made over a century ago, and never found a woman that I wanted to give it to." He watched her hold the box carefully. "Until now. Open it."

She slowly opened the box, and inside was a necklace made of navy blue opal. Or, that is what it looked like at first glance. It was a choker made of dragon scales set in platinum.

"Is this?"

"Yes."

"But these scales are tiny. Your scales are much larger." Her hands shook as she drew the choker out of the satin nest. She flicked her hair aside and fought to join the clasp.

"Let me." He moved to kneel behind her and fixed the choker into place.

"Those are my scales. They are from my member. They don't grow back."

"Your member…?" She looked down at his penis, and there, where she had never thought to look were tiny scars. "You would have had to have done it while in full form."

"Yes."

"It must have hurt like hell."

"Well, it is a necklace to mark my life mate. From the moment that I put it on her, my lifespan will be linked to hers. And hers to mine." There was a tiny snick and magic flowered around her.

A blossoming feeling of rightness ran through her. He was the one. The only one from now until she stopped drawing breath.

"Did I? Did you? Did we just…?" She was giddy with the magic, just like the first time.

He held her hands in his and caressed her palms with his thumbs. "Yes. We just did."

Her head fell forward, and their foreheads met. For long moments they simply sat still, letting the magic flow between them. "This has been one helluva week."

Chapter Nine

The day of Albina's wedding.

"DECKLYN, YOU'RE GOING TO HAVE TO COME WITH ME, OR LET ME OUT. ALBINA'S wedding is in two hours and I am going to be there. With or without you." Anryn stood and tapped her bare foot against the carpet. Decklyn was lounging in bed, glaring at her.

"You're pregnant, and not going anywhere without me."

"Then you'd better get dressed and get your ass moving, buddy. I am going to that wedding." She marched into the shower, scowling at the reflection of the blue tracery around her neck, just below the choker. The venom in his bite had found an eager recipient in her body, and she had begun to 'show' a week earlier. "I'm the freakin' maid of honour!"

He tried to enter the bathroom after her, and she glared at him in irritation, locking the door behind her. Dragons were notoriously possessive of their females when they were breeding. Decklyn was no exception. He wouldn't let her go to work, had begun corresponding his investments with his new executive assistantappily married harpy—and generally was taking over everything she did.

Her only comfort had been her mother, who was able to slip past the wards surrounding his estate. Mylawith had brought her junk food, trashy magazines and some of her clothes. Decklyn had found the clothes, the magazines and smelled the cheeseburger.

He then launched into a lengthy lecture on the evils of fat and constrictive clothing. As a result, Anryn had been running around naked for the last week. Now, enough was enough.

She made some calls. Delayed the wards at Morcalla's, talked to an extremely amused Albina, and made the final arrangements for the wedding in Realm. She faced the mirror and rapidly charged it for the transfer.

She heard the door to the bathroom splinter just as she crossed the threshold and as she looked back through the gateway, she saw him coming after her in fury.

She popped out of the mirror station in Realm and began to walk to the wedding tent. Astonished passers-by froze in their tracks as the naked dryad with obvious signs of a dragon's child wandered across the green fields.

Wedding guests that had arrived early and were from the groom's side, leered at her as she wandered in search of her family. The Warders and guests waved her to the Bride's tent.

"Anryn, for the love of the summer winds, get over here!" Mylawith was as surprised as her husband to see their daughter approaching them wearing nothing. She tucked her wrap around her daughter and herded her to the bride's tent, questioning her in hushed tones the whole way.

"Where the hell is Decklyn?"

"He was giving me a hard time about appearing in public, so I came without him."

"You broke his wards?"

"No. I just bent them out of shape to get my way."

"Ah, child. Where is he?" She shook her head at her daughter, then laughed. This was Anryn to a tea. Every time she didn't get her way, she just ploughed on through. You had to give in eventually.

"I think he got stuck in the transition. He'll probably arrive after the ceremony."

"Or he could be right behind you, Sweetness." Anryn's back stiffened at Decklyn's voice. She carefully kept from meeting his furious gaze and stayed with her mother.

"How do you do that? How is it that where ever I go, you are one step behind me?" She walked forward and kept her eyes on Albina's tent.

The other bridesmaids were inside and desperately trying to get all of the layers on the bride, without wrinkling the fabric. The fussy goblin supervising the process wasn't helping.

"Morcalla! Give it a rest, would you? Albina is nuts enough as it is." All eyes turned to Anryn, and kept going to Decklyn who had entered the tent behind her.

"Good gods, Anryn. You're not dressed yet." Morcalla was mortified and ran to the wardrobe on one side, gathering up armloads of fabric and approaching Anryn with the dresses. The nudity that she was currently sporting didn't faze her at all.

"Decklyn, I promise that you can punish me as much as you want, as soon as the reception is over. But, now, this is Albina's day, and I won't do anything to ruin it." She pressed herself to him, drawing his head down and mingling her breath with his. Slowly, and thoroughly he kissed her in response, letting her feel his teeth and pulling her hips into his with both hands.

There was no doubt that she would be 'punished' as soon as she let him get her alone. She could hardly wait.

"Uh, Anryn? I don't mean to wreck the moment for you, but your guy is naked, and I am getting married in an hour." Albina was serene, but a tiny frown puckered her brow. She was a blindingly beautiful bride. Each layer of fabric was gossamer, embroidered with delicate silk stitches. There would be twenty in all, to commemorate the number of species that the Warder women had mated with. It was a traditional djinn design, but with a Warder twist.

Her hair was wound with precious stones, and gold jewellery hung on every available piece of her. The necklaces alone must have weighed over ten pounds.

"Oh, I am sorry. Albina Ophelia Warder Lakin, this is Decklyn Ringler. Dragon and pain in the ass."

"Pleased to meet you." She reached out to shake his hand. Decklyn took one hand off his mate and took the ringed fingers in his own. The heavy scent of djinn magic was all over her, and he could make out the djinn marks behind the gossamer fabric on her breast.

"Congratulations on your wedding."

"Thank you. Now can you please get out of here before my fiancé gets wind of the fact that there is a naked dragon in the bride's tent?"

For the first time since she had met him, Decklyn blushed. "You're correct, I am sorry. Is there somewhere that I could get clothing? I seem to have forgotten to dress before charging after Anryn."

"You might want to try the other dragons."

"They won't help me. I am not exactly popular with the council." They had not been impressed with the Ariane situation. Not to mention the large bloodstain in the foyer.

"I'll handle it." Anryn walked to the flap of the tent. "Dad!"

"Yes?" Dominick appeared. His normally unflappable demeanour was a little ragged around the edges. It used to be his wife that he had to keep chasing and putting clothing on. Now his daughter was in on the action.

"Could you go to the groom's tent and get Imaran to whip up some clothes for Decklyn? We can't have him intimidating the djinn, now can we?" She carefully kept the flap over her body, not needing to traumatize her father any more than was necessary.

"Sure. C'mon, Decklyn." He grabbed the other male's arm and began to lead him away. "While we're out here, I think I'll explain the details of living with a Warder woman."

"What do you know, you married a dryad?" He was sullen. It was humiliating to be led about by a warlock when his chosen mate openly defied him.

"Ah, but my sisters are Warders. It takes a certain amount of stamina to deal with them." They were almost out of earshot now. "You see, they think that they're always right…"

Shaking her head, she turned to the group of giggling women, goblins and elves. First, she was bound to him, now he was following her nude around Realm. This was really more excitement than she had planned on when she agreed to be Albina's maid of honour.

She spread her arms in surrender. "Okay, Morcalla. Attack."

Chapter Ten

THE BRIDE WAS RADIANT, THE GROOM WAS SMUG, AND THE REST OF THE WEDDING WENT off without a hitch. Their powers and lives were bound in front of witnesses. The groom's family was elated, and the bride's family was looking forward to the party.

The instant that the photo's were finished, developed, and distributed, the reception began.

The band was a lively group of goblins and over half of the guests flooded the floor the moment that the bride and groom had finished the first dance. Anryn winked and waved at the drummer as the band started to play. He had really known how to use those extra appendages of his.

Goblin Rulz was doing an amazing job at getting the multiple races to dance. Even the djinn women were dancing in groups on the floor. The heady beats caused even the most subdued of creatures to start moving.

Anryn was hiding from her mate and answering questions from her cousin Ruana about her sex life, and the eating habits of her dragon.

After the first rounds of giggles between the girls, it settled into something old and familiar. Anryn's parents and Ruana's had always enjoyed the family events together.

The parents were currently over at the buffet table trying to get an elf to try a devilled egg. They weren't having much luck.

Ruana suddenly turned serious. "Anryn, are you aware that the Dragon Council used to send Decklyn to purge the dragon territories of werewolves."

"He mentioned it in passing."

"He used to eat them. The wolves that he killed." Ruana was a little concerned. She was a half werewolf, and going into heat soon. Anryn could tell, there was a flush to her cheeks and a heat to her gaze that was not normally there.

"Ah. Well he is a dragon."

"He won't eat me or Dad will he? Or any of the wolves in my area?"

"Not if he wants to live to see the next millennium." She pondered for a moment. "Or ever get laid again."

"Thanks, you put my mind at ease." She sipped from the soda she had gotten from the bar. "I am just a little more emotional than usual right now."

"I know Fuzzy. You are going into heat again."

"Yeah, but this time I have to break cover and find a mate. Even for a night. I just can't keep pretending everything is normal when it isn't." There were tears in her eyes. This was by far the scariest thing she had ever had to do. Even eating Anryn's cooking wasn't this scary.

"Yeah, I know. And sometimes, you just want to get laid." They giggled and then the wolf's expression sobered.

Ruana's face let her know who was behind her. "That would be my clue. But, Ruana, call me if things get ugly, okay?"

Before she could hear her cousin's response, Decklyn cut in.

"May I have this dance, my dear?" He looked good, better than good. The djinn fashions were very complementary on him. The loose trousers tucked into boots, held in place by a jewelled belt, and the open vest in a matching colour opened in the front and hung to his knees.

"Wow, you look great." She took his hand and let him lead her to the dance floor. The dancers parted for them and as he took her into his arms, she sighed with satisfaction. He was a great dancer.

"As do you. Imaran assisted me. He is quite the gentleman, but I do object to the way his relatives were looking at you. The lust in the eyes of the djinn almost drove me mad."

"Well, then maybe you shouldn't have hidden my clothing." Now, it was her turn to be smug.

"Well, maybe you shouldn't leave the house naked."

Her mouth opened to retort and his mouth swooped down to silence her. They continued to kiss and dance until the music changed. Then they slowly pulled their heads apart and left the dance floor in silence. She had never been good at silence.

"There will be family responsibilities that I have to take on. There is no way that I am going to stop doing it. It's part of what I am. And I want to work. I'll be all yours on the weekends and sleep with you every night, but I like my work. And not just the warding, the massage therapy is good practice for me. Are you willing to take this on?"

"The Dragon Council representatives cornered me. Since I have repented my wild ways by mating a Warder, my status has just been elevated. I may now attend the council meetings and have a right to be a representative if I should choose to put my name in the running."

He continued his offer. “I still don’t want you out of my sight, but I have a compromise. Open Relaxed Realms in my building. I have an extra set of offices that are not used, and you could move in there, rent-free. Provided that you work on-site only.”

“Let me think about that.” They walked in silence away from the wild dancers. A large portion was the male population of the attendees, trying to impress the Warders with their moves. A few alliances would happen tonight, some of them lasting for lifetimes.

“I have thought about it.” They were now near the woods that surrounded the meadow. She grabbed the front of his vest and dragged him off into the woods. She asked the greenery for a meadow, and one appeared before them.

“Anryn, where the hell are we going?”

“I don’t know about you my friend, but I am going down.” She dropped to her knees in front of him and tugged his trousers loose from the jewelled belt. His phallus drew free of the fabric easily. She began to caress him with her fingertips. Smiling as he responded, and his head fell back to expose his throat to the sky when her lips embraced the tip of his cock.

She sucked and flicked at the head of his cock, rubbing her tongue on the delicate underside, listening to the hiss of pleasure that her actions gave him. She cupped his balls in both hands and worked them with gentle and steady persistence.

Her mouth took him deeper, sucking and swirling her tongue around him as she dragged him to the back of her mouth, over and over again. Finally she felt the tightening that she had worked to bring forth, and she pulled her mouth away.

He looked down at her startled. Then understanding dawned as her skirts were raised above her waist and she climbed him. His hands came down to hold her buttocks in place as her hand reached between her thighs to open her to him completely. She slid down onto his cock and, with him supporting all of her weight, began to ride him.

She loved the feel of him deep inside her and rode him faster and harder until she screamed his name and came apart in his arms. Her body was damp with perspiration, and so was his. Her delicate skirts clung to his damp body as he let her slide to the ground and waited for her to get her balance.

She smiled brightly at him. “I think it’s a perfect idea. I’ll tell Bethany on Monday.”

He was dazed, “So this is what happens when you get your way?”

“Yep.”

"You may be right more often than I thought." They returned to the big party, his arms around his mate, and his mind at peace for the first time in centuries. Warders weren't as hard to deal with as everyone said. If he had known as much, he would have been on her as soon as the Dragon Council had given him her name as his perfect match. He could have had her under him for ten years already if he hadn't been so stubborn.

But since fate had insisted, he would accept his mate with grace, patience and enthusiasm. And be ready the next time she ran. He would follow her to the ends of the earth if necessary and through Realm every time duty called. That is what the scaled choker did. It tied them together so that he could track her anywhere.

He just hoped next time she would grab a shirt before she jumped through the portal.

The Warder's Wolf

Chapter One

RUANA'S HANDS SHOOK AS SHE FINISHED SMOOTHING HER DRESS OVER HER HIPS. HER friends were meeting her at the Howl and would no doubt give her a hard time for her choice of clothing. They tended to wear short leather skirts and even shorter tops. She had opted for a spring dress of cotton. It covered everything and fell to her knees.

Those knees buckled as another bolt of lust flared through her and left her panting. Over the last two days she had gone into heat, and her clit was trying to kill her. Never in her memory had she been this aroused and no amount of masturbation was taking the edge off. Her clit was sore and sensitive to the lightest touch, and yet she still couldn't cum. No. Not couldn't, wouldn't. Her body refused to obey her demands.

Well, if she could catch the attention of one of them tonight, then her little problem would be over.

Her friends had already arrived and taken root at the bar when she showed up. Ruana wandered over to them, letting her senses catch a glimpse of her prey. Good. There were at least four wolves in the crowd, if all went well, this might even be easy.

Keena introduced her to the bartender. Ruana extended her hand to shake his. Zan took her hand in his and raised it to his lips. As she waited to get her hand back, she felt his tongue flick across her skin and her legs nearly buckled under her. Her teeth bit her lip to stifle the moan that the tiny gesture had brought on. Meeting his eyes over her hand, she could see his wicked grin. Lord he was good looking. It was no wonder that her friends talked about him constantly.

"May I have my hand back now?" Her fingers wiggled to draw attention to their captivity, and he reluctantly let his prize be snatched away to its owner.

"This is your first time here." The low rumble of his speech carried through the higher pitched voices of all the women swarming the bar.

"Yes." It was all that needed to be said. She would have been here sooner, naked, if she had known that he smelled as good as he looked. His scent clung to the hand that he had touched, and she could still feel the warmth of his skin against hers.

"Make sure and tell me before you leave, wouldn't want to start a stampede." He gave her a serious look, then a wink.

She flashed him a small smile, and turned back to the flamboyant humans who had invited her. He watched her for a few moments and then got James to take over the bar. He had a few calls to make.

Three hours later, Ruana was beyond bored. Her friends were off dancing with the guys that they had picked up, but not one of the candidates she spotted had come anywhere near her. Six perfectly good werewolves scented a female in heat, and not one of them made a move. Her dress must be uglier than she thought.

She walked up to the bar and spoke to the bartender. He was blonde and attractive enough, but not her type. "Is Zan still here?"

He turned to her with a bored look, "I know you must be one of his many fans, but I am not going to tell you where he is sweetie." He took a close look at her, "And besides, a librarian isn't really his type."

She blushed furiously, and cursed the damned dress again. "It's okay, he just told me to let him know when I was leaving. Since he's the only guy who spoke to me tonight, I wanted to say thanks and goodnight." She gave him a short smile and headed for the door, and the cab that was always out front.

But when she got outside, the cab was gone. She turned to go back into the club, but her way was barred by three of the six possibilities she had identified.

She turned to run and found that the other three had taken up a flanking position. "Oh shit."

INSIDE THE HOWL, Zan finished his queries in the back room and came out, his eyes scanning the establishment for any signs of Ruana. The calls had taken longer than he had thought.

"Hey, James, did a girl come up here looking for me?"

"Can you narrow it down? About five from your fan club have been by- one to say that she was leaving without waiting to see your beautiful face again." James grimaced and loaded glasses onto a tray for a run through the dishwasher. All of his attention was on it, ignoring the women clamouring at the sight of Zan behind the bar once more.

"Mousy, in a plain cotton dress?"

"Yep, that's the one." James turned to look at his employer and took a step back at the fury in his eyes.

"How long ago?"

"Five minutes, maybe less? A few guys followed her out, but who could be that desperate?" James was talking to air as Zan vaulted over the bar and headed for the door at a breakneck pace.

"Uh, guys. I just want to take a cab home. No trouble." She spread her hands to her sides, and prepared to fire a defence spell. She was a little rusty and could probably only hit two of them, but she hoped it would slow them down.

"Choose, bitch." The three flanking her moved closer.

"Uh, choose what? What exactly are my options here?" Slowly she turned her head, and looked for another way out.

"You have to choose one of us to fuck, or we will choose for you. And we won't limit the number." This growl came from in front of her. One of the three blocking the entrance to the club. She saw a movement behind them and then, as she was thinking on how she could talk her way out of this one, she heard a howl.

All of her suitors froze. They shared frustrated glances between them and disappeared into the night. A minute after the howl, there was no hint of any danger left in the area. But Ruana couldn't move. She slowly backed toward the door of the club.

Fear at what had almost happened shook her to the core. This was why she had just stayed home the last five times that the heat had struck.

It was damned dangerous.

Out of the shadows Zan appeared. He walked casually up to her and asked, "So are you willing to take me on? It might beat the alternative."

"At this point, I would go with Satan if he said he had a place for me." Ruana noticed that she was actually shaking where she stood.

"Not too complimentary, but follow me." His easy saunter led them around to the back of the bar and a small employee parking lot. He wandered up to a small sporty car and opened the passenger door.

"Get in." He held open the door for her, and she slid into the embrace of the leather in the small black sports car.

Once he had gotten into the driver's seat, he locked the doors again. "No sense taking chances."

They drove for over an hour until they reached a whitewashed farmhouse on an enormous yard. The way he drove the car, Ruana wouldn't have been surprised to find that he and the machine were bonded on a genetic level.

"Here we are." He slid out from under the wheel and came around to her side of the car, holding the door for her once again. "C'mon out, I won't hurt you."

She forced herself out of her shock and surprise at what had occurred at the Howl, and sluggishly began to make her way out of the car. "I noticed that you didn't say that you don't bite."

He grinned at her, relieved that she seemed to be coming back to reality. "I don't make promises that I can't keep."

"Good to know."

"Come inside. I'll get you a glass of wine. You're way too tense."

He led the way into the farmhouse, and to her relief, turned on the lights as he entered each room.

The rooms were tidy, and lived in. The oak furnishings were gleaming in the light cast by the floor lamps. The couches were lightly scuffed and the drapes a soothing blue. The fading scent of sunlight was still in the room, the heat of the day combined with Zan's light musk to make a heady blend. This was his territory and she was a little nervous to be invited.

"So, um. Do you rescue a lot of girls like me?" She was wandering into the kitchen behind him and watching him open a bottle of wine.

"Nah, most know what they want, and who they want it from. As you know, the fact that you have no pack affiliation makes you an easy target." The cork came free with a soft 'pop' and he reached up to get a wine glass from the cupboard.

"How did you know that I don't belong to a pack?" She was wary once again, the throbbing in her lower body at the sight of him reaching for the glass, pushed aside for the moment.

"Easy." He turned and handed her the glass of wine. It was a delicate pink and smelled of flowers and berries. "I checked."

She thanked him and took a cautious sip. The flavours exploded on her tongue. The only thing that she could think that it tasted like was wild summer. Her breath came out in a shuddering sigh and she took another delicate sip. Wow.

As she met his grey eyes, she felt she had to ask, "Okay, I am new at this. Where exactly does that leave me? My not having a pack, I mean."

"Prey to any and all who want to take advantage of you. With no recourse and no one to protect you. Basically raw meat." He was matter of fact, but still watching her closely.

"Ah, I thought as much. If it hadn't gotten so bad, I would never have broken cover." She looked down and was surprised to find that she was at the bottom of her glass.

"If what hadn't gotten so bad?" His voice was distant, even though he was sitting across from her.

"If I hadn't gone into heat again." She shook her head to clear it. "The pounding in my blood is unbearable. My thighs are slick with my own juices, I want to touch myself, but it does no good, the fire only climbs higher."

His head cocked to one side. "How often has this happened? It doesn't seem like this is the first time you have gone into heat."

She blushed scarlet. "May I have some more wine? Thank you." She sipped again." Naw, this is the fifth or sixth time it's happened. The other times it started to go away after a few days, but this time, it just keeps getting stronger."

"What did you do the other times?" His voice seemed to be coming from another room, but he was still there in front of her.

"Oh, I masturbated until it felt like my fingers were going to fall off. Burned out a few pairs of batteries, that kind of thing." The wine was gone again. She giggled.

"Can I have some more wine? It tastes really good." She was incredibly relaxed right now, no cares in the world. And when Zan got up from the table she smiled at him. Not a grin, but a slow smile that started in her eyes and slowly drew her full lips away from her teeth. Her tongue darted out to wet her lips and she was amazed at the effect that it had on him.

One moment he was standing next to the table, and the next moment, she was on it. "Oh."

His eyes met hers as he slowly slid his hands under her skirt, and up her thighs. When he reached the molten heat between them, he let out a lurid curse and pulled her legs apart to stand between her knees.

Her panties tore away in his hands, and then she felt his fingers stroking the flesh and parting the lips of her sex. He returned one hand to his jeans and unsnapped and unzipped them while keeping his eyes on hers.

A furious blush had spread over Ruana- this was what she wanted, what she craved, but not something that she was used to. The last time she had felt a man's hard length moving inside her, it was just after high school and not all that pleasant. She sensed that this time, things would be different.

With a few small movements of his hand, he was free of the confining fabric. Ruana looked down and watched the angry purple head of his cock move toward her. Her weight was resting on her hands, and her thighs were spread wide on the table. Now, based on the determined look in his eyes, she was going to be seriously fucked.

Two fingers slid inside her and began to move, then he added a third. They slid in and out, hard and fast, and she squealed and arched against them. Just as her body was letting her find her rhythm, the fingers withdrew.

"No! More!" Her only coherent thoughts came out in a wail. Her hands fisted on the table and she whimpered.

Zan did not even respond to her, but pulled her hips to the edge of the table and set the head of his cock against her. Her slick heat embraced the head of his member with a relieved flutter. Slowly he moved deeper and deeper within her, until he was buried to the balls.

"Oh, God, yes!" She groaned in relief. Then he began to thrust.

He was very slow and extremely thorough. Each thrust rubbed the sensitive tissues within her pussy and caused her to arch toward him. He was taking her weight with his hands on her lower back and working her against his thrusts as he pushed and slid through her slick channel.

Without knowing it, her hands had moved to his shoulders, and her fingers were twisting in his hair. He began to pick up speed, and was beginning to pound her against his cock with each inward thrust.

She felt the spiral of tension build within her, and dropped one of her hands off of his shoulder to rub circles around her clit. The wetness that had spread out of her from their fucking had made it easy. In only a few passes, she felt the tension grow and heard him growl from above her. Her eyes flew up to meet his and one of his hands pulled hers aside, just when she was almost there!

"What?" No other words passed through the haze of pleasure as his wicked fingers took over from where she had left off.

"Mine." More of a grunt than a word, but its meaning was unmistakable.

His fingers circled, pinched and flicked at her clit as his cock slammed into her with renewed effort.

"Oh, hell!" She screamed and clutched at him as her back arched and her legs wrapped around his waist to hold him within her as she came. He continued to pound into her, against the tension surrounding his shaft, trying to hold him within her. Her orgasm went on and on, a fresh pulse of sensation with every plunge and withdrawal over her sensitive tissues.

When her release had run its course, she fell limply onto the table, feeling the mad rush of energy that now filled Zan's body. Every thrust took him to the hilt. Pounding away at her in a burst of motion that soon had him howling as his own orgasm claimed him.

Ruana felt his climax within her, and felt the wetness of his seed as it released in the depths of her belly. If she had had the energy, she might have held him when he collapsed on her, but she didn't. She lay on the heavy oak table and struggled to catch her breath, wondering if this was it, and she could go now.

She closed her eyes and took stock of her body. Beneath the throbbing satisfaction was the hunger for more. As if woken by her thoughts, the hunger began to grow again. The rest of her was ready for round two as well. She only had one tiny injury on her ass where Zan's fingers had bruised her.

Between her thighs she felt him stirring again and shuddered in response to the bolt of heat that went through her. Zan's head rested against her breast, and the nipple near his mouth came to swift attention as his breath blew over it through the thin layers of clothing. She squirmed gently under him, wanting more, but not sure how to ask for it. One of her hands slid through the dark silk of his hair, and caressed the back of his neck.

He raised his head. "Care for another round?" He kissed the tip of her nose and then kissed her lips for the first time. His hips rocked gently against her as his tongue slid into her mouth.

It seemed that they kissed and slowly moved together for hours, bodies sighing and clothing rustling against each other, but abruptly it was too much for Ruana. Her legs locked at the base of his spine and pulled him into her with all the force she possessed. He grunted in reaction and flipped, so that his back was now against the table and she was kneeling over him. Her hands braced against his stomach and she rode him like a wild thing, moving up and down on his bursting erection as he howled and arched under her. She continued to fuck herself on his arching body as she felt his balls empty within her. Her hands came up and clawed at her breasts through her dress and she pinched her nipples with a vicious grip.

The pain blended with the pleasure, she gasped and fell forward as another wave of ecstasy claimed her.

Zan wrapped his arms around her and smoothed her auburn hair off of her face. His heart was slowing under her and she started to laugh as she realized that they were both still fully clothed. It started as a little hiccup of giggles and when she felt him slip from her sore and soaked cunt, it turned into a howl of laughter.

He started to sit up, and as he did, she fell to one side. Then off of the table and onto the floor. Ruana landed with a thump. For a moment she was silent-then the hilarity gripped her once again. Tears streamed down her face as she gripped her ribs and curled into a ball of hysterics. Zan went over to the sink and tidied himself up, then came over to her with a washcloth in his hand.

The room smelled of heat and sex, with the unmistakable muskiness that the wer had as their own.

He turned her onto her back and forced her thighs apart with one hand while cleaning off the sticky evidence of their coupling with the other. When he was through he asked, "Are you ever going to stop laughing?" He was hunkered down next to her and looking at her with great attention to every detail of her writhing anatomy.

Her convulsive laughter must be the result of too long an abstinence. There was no other reason that she could think of to have collapsed with hilarity after the hottest sex of her life.

Still giggling, she tugged her skirt down once again and sat up.

"Dare I ask what was funny?" He gave her his hand and tugged her to her feet. Somewhere along the way she had lost her shoes. Her toes wiggled against the hardwood floor.

She grinned at him, "Well, aside from the messed up hair, you and I look like we just spent an evening playing scrabble." A giggle broke free once again. "Do you know where my shoes went?"

"Somewhere under the table. Hey, get back here." He was left talking to air as everything but her backside disappeared under the table. It was a very nice backside, but he would have to see it without clothing on to be sure.

"Aha! Got 'em." Brandishing the strappy sandals triumphantly she appeared on the other side of the table from him. Hopping from foot to foot she put the sandals back on.

"Ruana, we need to talk." Zan was serious, he knew what was coming, and was dreading it. The truth was, they were far from finished.

"No, Zan, we don't need to talk. Can I call a cab from here, or will you give me a ride back into town?" She brushed the front of her dress straight- then frowned. She could feel the evidence of his climax slowly making its way down her thighs. Her nose wrinkled at the scent and she turned back to him with an expectant look on her face.

"Oh, so now that you have what you need, you don't want me anymore. Very nice." He sat back at the table and crossed his arms over his chest, while crossing his legs at the ankle.

"So, can I get a ride or what?" She really had no frame of reference for this type of activity, but he looked offended. "I thought that you would be happy that I didn't want to stick around."

"Not really, we still need to talk. Have a seat." He gestured to the chair that she had previously occupied.

"Um, how about we talk another time, I really want to get home." She shifted from foot to foot.

"Well, be off with you then. You can't get a cab from here, but about an hour's walk down the road you should find a gas station, you can get a cab from there. If you make it." His eyes were hot, and she felt a frisson of fear as she noticed something rising behind his eyes that had not been there before.

"Oh crud." A trickle of sensation ran down her spine. Part of it was fear, but she was ashamed to admit that the heat was riding again. "How long are you going to give me?" She quickly flipped her shoes off and started to back out the door.

"You have ten minutes. I would go now if I were you." The wildness was rising in his eyes, and there was a flush to his skin that had not been there before. He seemed alive with energy, and it was barely contained. In a few moments, he was not going to bother containing his hunger at all.

She ran.

Chapter Two

SHE LEFT HER SHOES IN THE KITCHEN AND BOLTED OUT THE DOOR AS IF ALL THE HOUNDS of hell were on her heels. Down the driveway and into the woods, she ran. She tried to mask her scent as best as she could, but having quizzed her mother on the mating habits of werewolves, she knew that he could probably find her anywhere she went. Thanks to their earlier mating, she reeked of his musk.

She stumbled blindly in the dark, trees and branches snagging and tearing at her clothing. A branch whipped across her face and she flinched with pain, her heart pounding in her ears.

In the distance, she heard a howl, and ran faster. She tripped and fell into a stream. She got up, her hands bleeding from the rocks and moved down the stream as quickly as she could. As much as fear was riding her hard, arousal had started to creep into her flesh as well. Through the damp of her dress, she felt her nipples pushing at the confines of her bra. The wetness between her thighs was scalding hot, a sharp contrast to the icy cold of the water swirling around her ankles.

She heard another howl and froze in place. It seemed close. Really close. She held her breath and listened with everything in her. The wind shifted and she could smell him. He had not transformed completely, there was man mixed in with the wolf, and she shuddered with arousal once again. It meant that he intended to fuck her when he found her- that was not even a question. It was the only reason that he would not have changed all the way. In wolf form, he may have tormented her, bit her and chased her, perhaps even killed her. The partial form was only good for being able to move and act as a man, at the same time that he took on the most effective tracking abilities given to him by the wolf within.

She was in serious trouble.

Ruana left the stream and ran on numb feet through the woods once again, stumbling, crashing into trees and brambles. She fell. Her arms moved under her to push her up and she heard him. She listened to the careful steps coming toward her. Her body shook with panic as she thought of what she could do next.

Desperate for cover, she rolled under a nearby bush and tried to tuck her arms and legs against her body. She could hear his footsteps coming closer and tried to hold her breath and quiet her heartbeat. Her eyes closed and she listened to his steps pass her hiding place, she could hear him scenting the air, snuffling through his extended muzzle. She kept herself completely still, and did not even breathe the sigh of relief that she felt burning within her when he kept going.

Her breath blasted out of her when a clawed, furred hand, wrapped around one ankle and dragged her out from under the bush. She screamed in panic and flipped to her back, to find a grey muzzle and burning amber eyes boring into her own.

With casual brutality his claws tore through her dress and shredded her bra. She was left sitting in scraps of fabric where her dress used to be, her breasts heaving as her lungs fought for air through the constriction of panic.

She slowly edged back from her suitor, stopping when he growled in protest. His eyes roamed over her body slowly and his hands took hold of her hips to bring her under him. She kept as still as possible as the muzzle went over her from head to toe, pausing to carefully inspect the scent of their earlier mating. Her body was shaking, partially due to her fear. There was also the animal part of her that was awakening with lust at his presence.

He lifted her off of the dirt and bracken covering the forest floor, and turned her onto her knees. His hands stroked her from neck to hips in a soothing motion, only occasionally drawing blood with his claws. When her shaking had stilled, he began to lick her. First at the back of her neck, then across her shoulders. His hot tongue constantly moving and tasting her flesh. The wet expanse of his tongue triggered an answering warm wetness between her thighs. She clenched them together as if to deny her response.

His snarl and his hand separating her thighs let her know in no uncertain terms that she was not to deny him. Her head fell forward and she let him have free reign of her body.

He tasted every portion of her flesh, his muzzle and tongue lapping between her buttocks, across her anus and down to her weeping flesh. A shiver started in her core and her muscles tensed for battle. She felt his teeth on the inside of her thigh and she snapped.

Naked and aroused she leapt to her feet and tried to escape. She had no chance. She had only managed to run a few yards when the warm, furred body slammed into her and bore her to the ground. She whimpered and fought him, pushing away from the ground and lifting them both with strength that she didn't know she possessed. He forced her down once again with his weight and closed his teeth on her neck. She stilled.

Giving in to the inevitable, she relaxed against him. He loosened his jaws and she rolled to her back and then offered her neck to him.

The golden eyes above his muzzle gleamed in the darkness, reflecting all available light. His teeth gently closed against her throat as she arched her neck into his jaws, and he bit her hard enough to break the skin. A pleased rumble left his throat and he released her neck to lick at her chin.

Her hands found his shoulders and she caressed the fur and muscle, reminding herself of the man behind the monster. His teeth found her nipples and she shivered again. Then, almost came as the darts of sensation ran through her. His muzzle nipped, licked and tormented her breasts. Pain and pleasure drawing together. On her own, playing with her nipples had always gotten her wet, but what he was doing now was almost criminal. She sobbed, twisting against him, and he moved on.

His lapping tongue found the hollow of her belly, and delved lower, between the thighs that she spread for him as he made his way to her core.

When he discovered her flowing honey he snarled his approval and once again flipped her to her belly, then drew her up to her knees. This time he acted immediately, the large stiff head of his erection prodding at her entrance. He rubbed himself against her from her clitoris to her open warmth-then thrust his hips forward.

She grunted at the first impact on her delicate flesh, the bulbous head moved into her an inch, then withdrew and moved forward again. In this form he was quite a bit larger than as a human. She hissed her discomfort, then moaned her pleasure as he continued to work his way into her.

Inch by inch, he buried himself in her, then began rapid fire piston-like thrusts. Drawing out, then hammering forward, throwing her onto her elbows just to maintain her balance. His clawed hands dug into her hips and pulled her onto him. Fucking her with savage ferocity that left her breathless as the spiral of tension in her body drew tight, then snapped.

She screamed, her voice transforming to a howl of satisfaction as his voice joined hers. Distantly, she heard his howl of triumph as it echoed through the trees. His body pumped violently into hers and she heard his final grunt of satisfaction as he shoved himself into her one last time, then withdrew to drip the last of his cum onto the woodland carpet of moss. For the first time in her life, Ruana fainted.

SHE DREAMED. DREAMED of being hunted through the forest, being chased by a wolf. Her heart was pounding, and she couldn't see. He was right behind her. He would be on her any second.

Ruana woke, gasping for air, her heart beating like a drum.

"Oh, thank God." She fell back into her sheets and stretched under her comforter. It had all been a dream. The whole thing. Probably brought on by her going into heat again. She laughed at herself, like she would ever be desperate enough to go to a bar, to pick up a werewolf to satisfy her cravings. This morning though, the heat seemed to be over. She felt rested, relaxed and the pounding arousal was finally gone. Maybe the dream had done it for her.

She checked her alarm. "Damn." She had overslept. Seriously overslept. She was due to meet her parents for Sunday dinner at four, and it was almost two.

She flipped the blankets and sheets aside, swung her legs out of bed and stood up. And promptly collapsed. Her legs would not hold her, the muscles were sore and unprepared to bear her weight.

"What the hell?" Then she froze. Coating the insides of her thighs were evidence of her nocturnal activities, a strong musky scent came to her as she examined herself.

Pushing herself upright with the bed, she wobbled to the bathroom and surveyed her devastation for herself. Claw marks covered her skin, tracing red over the pale flesh. Welts had formed on her neck from the bite, and her hands were covered with dirt. "Oh, shit."

She jumped into the shower and started to scrub. As much to remove the dirt as to banish the memories of the night.

She finished her ablutions and got dressed, choosing a high-necked shirt to camouflage the marks on her neck. She tried to put on a pair of jeans, but found the fabric too abrasive on her sore flesh. She opted for a denim skirt instead.

Her face seemed a little flushed, so she applied her 'five-minute makeover' then was out the door and off to meet her parents for dinner.

Her mom was gracious as always, but her father was a little stilted when he hugged her. She sighed. He could smell Zan on her. She didn't even question it.

When her mother left them alone to get some dessert from the kitchen he pulled her into the other room and asked her, "Okay. Ruana, who was it? I need to know."

"His name was Zan, Dad. That's all I know." She kept her voice to a whisper, so that her mother wouldn't hear. Her mom never wanted to listen to Ruana's comments on being a half werewolf. She liked to pretend that her little girl was completely normal, and the only supernatural items that she had inherited came from the witch blood on her own side of the family.

"I can't believe this. Did you get a last name?" His whisper was just as urgent as hers.

"No, you see, there were these six other werewolves who had kind of cornered me…" Ruana's mother came back in and that was the end of that discussion for now, but the way her dad's eyes had bugged out, she knew she was in for a phone call.

Just because he had left the pack to marry her mother, didn't mean that he had given up on their traditions. Some male messing with his daughter would not be tolerated. He still had his family to call on if he needed it. Ruana was hoping that he didn't.

She left her parents' house after she washed the dinner dishes. She had been home for three whole minutes before the phone rang, and she filled her father in on the pertinent details. No, she didn't get his last name. Yes, six other wolves had cornered her. Yes, Zan had come to her rescue. No, she didn't know where he lived. Yes, she was fine and her heat seemed to be over. Yes, she loved him too. Goodbye.

Slowly and methodically she thumped her head against the wall next to the phone. She could not believe the chain of events that had led her to that discussion with her father. Wasn't sex with strangers supposed to be all the rage? Her dad was raging all right. So much for hoping for a quiet solution.

Ah well. There was always tomorrow. A whole new chance to humiliate herself awaited.

Chapter Three

SHE CAREFULLY LAID OUT HER CLOTHING FOR THE NEXT DAY AT WORK, WATCHED A MOVIE, and then went to bed after changing the sheets. Dirt and cum had crusted on the bedding. She could not bear to climb into that mess. She carefully set her alarm and went to sleep.

She had the same dream, but this time when she woke up there was no pressure on her legs, no twinges in her thighs and no strange musky scents on her body.

She got dressed in slacks and a long-sleeved, button down shirt, and went to work. Keena met her at her desk. "So, where did you get off to on Saturday? Find a hot guy?"

Her friend was relentless, so Ruana compromised. "Yeah, I found a hot stud on Saturday, got laid and here I am." It was true, lacking in details, but true.

"Wow, you're so lucky. All of the good looking guys disappeared around eleven, and after that it was just poor guys whose wives had kicked them out for the night." Keena did not seem upset by the circumstance and Ruana got the feeling that one of those 'poor guys' had gotten lucky as well.

"The boss wants to see you at ten. His wife is in as well. Must be some kind of internal audit." Keena walked away, sashaying for the benefit of the guy from the mailroom that had wandered onto their floor.

Paperwork of the endless variety that piled up on the average clerk's desk kept her busy until ten, at which point she stood, walked down to the CEO's door and knocked. The door said Maxwell Masters, but everyone called him Max.

"Come in, Ruana." Max's voice was unmistakable. It was a bass rumble that usually held a trace of amusement, but could occasionally rise to a cold roar that sent employees scurrying for cover. His wife had a gentling effect on him, but that was when the cold intelligence rose to the surface.

"Hey Max, you wanted to see me?" She sauntered into the room. Arissa was there as expected, but the second guest in the room caused her to stumble and almost fall.

As Zan's steadying arm came around her, she looked wildly at her boss. "Oh, God." The signs of the werewolf were easy to see, now that she was looking for them. Arissa as well. Damn.

"It was a set-up. The whole thing was a set-up." Zan helped her into a chair and she buried her face in her hands. She was not upset, she was mortified. Humiliated.

Her voice was muffled behind her hands, "Max, you were the one who told Keena to take me to the Howl." It was a statement. She had finally put two and two together.

"Actually, it was me." Arissa's smooth and low voice was gentle. "You were in heat, Ruana. If we didn't send you into a controlled situation, you could have been hurt."

"You didn't tell them about my fan club?" She looked at Zan, her voice almost hysterical. She knew that the whites of her eyes were showing, like a panicked deer. Ruana had never felt more like herded prey in her life.

"How many?" Max's voice was grim. Ruana was afraid to look up, but she could *feel* the hunter rising behind that desk. Now that she had physically contacted with a werewolf, her senses were going on overdrive.

"Six. They followed her out of the club. Despite the ugly dress." Her head lifted, and a startled laugh left her before she could stop it. Zan was watching for her reaction and tried to send her a soothing smile. It was more of a grimace, but he did try.

Max tapped his hand against the desk to regain their attention. "Any clan members among them?"

"All of them. I scared them off, but they're going to petition for her." Zan was just as grim as his brother.

His brother's eyes closed in resignation. "Ah hell. Are you ready for the challenges? Will you take them or let them have her?"

She was indignant, "Hey!"

"I will take them." Zan's voice was implacable.

"Arissa, what the hell are they talking about?" She knew she sounded shrill, but this was not the kind of meeting she had been braced for. She had spent her morning memorizing inventory questions that he might ask.

Arissa sighed and looked at her husband. At his nod, she began to fill Ruana in. "Okay, now you know your father left the clans when he married your mother. Right?" At Ru's nod she kept going.

"You were born of mixed blood, this usually results in a girl being born without any attributes of a werewolf at all." Arissa smiled kindly, "Not so with you. You may not be able to change shape, but you have the strength, the reflexes and the intelligence of the highest werewolf families. You also do something that only one in twenty full blood wer female's do. You go into heat. Frequently, and obviously. The long and short of it is that you can have fully powered sons and daughters, who are just about guaranteed to be Alphas, the highest ranking in the clans."

"Offspring of a female in heat are stronger, faster, and more intelligent than that of the average werewolf female. This makes you a valuable bargaining chip. The various clans are bidding on any female with this particular trait. Once discovered, you have nowhere to hide."

"I am only sorry that our little plan to get you to Zan at that time caused you to become exposed to the rest of the clans. The bidding war has already started. Zan will be challenged for the right to be your lover until you conceive. Then the next clan will be in line, after that first child is born."

"...And on and on, until I die in childbirth. Not a very pleasant future." Tears seeped from he eyes as she contemplated her fate. Endless mating with strangers to produce children that could literally bite your head off. "Is there any way out of this? Anywhere I can hide?"

"No. Once you were spotted, an alarm went out trying to find your identity. Your erstwhile suitors were very excited to come across one of your type with no clan protection. But there is something that you can do." Arissa's voice was soft, and she looked like she wanted to cry herself.

Ruana was desperate. Tears were slowly tracking down her cheeks. The only outlet for emotions that made her want to scream in anger. "What? Anything. You name it and I am there."

Zan took over the conversation. "What Max wants us to try is a little complicated. You become my mate. Permanently. We marry and register it with the state. Not one clan can challenge our relationship after that. You will belong to me, and I to you. And hey! You can stop working for this tyrant." Across the room, Max smiled at that. Well, she thought it was a smile, he bared his teeth.

"Wait a minute- we still have your clan to contend with. Don't we?" She was finally coming around into the planning stages.

"I'll start making calls. Zan, you get her out of here. Anyone of those who saw you could identify you and come to find her here. They all know where I am and that you are my brother."

Zan tugged her to her feet and was halfway out the door with Ruana before she added "Hey, you still have to pay me for working today."

The door closed on their laughter, and she took Zan's arm as he led her out of the office and to his car. The secretaries giggled and pointed at them as they walked the halls. It was an occasion of monumental proportions that the 'little librarian' had a man. And the boss's brother, wow. The sports car was a devastating blue in the daylight. She was amazed. Last night it had looked black.

She had always been a sucker for blue. "Your car is wonderful."

"Thanks." He opened the passenger door for her.

She nervously drew her shaking hands across the seats. "Mm, leather interior. Nice."

He slid into the driver's seat and started the car. "You are chatty today. On Saturday you hardly said a word."

"On Saturday I was scared out of my wits. I hadn't ever done that before."

"What, picked up a guy in a bar and fucked him senseless? You were very good at it." He smiled over at her as he headed for the highway.

"Thanks. You know I never thought that what came afterward would be so, pleasant." Her face was completely bland, but she knew that that would get a rise out of him.

"You enjoyed being chased through the woods, almost torn apart and mauled by a wild beast?"

"It had its moments." She glanced over at his crotch and noticed the bulge that seemed to be growing behind the fabric. "Like when you pinned me to the ground with your body, and I felt your enormous cock pressing into my ass as I lay helpless."

A few beads of sweat had formed on his brow, and the bulge in his trousers was no longer small.

"While I am driving, could we please talk about the weather?" It was a barely human snarl, but she understood it.

"Okay, new topic. How did you get me into my house?"

He gave her a sardonic look. "You left your purse in my kitchen. I can read a drivers license, and use a key."

She felt her face heat. "Why did you take me home then?"

"So you would have familiar things around you when you woke up. I knew what would happen on Monday. Max had invited me to the meeting when Arissa had them bring you to me."

Ruana was silent. She carefully watched the route that he took into the farming areas around the city. They passed the Howl, the bar lying dormant in the sun, and she averted her gaze. She watched the countryside fly by the window once again.

"Why did you let them convince you to go to the Howl on Saturday? You really don't seem the type." He broke the silence after a few miles had passed.

She turned her face toward the window and kept her mouth shut. She had been kicking herself since the moment she had walked into the bar, and she wasn't about to let him know that. He was nice enough for a werewolf, but she could not forget her father's admonishing words about wer. Basic instinct was valued over intellect, and the most cruel and violent of behaviours were applauded if they helped you move through the ranks of the clan.

Zan may have helped her out by separating her from the others, but he was just as capable as they were of taking what he wanted, should she protest.

She sighed and broke the silence. "So what is the type that frequents the Howl?"

"Usually women in short skirts and tops slit down to the navel so that their tits hang out. They come in, get hammered, drool over the wolves that are in the bar, pick one up, and get hammered all over again." He grinned and winked at her as she turned to stare at him in appalled amazement.

"So, what you are saying is that I stuck out the second that I walked through the door." She sank further into the embrace of the leather and squirmed uncomfortably.

He let out a harsh bark of laughter. "No, I stuck out the second that you walked through the door. Damned uncomfortable in those jeans, I will have you know."

"You know, I never expected Max's brother to be so...crude. He's so polite at the office." She was trying hard not to smile, and failing miserably.

She smiled at his wicked chuckle. "Most men are fairly crude given the opportunity. It's only the formal bonds of normal society that keep us from making all kinds of unfortunate statements and noises in public." He smiled. "And some of us do it anyway, but Max has his business to run. He had higher priorities the whole time we were growing up."

"Is he the older brother?"

"Naw, my younger by about three years. I taught him everything he knows, including how to run a business. We are both of alpha standing, but have no urge to run the clan. Too much politics."

His hands were steady on the wheel, his eyes distant. He was obviously lost in some kind of memory. The grim set of his mouth was an indication that it was not a pleasant scene that he was recalling.

Silence fell again.

"Is there going to be trouble because of me? Because if there is, can I make a few calls?"

"By the time we get you safely stashed at my farmhouse, half of the clans will know that there is a breeding female available, and the smart ones will know that you have no protection." He sounded as if he were talking to a child. Explaining the facts to her in simple terms.

"Fine. But can I call someone that can help? Yes or no?" She waited. And waited.

From inside his coat pocket, he brought out a cell phone. "Fine, call anyone you want. But the clans will handle this."

Ruana flipped open the tiny phone and dialled her mother's number at work. When she was put through she told her mother everything as quickly as she could. Her mother sat in stony silence on the other end of the call.

Finally, "Mom, do you think you can call out some of the cousins for this? Does it fall within Warder jurisdiction? Great, Mom. Thanks. And can you make the call to Anryn? I think she would really get a kick out of this."

Zan had been listening carefully. "What is a Warder? And who all is coming?"

"Long story on the clan, but currently it is a network of witches and warlocks related by blood who specialize in defensive magic. There is a clan that I belong to, The Warders."

"And the Warders will use all means to defend my choice of mate, but only once. So you had better have a detailed stock portfolio ready for my mom and the elders to go over, or kiss your ass goodbye." For the first time in days, Ruana felt confidant.

Her mother had been surprised, but not shocked, and had swiftly realized the peril that her daughter was in. Calling in the clan was standard procedure, and would surprise the hell out of the werewolves coming after her.

"Mom is going to call me back in a few minutes. I gave her your cell number. The clan should start arriving this afternoon, I think you have enough room for them to camp out."

"What clan? I thought that your father had left his clan associations behind." Zan was a little confused by the conversation that he had overheard.

Ruana started to snicker. "Not my father's clan. They won't have anything to do with us." She paused for a few moments, then dropped the bomb. "My mother's."

"Your mom is a wer?"

A short bark of laughter answered him. "No. My mom is a witch. Of the

Warder clan. We are the largest and least respected of all of the magical clans in Realm." She looked perversely smug as she described her family.

"Realm? There are clan legends and histories, but none of us have been there." He was looking a little white around the eyes. "So, your mom is a witch?"

"One of the best Warders of the last generation." Her chest puffed up with pride. "That was how my parents met. She laid a trap for him, and caught him."

"What kind of a trap?"

"Nothing invasive. Just a set of standing stones. She needed his help tracking down a rogue wer from his clan. He refused to participate willingly, so she trapped him." Then seduced him, but she was not about to tell Zan that. The slightly trampy behaviour of her relatives was not something she was particularly proud of.

Mind you, last weekend hadn't been all-bad. Perhaps she could see the attraction in jumping guys after all. Well, Zan anyway.

The car turned into the farmhouse's drive. She smiled at the whitewashed porch and expansive lawn. There was serenity in the expanse of greenery surrounding the house in the woods. She felt part of her relax. It was the same part of her that hated the congestion of the city, longed for the hunt, the chase and bringing down her prey.

Ruana shook her head. She had never hunted. She looked over at Zan and noted the relaxed, blissful look on his face as he took in the sight of his home. Her mind probed at the emotions that were rising within her, and she noted the distinctly masculine tone that they were taking on.

Aw, hell. They were bonding.

Chapter Four

Zan's cell phone rang. Ruana grabbed at it and checked the caller ID. It was her mom. Thank God.

"Hi, Mom. What's the verdict?" She listened carefully and looked over at Zan's attentive expression. He was obviously puzzled at the turn of events that she was pulling on him, and slightly off balance.

Her mother's voice came through clearly. "We can have Anryn there as soon as you get a four foot reflective surface ready. The rest of the available clan members will be there by nightfall."

Ruana covered the lower portion of the phone with her hand and asked him, "Do you have a large mirror in the house?"

"How large?" He placed one of his hands on her lower back and steered her to the front door.

"About four feet." She turned back to the phone. "Four feet. Right, Mom?"

"Yes, dear. Just lay your hand on it, and she will come through. She's waiting for you." Her voice dropped to a hushed level. "Are you sure that he's the one, sweetie? It isn't too late to have you pulled out of there."

"Mom, he's willing to take on the rest of the clan champions to keep me. So, yeah. He's the one." Saying it out loud made it final. No matter what happened later this evening, she wanted Zan.

"Well, Ru, as long as he's the one you want. I am sure that your father and I will get along fine with him. We should be there after your dad gets off work. Anryn will bring us through Realm for the engagement ceremony." Victoria paused for a moment. "Be careful, Ruana. I love you."

"Love you too, Mom. Goodbye." With a punch of her thumb, she disconnected the call and then turned to the mirror that Zan had led her to.

Zan had grinned when she said that he was the one, but now he sobered. "So, how is your mother taking this?" His concern was obvious.

"Pretty well, considering that this is something she has always dreaded actually happening." Ruana shrugged and looked around her.

It was obviously his bedroom. The king-sized bed gave it away. The room had the same lived-in feeling as the parts of his house that she had already seen. It was also spotless.

Great, he was a neat freak. This was boding ill for the future.

"Ruana, the mirror?" He stood aside. "What are you going to do with it?"

"Me. Nothing. My cousin Anryn however is going to use it as a gateway. Better stand a little further to one side. She tends to come through running." She held her hand over the mirror's surface, tingling warmth jumping from the glass to her skin.

"Okay, I am going to give you the short course here." Ruana drew her hand back and took his to drag him over to have a seat on the bed. "If you don't want to be involved with me after you see my family, you can just let me go. My family is magic. My mother is a descendent of one of the oldest bloodlines of magical humans."

She drew a deep breath and continued. "We have a family curse that keeps us from being accepted in the regular society of Realm. Realm is an alternate dimension that acts as a haven and a training ground for those of magical families. And all the non-human races, of course."

"Because of my family's stigma, we are not usually welcomed as in-laws by the other families, so we find mates elsewhere. Usually in the non-human races. My cousin Anryn is half-dryad. I myself have more mixed blood in me than human. Our talents are varied, but one thing is certain. We can all cast wards. Magical barriers that keep out whatever we tell them to. Kinda like your computer's firewall."

"Anryn is coming for two reasons. One is that she is currently the most powerful Warder that we have. Two is because her husband will be hot on her heels, and he will probably give an entire werewolf clan a run for its money." She smiled brightly at his stunned face. "Ready?"

"As I could ever be. Invite your cousin." He sat still, watching carefully as her hand hovered over the surface of the glass once more.

"Here we go." Ruana's hand plunged into the glass, with only the briefest of hesitation. It rippled, and in the movement Zan could make out a figure, getting larger.

Seconds later, two hands plunged free of the mirror with the rest of the body soon following. The female figure tucked and rolled to a stop against the bed. "Close the mirror!"

Startled, Ruana began to pull her hand away from the rippled surface. It was stuck. She looked into the mirror and saw burning golden eyes glaring at her. They belonged to the clawed hand that was wrapped around her wrist, holding her in place.

"Ruana!" Zan was on his feet the second that Anryn had tumbled through, he grabbed the hand that was holding her, and wrenched it off. His arms swiftly wrapped around her and drew her from the mirror's surface as the golden eyes faded away.

"Are you okay, Ruana? Sorry, he was really close behind me." Anryn stood and stretched. Her olive skin pulling over her smooth muscles.

"Yeah, I'm fine. What is up with Decklyn?" Ruana relaxed into his grip and leaned against the strong wall of his chest. "He looked mad."

"Well, we kind of had an argument about me coming here. He has gotten really paranoid lately about my safety." She flipped her hair over one nude shoulder, and twisted.

"Why just lately?"

"Ah, something to do with the pregnancy. He thinks I might put myself in danger." Anryn finished stretching. "Introductions please?" She wandered over to where Zan still had Ruana in his grip, still unabashedly naked after her trip through the mirror. The only thing she was wearing was a tattoo and a choker of dark blue opal. It pulsed gently, glowing from within.

"My name is Anryn Warder. You would be the werewolf who slept with my cousin?" Anryn's brow arched over her bright green eyes. At first glance her skin appeared to be an olive tone, but upon closer inspection, she was actually green. A deep blue tattoo with an intricate pattern ran across her neck and collarbone. The tone set off her midnight hair, which was the only thing she was wearing over her form.

He set Ruana off to the side and bowed. "Aleczander Masters, please to meet you. May I offer you some clothing?"

"Gentlemanly conduct. Oh, he's a keeper. Yeah, a shirt or something would be great." She crossed her arms over her breasts and waited while he rummaged through the closet behind the mirror.

She caught the white dress shirt that he threw at her. A delicate sniff told her that it had just come back from the cleaners. Great, one less thing for Decklyn to get upset over. The less she irritated her husband the better. The last time she had been grounded for a week. That was when he had discovered her ticklish spots.

"Thanks." She shrugged into it and then straightened her shoulders. "Okay, shall we go downstairs and plan the defence, or do you want to have some private time together?"

Both of them looked longingly over at the bed, then at each other. Zan made the decision. "Downstairs. I think it's time for lunch anyway." He ushered them out of the room and down the stairway to the kitchen.

The ladies sat on the kitchen stools and watched him prepare a selection of sandwiches. There had been at least four minutes of silence when it finally clicked. Ruana jumped to her feet and shrieked in delight as she embraced her cousin. "You're pregnant! Congratulations! How long? When are you due?"

"Enough, enough. I am just ending my first month. Hopefully, the little one will keep to mommy's biology and not daddy's." She patted her softly curved belly gently. There was no hint of her pregnancy in her body yet, but the glow surrounding her proved it.

"Do you know if it's a boy or girl?"

"It's a boy. But I saw that one coming even before I met Decklyn, remember?" She was referring of course to a bunch of the cousins sneaking into Realm to go to the Vision Falls. It was to find out if they would fall for humans, or something else. Decklyn definitely qualified in the second category.

"Oh, of course. You know, I had forgotten all about that." She looked over at Zan where he was still busy pursuing the last of the mayonnaise. A brilliant smile broke over her features.

She crouched down to whisper. "So, if Zan agrees, can you do it? The hand-fasting I mean."

Anryn whispered back, "As soon as I get Albina and her Djinn here. Just let me have lunch first."

"Lunch is ready. You might want to eat it now." Zan's whisper caused Anryn to blink then laugh out loud. He had leaned in over the table and was only inches from their hushed conversation.

"Right, let's eat." Without further ado, she grabbed one of the sandwiches and began to devour it in a manner most disturbing to the couple watching her.

With a muffled "Sorry." she kept stuffing her face until the sandwich, a plate of pickles, and half of a bag of chips had been demolished.

Ruana carefully kept her food out of her cousin's reach. She ate slowly, knowing that a second meal that day would not be likely. Zan followed her example, hoarding his food away from the remorseless eating machine that was sharing the table with them.

Finally, brushing crumbs and debris from her lips, Anryn faced them. "Okay. Now I need to know before we go any further, are you two willing to spend the rest of your lives together? Divorce won't kill this bond. You will in effect become one soul." She burped delicately. "Zan, I know that this is coming on you kinda fast, but you're going to have to keep up."

"You agreed to marry Ruana to protect her from the werewolf clans that are bidding on her. There is no need for that. Her clan can protect her and you for that matter. But if you truly want to have her in your care for the rest of your life, we can hand-fast you today. It is a legally binding ceremony, and will let you call on the Warder clan as you need it."

"You can think it over, but don't take too long. There are delegations from three of the werewolf clans on their way here at this moment, and they will be here in three hours. Fortunately, my husband will arrive here in two."

"Oh, and just so you are clear on this. The hand fasting is only temporary. You'll need to suffer through an official Realm wedding before you can get her pregnant. But have fun practicing." She gave Zan a brilliant smile and he actually blushed in response to her frank appraisal.

She stopped to take a deep breath. "I'm going to set a few wards around your property. I'll be back in about an hour and a half. Talk it over." Giving Ruana a peck on the cheek, and Zan a clap on the shoulder, she left the farmhouse to give them some privacy.

Idly she walked through the yard and picked up pebbles. With a flick of her mind she charged them with warding power and then padded barefoot into the woods.

ZAN LOOKED OVER at Ruana, "Whew. Your cousin is a little, hmm… focused. And green. She is definitely green."

Ruana was tidying up the lunch dishes. "I told you that she was half dryad. Didn't you believe me?"

"Well, she was more than I expected. What exactly is her husband? He didn't look human either." Zan moved to help her, drying and putting the dishes away as she washed them.

Amusement crossed her face. "Oh, I don't want to spoil the surprise. Besides, you'll meet him soon enough. He should be here this afternoon." She paused for a moment. "I hope that he remembers to shield his presence. He might scare your neighbours."

With hands dripping with foam and water she turned to him, "Zan, are you sure about me? I mean, we only just met."

"Yes, I am sure. I was prepared to fight the other wer clans to keep you, remember?" His hands gripped her hips and pulled her to him. He drew his head down to her neck and inhaled deeply. "Are you sure that your family will be able to convince them to leave you with me?"

Her head fell back, her wet hands grabbing his shoulders for support. "Trust me, they won't be able to touch me once we've been hand-fasted." Her actions exposed the bite marks on her neck. He snarled his approval at the marks of his possession on her body.

Ravenous, his eyes burning with heat, he took her mouth with his. Her fingers slid up to twine in his hair and hold his mouth against hers as he ravaged her. She lifted her legs to wrap around his waist and, using the counter at her back to brace herself, rubbed herself slowly against him.

The air came out of him in a shuddering groan. His hands held her hips against him, taking her weight, and began to walk to his bedroom with her twined around him.

Ruana began to shake in his grasp. Lust fired along every nerve. This was far different than the uncontrollable heat of the week before. This was deliberate arousal, surrendering to her desires for the first time by her own choice.

As he took her to his bed, she hoped that she wasn't making the biggest mistake of her life.

Chapter Five

RUANA VERY SWIFTLY FOUND THE DIFFERENCE BETWEEN LAST WEEK AND NOW. THEN IT was sex, a violent drive to release and satisfaction. Now, it was making love. Forging a bond between them, as Zan slowly peeled her clothing from her to place it neatly on a nearby chair. Neat freak. As he uncovered each inch of delicate flesh, he tasted it. Pressing his mouth against her in a kiss that had her sighing in enjoyment.

She tried to return the favour, reaching for the buttons on his shirt and undoing two of them before his hands drew hers aside.

"Next time, I promise. This time let me." His kiss found the sensitive spot on the side of her neck, and her head tilted to allow him to make use of his discovery.

As he progressed with his unveiling, she moaned, panted and whimpered in turn. At last she stood before him, clad only in quivering eagerness. This too, was far different from the last time. She had not been unclothed to his human eyes. Nor he to hers.

His eyes devoured her from head to toe. Pausing at her neck, breasts, hips and caressing her legs in a burning path that raised goose bumps on her. "I had no idea," was all that he said.

They would be the last words spoken for an hour.

With impatient movements he pulled his own clothing off. Sparing none of the care that he had shown while undressing her. His shirt flew off in one direction, his pants in another. His shoes disappeared and his socks evaporated. When his hands began to draw off his briefs, Ruana flushed and looked away. She had not seen him nude before, only felt him.

With a smile and eager hands he reached for her, drawing her against him. She felt the hard length of his cock against her belly, and shifted her hips to rub her soft skin against him. He grunted in response to the caress and lifted her onto the bed. Laying her out on her back and hovering over her on raised arms. His body completely shielded hers from the daylight, and she could only make out the shadows of his face above her, surrounded as he was by the afternoon sun.

Deliberately, he lowered his body onto hers. Murmuring in pleasure at the contact of her soft flesh, the slide of her thighs parting to accommodate him. She felt the liquid heat leaking from her, wetting the curls at the juncture of her thighs. As his weight settled on her, her hips arched against him, seeking more thorough contact. Her thighs lifted high against his hips opening her body wide in invitation to the fiery shaft that waited just outside her reach.

He moved to lodge his cock within her entrance, then waited. Her body squirmed, unable to impale herself without his assistance. She met his eyes, finally opening her eyes after closing them to sensation. As her eyes locked with his, he slowly drove his flesh into hers. Every time she closed her eyes, he stopped until she opened them again.

She bit her lip and moaned as he was finally, fully within her. She kept her gaze on him as he began to thrust gently, and experimentally closed her eyes to have him stop once again.

She laughed gently, then focused on his face as he made love to her, her hands moving into his hair and stroking his shoulders. Time slowed. All too soon she felt the shivers of her release beginning within her. Breathy cries flew out of her throat, her hands turned to claws, digging into Zan's flesh as he buried himself within hers.

She began to buck against him with every thrust, keeping her gaze on his face, though her eyes had gone blind with pleasure. A howl burst from her throat as she lifted them both off the bed with her orgasm. Her back arched, all of their weight borne on her shoulders as her channel pulsed around him, until she slumped with boneless exhaustion back onto the sheets.

He stopped again. She lifted heavy lashes to see the satisfaction and masculine pleasure on his face at her obvious exhaustion. Once she had opened her eyes, he began to thrust again. In less than a dozen strokes, she felt him shudder and his own howl of release rent the air. The sticky pearls of semen broadcasted into their new home. Zan's eyes had gone blind during his orgasm as well, his body and mind focused on the divine release of pleasure. Her aftershocks milked him as he slowly collapsed against her, burying his face in the pillow, resting his weight on her warm, sated body.

Minutes passed, Ruana lay fighting to regain her breath. His weight on her was not helping. He seemed to figure it out though, and shifted to the side, pulling free of her body with a sigh of regret.

Still not speaking, he cuddled her against him, and breathed deeply of their combined scents. The silence stretched between them. Finally, he spoke again. "Yes, Ruana. I am sure."

Tilting her head back, she saw the truth in his eyes. She moved and kissed his lips gently, "So am I, Zan. So am I."

Slow and rhythmic applause broke out. Zan flipped quickly to put himself between Ru and the intruder. Anryn stood in the doorway, leaning against the frame of the open door, her hands making a loud noise in the empty hallway.

"Very impressive cousin." Anryn walked into the room, the borrowed shirt as pristine as when she had first put it on. It did not look at all like she had been wandering in the woods. Unless of course, one looked at her feet, which were stained with dirt and leaves.

"Is he as good as he looks?" Unabashed, she perched on the side of the bed and looked at her satisfied and blushing cousin.

"Anryn, could you give us some privacy. Please." Ruana's voice was husky from her screams, she tried to tug the sheets up to cover herself, but Zan was sitting on them.

"Already did, Ru. Two hours worth. Albina and Imaran are downstairs." She got off the bed and sauntered to the door. "Decklyn is only ten minutes away, you might want to be dressed when he arrives." With a short laugh, she disappeared. "It wouldn't do to look like prey."

Ruana looked over at Zan. "Two hours?" Her voice was weak.

"It only seemed like a few minutes to me as well." He shook off his bemusement. By nature he was territorial, but now his new mate's family was invading his territory. The sacrifices he was willing to make. He rose to his feet and scooped her off the tangled sheets.

Moving swiftly, he herded her into the en suite bathroom and shoved them both into the shower. As his hands moved over her curves, he promised himself that the next time that they were together, they would take their time.

He soaped and rinsed them both, then wrapped a towel around his hips, where a tent belied his interest in her naked form, and dried her swiftly with another.

She looked longingly at the erection that had so obviously been caused by the close contact in the shower. "You know, sometimes, I hate my family."

Zan just laughed. A strained sound that echoed off of the bathroom tiles. "Let's just get dressed, and get this over with." He looked over at the devastation in the bedroom and shook his head. Wandering over to the dresser, he opened a drawer and pulled out some briefs for himself.

"I can't wait to see how you get into those." Ruana took a longing look once more at his erection as he attempted to wedge it behind the cotton fabric. Her clothes were all located on the chair where he had put them. Her dressing was quick and painless, but she caught him grimacing out of the corner of her eye as he zipped his jeans up over his briefs.

"Am I decent?" She checked the mirror once more, to make sure that everything was tucked into its proper place. His arms wrapped around her and he murmured into her ear. "I would say that you were fantastic. Not just decent."

He had pulled on a shirt, but not done up the buttons. His skin radiated heat and she snuggled into his embrace, revelling in the contact. She inhaled deeply and the scent of their coupling was still hanging in the air.

"Do me a favour, Zan?"

"Sure, Ruana. What do you need?"

"Don't go too far, okay? I don't want Decklyn to eat you." A tiny laugh escaped her lips, but he gave her a startled squeeze as her reflection told him that she wasn't kidding.

Heavy wing beats filled the air. "He's here. Stay close."

"What the hell?" But he was talking to air as she slipped from his grasp to make her way to the door.

"Coming? Time to meet the in-laws." Ruana skipped out of the room and made her way down the stairs to the front door, Zan hard on her heels.

"Holy shit!" There was no other word that sprang to mind as he watched a dragon land in the yard outside the door.

Over forty-five feet long, Decklyn had navy scales and golden eyes. Zan was soon to learn that those eyes followed him in all forms.

Anryn wandered out of the house and straight up to the ferocious beast that was snorting smoke in agitation.

"Hey honey! You made good time." She reached up and stroked her hand down his scaled, reptilian neck. He let out a snort and pulled away from the caress. "Why don't you shift forms and I can introduce you to Ruana's choice."

Her hand reached out once again, this time to scratch him under his chin. "C'mon honey. Let's be civil about this. The baby is fine, and I'm not going to spend the next nine months chained to your bed." An evil leer lit her face, "As much fun as that has been."

A resigned huff flew out of the dragon's mouth and he shook his enormous head in frustration. Slowly he began to shrink, taking the shape of a man, but retaining the wings and claws that he had possessed in his earlier form. He was handsome enough. His features hewn by a rough hand, his scales almost imperceptible in the human form. He was also naked.

"Don't ever run from me again, Anryn." His hands grabbed her arms and he lifted her effortlessly to hold her eye to eye with him. His golden slitted eyes burning into her green and black gaze. She dangled in the air unconcerned, waiting. Finally he sighed and brought her in for a gentle kiss. Her hands came up to cup his face and soon she was sliding down to stand on her own two feet once again.

"You know that when the clan needs me, I'm there. It would be best in the future if you put aside your anti-social behaviour patterns and just came with me." Her hands restlessly stroked his shoulders and chest. Petting and soothing him.

His arms wrapped around her and held her close. Breathing in her scent, resigning himself to a lifetime of chasing this woman around the globe. Not the worst fate he could have imagined. At least the view from behind was pleasant.

Decklyn grinned then, exposing his teeth, causing Zan to flinch. Those were some serious fangs.

"Decklyn, I would like to introduce you to Ruana's wolf, Zan. Zan, this is Decklyn." How she could make herself understood while mashed against the enormous chest was beyond Zan, but her voice chimed out clearly.

"Please to meet you." Decklyn reluctantly released his mate and extended his hand to Zan. He took it in a handshake that was polite and controlled on both their parts.

Ruana hovered nervously nearby. She did know that Decklyn had, at some point in the past, hunted members of wer clans for sport. She hoped that he would be polite.

"You as well, please come inside. I'll see if I can find you something to wear."

"Wear? Oh, right." He shrugged and followed Zan into the house. Each male keeping his female within his embrace as they entered the house.

Zan was brought up short as he saw the other members of the Warder clan that Anryn had mentioned earlier.

"Albina and Imaran I presume?" The pale woman with white hair stood next to a man with obvious exotic ancestors. He sighed and shook his head, then walked forward to take their hands. He would have to ask Ruana about warding his house to keep out her family after this was all over. The intrusions to his territory were setting his nerves on edge.

"I'm sorry, we would have introduced ourselves when we arrived, but you were…occupied." Albina's voice was quiet. Everything about her was so serene it was unnerving. The only spot of colour in her face were her blue eyes and the red flower of her mouth.

In contrast her companion was a study in the harsh colours of the desert. Mahogany skin, black hair and deep black eyes took Zan's measure as he approached them.

Satisfied with what he saw, Imaran offered his assistance. "I see that Anryn and Decklyn have been traveling without clothing again." He clapped his hands together, and where an afghan had lain against the couch, clothing for the couple appeared.

"I think I need a cup of coffee." Zan walked swiftly to the kitchen, still keeping Ruana in tow.

"Zan, could you let go now? I promise not to take off." She spoke to him in low tones, knowing that his nerves had had enough of a jolt for the moment.

"Huh? Oh sure." He filled the carafe with water and began the mundane activity of making coffee for the oddest group of beings that he had ever imagined.

And he had just signed on to join the family.

Chapter Six

THE COFFEE MAKER CHUGGED AWAY, THE DRIPPING AND CHIRPING OF THE MECHANISM the only noise in the silence surrounding Zan. The smell crept through the kitchen with the insidious insistence endemic to the beverage.

"A little overwhelming aren't they? You are regretting your decision now aren't you?" Ruana was miserable, tears welling in her eyes. Her fingers picked at the tabletop, shaking slightly.

"Ruana, just give me a moment, okay?" His hand reached out to grasp hers across the table, his thumb began to rub against her palm, giving her what comfort he could. His mind was still grappling with dragons, djinn, dryads and witches. Well, he was a werewolf, so why not?

Seeking comfort, Ru moved over to sit in his lap, cuddling against him. She could feel his confusion battering at her mind. The bonding was something that she was not going to tell him about until…well, maybe in ten years. She figured that he might have come out of his shock by then. She dug deeper into the emotions that were leaking into her mind, and she found his resolve to have her. He still hadn't changed his mind. She sighed in relief and snuggled closer as she let his mind work through the new information that challenged everything he had ever believed.

"SO, HOW DO you think he's taking it?" Imaran conjured drinks for them all.

"Fairly well, I think." Anryn frowned at Decklyn as he took her wine away. "I can occasionally have a glass you know."

"Best to abstain until the baby arrives. I read it in a women's magazine." Albina started laughing. The air of authority that the dragon assumed was almost ridiculous, until Anryn added her two cents.

"He's not kidding. He has read every damned book on modern pregnancy and the appropriate diet for me that it's no wonder I ran." Despite her acerbic comments, she snuggled against her mate and pulled his arm around her. The clothing that Imaran had provided was comfortable, but covered less than Zan's shirt. The halter-top and sarong were made of a gossamer fabric.

Fortunately Decklyn gave off a lot of heat. He was wearing a similar outfit, a loose vest that left his wings free, with a wrap kilt. The fabric was nice and soft. She breathed deeply and slowly, nodding into one of the naps that she had become infamous for since she had become pregnant.

"Imaran, may I compliment you on your choice of clothing?" Decklyn's voice was deep and soft, carefully not waking Anryn. "She hasn't cuddled with me like this since the first week we were together."

Imaran dropped his own voice to a whisper. "You mean the week when you used your talents to knock her out, then seduced her?" A dark chuckle rolled over the sleeping dryad and she stirred and shifted restlessly.

Decklyn resettled her quickly, stroking her arms and thigh to calm her. "Yes, that week."

TWISTING IN HIS chair, Zan filled the coffee cup he had put on the counter. He slowly sipped the dark, bracing brew. Ruana kept her head clear of the mug. He seemed to really need that coffee.

"So, you take your coffee black?" Idle chitchat seemed the way to go.

He seemed willing to play along. "Yes, how do you take yours?"

"Three cream, three sugars, more like syrup than coffee." She paused for a moment. "Do you think that we could rejoin the others in the living room? We need to make some plans."

"Are there any more of your clan joining us today?"

"Only my mom and dad, possibly one other. Are you expecting yours?"

"Max and Arissa. Our pack Alpha, Merlin. Oh, and his bodyguards. Anyone else will be an uninvited guest."

"Okay. My troops are ready." Ruana thought for a moment. "Oh, hell." In an instant she was out of his lap and heading for the living room. Entering the room to find Anryn snoring gently in Decklyn's arms, she stopped short, Zan right behind her.

Whispering, "When is she going to wake up?" she crept closer to the couples making themselves at home.

In about ten minutes, what's up? It was not the first time that she had heard Albina's inner voice, but the strength of it always surprised her. It was at such odds with her delicate appearance.

Zan has some relatives coming to the house today. I am afraid that the wards will hurt them, or leave them vulnerable. A rough start with his pack is not what I need right now.

I'll have Decklyn wake her then. She can nap later. A smile lit Albina's face. *Actually, now that she's pregnant, she can nap right after she alters the wards.*

Decklyn frowned for a moment and then slowly began to rub Anryn's back. Less than a minute later, she was sitting up and rubbing her eyes.

Ruana explained the situation, Zan standing behind her, his alarm creeping into her mind. Anryn yawned, rose and stumbled for the door. She missed.

Decklyn rose up off the couch and sighed as he steered her out the door and down the driveway.

The rest of them sat in silence after Ruana had fetched coffee and cream for them. Ten minutes later, looking considerably more alert, Anryn walked through the door, Decklyn on her heels.

"Well, I'm glad you woke me up. Not only was your family on their way, but there were three werewolves snagged in the outer ward. Decklyn scared them off." She didn't go into detail, but resumed her seat on the couch, then scooted over as her husband sat next to her, carefully settling his wings over the back of the couch once again.

Albina perked up, "Perfect timing. Ruana, your parents are here." As she finished speaking, the door shuddered under the knocking of David's fist.

Zan went to the door, to meet his soon-to-be father-in-law. The two wolves sized each other up. Each glaring at the other to assert their superiority.

"Mom! Call him off!" Ruana went to Zan's side, and Victoria went to David's. Each female broke the eye contact that the males had going by the simple expedience of stepping between them.

With no respect for the traditions of the werewolf way of life, the women dragged the men into the living room.

"Sit down, David! Behave or I'll send you home." Victoria was much more aggressive than usual, but after all, her baby's happiness was at stake. Stupid macho posturing was not going to wreck it.

He sat. The sullen expression on his face would have made her laugh, if Zan had not been wearing its twin.

"Dad, this is Aleczander Masters. Brother to Maxwell Masters, of the Silverfang clan. Zan this is my father, David Weldon, and my mother Victoria."

"Call me Vicky, dear."

"Pleased to meet you both. Be welcome in my house."

David relaxed into the couch and smiled ruefully at Zan, then glanced over to his daughter. "Well, at least you had the sense to choose someone who could protect you."

He didn't get the chance to elaborate on that point as the door swung open to admit Max, Arissa and a man whom she could only guess was Merlin. It was rather funny, as Merlin bore a startling resemblance to both Max and Zan. Only he was an older version.

Zan jumped to attention and hastened to make the introductions. "Ruana Weldon, this is the Alpha of the Silverfang clan, Merlin Masters. My father."

Chapter Seven

"I am pleased to welcome you to our clan, Ruana. Max has spoken well of you." Merlin was as handsome as his sons, the silver streaks running through his hair the only indicator of greater age.

"I am honoured to meet you as well." She went up to him and placed her forehead in the centre of his chest, neck bent in submission. His hand came up to close on the back of her neck, and she felt the pressure of his grip. She didn't move. She kept her breathing even, despite the pain that was beginning to radiate from her neck. Minutes flew by in silence as he applied sufficient pressure to crush the neck of a regular human. Finally, she reached her threshold and her legs buckled under her.

Merlin caught her and raised her back to a standing position and held her at arms length until her legs would once again hold her weight.

Zan was right behind her to take her from Merlin as he handed her over.

"You have a strong one there, Zan. Take care of her." Merlin looked extremely pleased.

"My turn." Victoria stood and addressed the members of the Warder clan that were in attendance. "Do any of you have reservations about welcoming Zan into our clan?"

Silence. The werewolves looked vaguely puzzled. None of the Warder clan members who had arrived had any objections to the match. They had all discreetly tested and probed him with magic as soon as they had arrived. He passed the tests. With the added bonus of his not running screaming from the farmhouse when he met them.

"Will you defend Ruana's choice?"

"Aye." Five voices spoke as one, David adding to the crowd.

"Will you witness the hand-fasting? Right here...right now?"

"Aye."

A grin broke over Victoria's face. "Anryn, open a gateway to Realm. I think we have a final guest."

The rest of the Warder clan burst into laughter. They knew what was coming, or more to the point who.

Anryn wandered out the door once again, completely oblivious to the admiring looks from Merlin and Max. Decklyn was not. His fangs came out, gleaming and vicious. The two wolves took a good look at the dragon following his wife out the door and kept their eyes to themselves.

The rest of the crowd trailed them out, the wolves puzzled and the Warders laughing. Anryn took up a position between two trees and stretched her arms out from her sides.

Ruana took Zan's hand and whispered, "Watch this."

A shimmering light surrounded Anryn, building swiftly to a blinding glow that had the wolves yelping in confusion. A circle of light shot from her to the two trees she had selected. It formed a web between them, thickening in width until a shimmering doorway was visible.

From the doorway, a figure emerged. Graceful, tall and garbed in flowing robes, it was impossible to determine the sex of the figure. As it cleared the gateway, Anryn closed it. Decklyn moved in and caught her in his arms as she slumped forward. "You're done for today."

"Eylonwy!" Ruana rushed forward and threw her arms around the figure.

As the light faded behind it, the figure was shown to be female. With extremely pointy ears. She hugged Ruana in return and walked forward to greet the rest of the clan members. After a round of hugs all around she turned to be introduced to the others.

"Eylonwy Warder, this is the Alpha of the Silverfang clan, Merlin Masters, his daughter-in-law Arissa Masters, and his sons Maxwell and Aleczander." Victoria made the introductions. "Members of the Silverfang clan, this is our elder Eylonwy Warder. She oversees all unions of our clan members. She also has the ability to bind magic into the union, defending both members against all attacks."

Eylonwy smiled graciously and shook the hands of the Masters family, one by one. At Zan she stopped. "Are you ready to join our little circus?" Her full lips parted in a grin.

He took a deep breath and looked at the expectant faces around him, "I am."

"Then shall we?" A graceful hand swept forward and flowers bloomed around the two trees that had housed the gateway. In a matter of moments that corner of the yard was covered in a riot of colour that created a beautiful and natural setting for the ceremony.

"Zan, Ruana, will you step forward? Anryn, Merlin. You as well." Eylonwy backed into position, her rainbow robes flowing around her graceful form as she moved. "Sorry for the hurry people, but we are under the gun here. I can feel them coming."

From the air, it seemed, she drew a length of red silk cord between her fingers. She gestured for Ruana and Zan to take each other's hands. Silently she bound their hands together.

"Bride, do you give yourself of your own free will?"

With a long look at Zan, "I do."

"Groom, do you give yourself of your own free will?"

Zan looked to their joined hands, around at her family and his, then, "I do."

Another cord appeared in her hand and Eylonwy wrapped it around the first. "I call upon the Air to witness." A gentle wind blew through the bower, ruffling the petals of the flowers and scenting the area with perfume.

"I call upon the Earth to witness." Another cord tied into place, as a rose bush sprang up between the couple.

"I call upon Fire to witness." Another cord appeared, and a rock near the couple burst into flame.

"I call upon Water to witness." Dew formed on the roses as the next cord went on.

"Warders, please surround the couple. Join hands. I call upon the Warders to bind, witness and protect." As she finished speaking, power flared between the joined hands of the women surrounding the couple. The bindings disappeared, becoming one with the two who had just sworn their joining. Eylonwy smiled as the hand fasting completed. It was her specialty, and her natural magic lent itself well to the joining of lives. After five hundred years, she still loved her job.

Zan and Ruana staggered back as the flash faded. They stood blinking in the rush of power that was flowing through them. "It is finished. They are bound as one for a year and a day. Let no one try to put the union asunder." Eylonwy raised her hands in the air, and then released them all with a gesture.

The husbands came forward to collect their wives, and Eylonwy wandered over to Anryn. Placing glowing hands on her shoulders, improving her colour and earning a look of thanks from Decklyn. She transferred her power to her cousin in a few seconds, then stood with a grim look on her elegant face.

"Alright, Anryn, drop the wards. Let them come."

THE WOLVES DID not know what was holding them at bay. The three of the

Yellowpaw clan that had attacked earlier had run back to their clans with tales of monsters.

If the Silverfangs had been willing to bargain for the bitch, this would not have happened. But even allowing them the first child from the bitch had not been enough. They wanted to keep her. That was not going to happen. They wanted that bitch for their clans, and they were willing to kill the Silverfangs to get her. There were only three there, after all.

They felt the instant that the barrier melted and surged forward in a wave. Sixteen members of the Goldeneye clan were involved in the attack. Eight members of the Fightinghart clan were with them.

As one they rushed through the woods, never questioning that they were all taking the same path to the farmhouse. They could hear voices in the light of the farmhouse ahead and moved faster.

Chapter Eight

THE WARDERS FACED THE ATTACKING WOLVES. SEVERAL OF THE WEREWOLVES HAD transferred into the half-change form that would give them the most power during an attack. The others figured that they had the Silverfangs outnumbered.

The Warders took up flanking position on Ruana and Zan. The newly bonded couple was front and centre when the attackers broke through the cover of the trees. Hitting the wall of power, that Anryn had laid down earlier on Ruana's behalf, caused some of them to flip through the air at the impact.

Ruana heard a few bones break as they hit the ground and took a deep breath then asked the question that they had to answer. "What do you want here?"

"We have come for you bitch. The next time you go into heat, one of us will fuck you until you pop pregnant. Then we will wait for the next time. The same thing will happen again. Hey, we might even have a lottery to see who ploughs you next…maybe a raffle?" His voice dissolved into twisted laughter.

"You may not have her. By the decrees of her clan and mine. She and I are married in front of witnesses." Zan's voice was strong, but he edged her back behind him. She stepped aside, then moved around him.

Decklyn was suddenly behind Zan, restraining him. "Let her do this. It's what she does best."

With an inviting smile on her lips, Ruana walked forward swinging her hips. "If you want me, try to take me." Her arms raised, palms up and she waited.

It didn't take long. The first wer to grab her wrist and tug with a leer in his eyes, screamed as a lightning bolt of power went through him. His body flipped backward and he lay moaning and smoking gently. The second went the way of the first.

The third came up behind her and had to be peeled off of her as the shock had locked his muscles into rigor.

"Are you getting the hint yet? I am not up for grabs. I can destroy anyone who dares to touch me. I belong only to Zan, only to the Silverfang clan, and only to the Warder clan. You can take that back to your Alpha's and let them know that hunting season is over."

Shocked and confused, they only paused a moment before dragging their wounded off of the yard and down the road.

"You mean, you could have done that at any time?" Zan's voice was a gentle whisper as he held her close, trying to stop her shaking.

"No, the hand-fasting gave me the extra power I needed. No one can touch me with lust now but you." She turned into his arms and started to cry. At first it was a gentle sobbing, but soon it grew into uncontrollable wrenching hysterics. He lifted her into his arms and began to walk back into the house.

Eylonwy stepped in front of him, "I will see everyone safely home." She leaned forward and gave him a gentle kiss on his forehead. "Don't worry, she always cries at weddings." He smiled at her and took his sobbing bride into the house one more time. Only to be thwarted by his brother, "What the hell just happened here?"

"I'll explain tomorrow, now get out of my way or I'll go through you." He was no longer smiling, as Ruana's crying seemed to get weaker with every passing moment.

Hurriedly he carried her up the stairs and into his bedroom once again. Carefully turning the mirror against the wall as soon as he laid her down on the bed.

She looked up at him with eyes red and swollen, "I hurt them. I never meant to hurt them. I only wanted to stun them enough to make them back off."

Oh, so that was the problem. He removed his clothes, then started on hers. She was limp in his arms as he peeled off her shirt and pants. Her white bra and panties glowed in the dim light of the tiny lamp next to the bed. It was wired to the light switch, he usually did not need a lot of light in the dark, but tonight he wanted the light of a thousand candles.

Her bra closed in back so he had to release the clasp by reaching around her and she quickly grabbed him and held him close. She wanted comfort, and was willing to tackle him to get it.

She had been so passive in his arms that her sudden movement caught him off guard, and off balance. He fell to his back and a second later she had discarded both her bra and the matching prim panties.

"My turn." She braced her hands next to his shoulders and slowly drew her body against his. Over and over she repeated the caress of her flesh against him. Her nipples had hardened to points and she shivered in response as they dragged through his chest hair. Her knees were astride his hips rubbing her pelvis against his hardening erection with every twisted push-up she did. She moved forward a few inches more, to let his hard hot cock rest against the sopping wetness of her open cunt.

She continued to rock against him, driving the flames in her loins higher and higher. He started to groan with every stroke. On shaking arms, she pushed herself astride him. Pulling her knees in beside his hips, his engorged cock brushed against the weeping channel between her thighs. Taking a deep and shuddering breath, she began to slowly and cautiously lower herself onto him.

As he slid home she drew a sighing breath of relief. Oh God, it felt good. She inhaled his scent as she began to move on him. Her head tilted back and her eyes closed as she rose and fell on him, revelling in the slow slide of his pulsing flesh within her slick walls. She moved faster and faster, driving for her own release, taking Zan along for the ride.

She felt her orgasm approaching, and felt his hands on her breasts as her hips began to stutter in their rhythm. Ruana's eyes opened, she moved her head to meet his gaze as his devilish fingers twisted and kneaded the flushed mounds of her breasts. Their eyes remained locked as he trailed one hand down to twist his middle finger against her clit in a short circular motion. Her breath rushed out of her and she froze as she came with the twist of his hand.

As her back arched, she felt him begin to come within her, his eyes glowing into hers in the darkness. Ruana's body shook as it milked Zan's cock of its payload, the delicate palpitations of her flesh caressing him with gentle insistence. She dropped forward, crawling onto his chest as he slipped from within her welcoming heat.

"Mmm. Nice." She burrowed her nose in the join between his neck and shoulder. She inhaled deeply, enjoying their scents twined together.

It seemed eons before Zan commented as well, but perhaps it took him that long to recover. "I heartily agree."

A sudden realization made her raise her head. "Hey, wait a minute. Did I just do all the work?"

Her comfortable resting spot was suddenly undergoing an earthquake. He stopped laughing for a moment. "Yep. And I look forward to you doing it again. Soon."

She groaned and put her face into the pillow next to him. "Mf, tngt m dmt."

"What?" He tugged at her hair, lifting her face away from her muffler.

She glared at him as well as she could with the sated pulse flowing through her veins. “Not tonight you don’t. I need a nap.”

He chuckled again and then cuddled her against him. He flipped a sheet over them both, and laid back, breathing deeply. “This has been a very eventful day. I think we both need our rest.” He pressed a sweet kiss against her forehead and held her close as her breathing slowed into the even rhythm of sleep.

As he drifted off to his own rest, his voice issued a thin wave of sound. “Ruana, thanks for wearing that damned ugly dress.”

The Warder's Vampire

PROLOGUE

"C'MON MITZY, WHAT DO YOU NEED? YOU KNOW I'M NOCTURNAL." SERAFINA Zenecar rubbed her eyes as her sister fidgeted with a teacup across from her. Her eyes were sensitive to daylight, it was just easier to do her work and socializing after the sun went down.

"I am so sorry to wake you, Sera, but I need your help." She put her teacup down with a clatter that startled her half-sister into gripping her hand to steady her.

"What is it? You know that I would do anything for you, but what do you need from me that Mom or Symon can't do?"

Mitzy took a shuddering breath and blurted, "I need you to take my shift at the Repository this All Hallows Eve."

Sera blinked in astonishment. It was Mitzy's source of pride that she had been the Warder chosen to guard the Repository of Magical Artefacts in Realm for the last five years. She wouldn't give it up unless... "How pregnant are you?"

"Three months. I haven't told mother yet. I was waiting until Thanksgiving." She sighed deeply and looked over at her half-sister, so different from the rest of the family.

Serafina had always been pale, a creamy ivory that set off her deep chestnut hair and pine green eyes. It was her pointed teeth and slightly pointed ears that gave a hint as to her father's nature. That, plus her sensitivity to sunlight.

The story that their mother told was that a stranger named Zenecar had seduced her at a Yule celebration, and left her with child. The Warders and the councils of Realm determined that the father had been a vampire, leaving poor Serafina to be the only Dhampir to be female in eight hundred years. The half-vamps were male as a rule.

Zenecar's appearance in Realm was itself unusual. The vamps left when the wolves did. Sure that they could make their own way in the human world without the interference of councils, they locked themselves out of Realm with blood and salt.

"Wow, a grandkid. Definitely something to be thankful for." She smiled brightly, showing her fangs, "Hey, I am going to be an Aunty! C'mere you."

She surged to her feet and moved with unnatural speed to hug her sister in a firm but delicate embrace. She had learned years ago that she could be hard on people if she was careless.

She pulled away and held her sister at arm's length. "Wait. Who is the father?"

The blush that had been building earlier flared into full bloom. "Well, you know the band Goblin Rulz?"

"Yep."

"The lead singer, Haruki. He is delighted, but I haven't been able to tell Mom or Dad yet. They aren't that fond of goblins."

Sera thought of her stepfather's stringent attitudes towards other magical species and winced. "Especially ones that can't pass for human."

"Exactly." Tears welled in her eyes. "I didn't even tell them we were dating."

"Symon should know that you had to mate with a non-human. It is one of the Warder bindings. We can't get out of it."

"Yes, well. He has been trying to make connections for me in the Magus guild. Dad wanted me to make a 'proper' match with a magus or wizard of his choosing." Mitzy blushed again. "He thinks that because Mom had you, the curse was satisfied for this generation."

"Oh, come on, Mittens. You know it doesn't work that way."

"I don't think he believed it himself, but he has the normal prejudice towards the non-human races."

"Normal for the Magus guild, you mean."

"Well yeah." Mitzy hesitated for a moment. "Can you tell me what it is?"

"What what is?"

"The baby, whether it is a boy or girl?" Her eyes filled with entreaty, and Sera sighed heavily.

"Are you sure? I can't take it back once you know."

"I'm sure. Haruki wants a little girl, and given the Warder birthrate, I know that it is an eighty percent chance, but I still want to know for sure."

"Alright. Give me a moment." Serafina closed her eyes for a moment and when she opened them her green orbs had changed into her hunting eyes. Slitted red pupils were ensconced in amber irises. Her teeth extended as her mouth opened and magic crackled around her.

Kneeling before her sister, she leaned forward until her face was inches from Mitzy's belly. An exhalation of magic swirled around the fabric of Mitzy's shirt and seconds later Sera stood, patted the abdomen she had just examined for life and looked expectantly at her sister.

"The little one is strong and healthy. Are you sure that you want to know the gender?"

"Please, Sera. This is hard enough without having all the information that I can."

"Alright, Symon will be happy. It is a little boy."

Mitzy's expression crumpled in disappointment. "Not a girl?"

"Well, you have one of those as well. A little girl with the mahogany skin and green tinted hair of her father's people who will carry on the line of the Warders, and a little boy with fair skin and black hair who carries on the Magus line."

A whisper of sound, "Twins?"

"Twins," she confirmed, then Sera darted forward to catch her sister as she fainted. Good thing she had fast reflexes.

She put Mitzy on the couch and set about preparing her special tea.

Using magic always gave her a craving for blood, and reading a pregnancy was no exception. The tea stopped her cravings and let her interact with normal beings on a regular basis without eating them or draining them dry. It came in handy at family gatherings.

By the time the tea was steeping, Mitzy was stirring. "Oh. What the heck happened?"

"I told you that you were having twins and you passed out. A sudden rearrangement of blood in your body. Happens occasionally during a pregnancy I'm told."

"You aren't joking? There are really two of them in here?" Her hands pressed against her abdomen and she looked at her belly in wonder.

"You won't be able to see them like that. Get a sonogram." Sera sipped at her tea and smiled at the bemused glow that was spreading across her sister's features. Her Mediterranean good looks came from their mother, her height from her father.

"Haruki will be so happy."

"So you are going to introduce him to Mom and Symon?"

"Of course. Now that I have inside information." She winked, then wrinkled her nose at the smell of the tea. "You still have to drink that stuff?"

"Yep. Every time I use magic. I will bring a thermos along when I go to the Repository on Halloween. Charging those wards against all that energy is going to be tiring."

Relief lit Mitzy's features. "So, you'll do it?"

"Of course. We can't put my niece and nephew at risk now, can we?" She quickly set her tea down as her sister hurled herself into her arms. She caught her in a gentle hug and smiled into her hair, being a big sister had its fun moments. Doing a favour for her little sister was one of them.

Chapter One

Serafina went over the checklist that Anryn Warder had given her. Books, ward stones, MP3 player, batteries, sandwiches, tea, and a few litres of soda.

Anryn had been the guardian of the Repository for three years until she got a part-time job as a teenager that kept her working on Halloween. The honour and duty had passed through three different warders since, but none that Sera trusted more.

Anryn was currently running her massage therapy business out of her husband's office building. She was also Sera's employer. It made her easy to find.

Now in the sixth month of her own pregnancy, Anryn was stuck in an administrative capacity at the business. Sera was taking on all of the evening clients. She was not the only nocturnal creature living in the mundane world with ties to Realm.

She double checked her supplies and powered up the mirror that would take her to Realm. Taking a deep breath, she stepped through and waited for the magic to carry her to the other side in a swirl of quicksilver and fire.

Realm, the warm rays of the sun combined with the magical pulse of the very air, welcomed her home. It was the only place that she traveled to where the sun welcomed instead of irritated her.

She breathed deeply and stepped off the mirrored platform to greet the guard.

Arov grinned widely as he spoke the ritual words, "Greetings to she who will guard the Repository of Magical Artefacts."

She bowed low and responded, "Greetings to the Guardian of the Gateway on this, the night of spirits."

She stood aside and made sure that no one else was on their way through the mirrors and asked him, "So, how is Albina?"

"Irritated with me. She wanted to attend the festivities, and I am not to be relieved until midnight. She had to choose between my family and hers for the evening."

Sera grinned at that. "So, she is with the cousins?"

"Yes, the werewolves have sent representatives for the festivities for the first time in centuries. I believe that she is with them just to watch their faces."

"Yeah, that does sound like fun." She grimaced, "Well, I had better get to work. The curator will be having a canary by now."

She bowed in response to his formal acknowledgement and set off to the small stand of buildings about half a kilometre away.

It took her only a few minutes and she was able to see the preparations for the great bonfires and the set-up of the stage and buffet tables.

Realm pulled out all the stops for All Hallows Eve. The magic flowed wildly, spirits flew unchecked and the Magus guild called a special service to hold solemn ceremonies. In response to that formality, the other creatures held a huge party.

Sera saw Mitzy in the distance, under the arm of a rather handsome goblin. It must be Haruki, she thought. No one else would have the nerve to keep their arm around her in an area filling up with her family.

Her opinion of the male that had won her sister went up a notch. Apparently he was willing and ready to force Mitzy's hand on making their relationship public.

She turned her mind back to the task at hand and noted the fading of the light. The Repository steps were black granite that glowed as her feet touched it. It acknowledged the magical blood in her veins and the door swung open to welcome her.

"Where have you been? I have been waiting for hours…oh. It's you." The curator was an officious little troll. *Literally*. Asgoth had been curator for the last two hundred years, after a warder had freed him from the confines of a bridge in Germany.

"Yes, Asgoth. It is I. Let's keep the animosity to a minimum, shall we? I need to set up." She dropped her pack to the ground and removed the first five warding crystals.

"Yes, yes, of course. I will be going. You hereby have responsibility for all of the objects in the Repository of Magical Artefacts. Please leave a drop of your blood on the ledger. There is a lancet on the table." Asgoth left through the main doorway and the Repository locked its doors behind him.

As the sun went down, she placed twenty-five ward stones around the building. One in each gallery of the twenty main species of Realm. She then placed one in front of the large mirror, the first traveling mirror designed by

Kesler and Celestyn Warder. It would transport the user to any reflective surface. Even the eye of a dragon.

It was extremely powerful, but not very well controlled, as were most of the artefacts of the Repository. She laughed to herself. As were most of the Warders, if she was honest.

The other four stones went in front of the underground passage, the window in the main hall and two in front of the doors.

Once they were all in place she went into the centre of the building and charged the wards. The stones gleamed in response to her power. She could see the magic coating and locking together the walls of the building. Nothing could come through a door, window, wall, or mirror with the wards up.

Time to have some of her tea, listen to music, and get ready for the four-hour mark when she had to recharge the wards.

As she sipped the brew from her thermos she thought about all of the races whose bloodlines ran through her veins. It had to be almost all of the major races by now, though the dragons tended to try and reclaim their granddaughters every few generations.

That a vampire had sired her was only supposition. No actual testing had ever been done on her, at Symon's insistence. She was an embarrassment to him. His wife's freaky bastard.

She sighed deeply and took another sip. Perhaps she needed to learn more about her so-called father. Since she was already in the Repository she may as well start now.

The halls of the building were made of the same power sensitive granite and marble as the stairs. The glow of her power was reflected in the radiance from the panels beneath her feet. The rooms were as bright as daylight as she passed them.

She stood on the threshold of the vampire collection and tried to see the articles stored there without actually going inside. It was no use. She could see nothing from where she was, only a collection of books and small articles were visible from the doorway.

She would have to go in.

Steeling herself she took a few steps forward, she gasped in amazement at the tapestries and works of art, which hung on the walls. Warriors and their ladies from over two thousand years in the past stared at her. One warrior in particular caught her attention.

He was without a lady by his side and holding a sword hilt in either hand. Obviously a warrior vampire. Trained and bred to lead and conquer.

A shiver went through her at the hint of arousal that followed the last thought and she looked quickly away from the hypnotic eyes that seemed to be calling her into the portrait.

Chapter Two

She shook her head and wandered through the vampire artefacts. She idly picked up daggers, opened chests, and tried on armour. There were no mirrors in the Vampire Gallery but she could see her reflection in the panels of glass guarding the dangerous artefacts. Before she knew it, it was time to recharge the wards.

Serafina wandered back into the centre of the building and poured her power into the stones. She was staggering slightly and had to take a break at the information desk. The lancet and the book lay open and ready for her.

She sighed heavily and pricked her finger, marking the book, and watching her designation in magical script come to life as it sprung from her blood. No other being had magic that would make the same mark, and she watched the graceful calligraphy that was uniquely hers with pride.

All the colours of the rainbow, and some that were not, flowed through her blood.

She tore herself away from the fascination with her own magic and energy to slowly make her way through the halls and to the Warder's cupboard. It was not common knowledge, but hundreds of years earlier Calliope Warder had created a dimensional portal for the express purpose of holding the soul stones of the Warder family.

The stones were far too precious to leave in any one person's hand and with the increase in the size of the family it was only prudent to put them somewhere safe. What could be safer than the Repository in Realm?

A touch of her hand opened a section of wall that the curator was not aware of and into it she went. A small flare of magic created light that allowed her to see that arranged on the walls was the history of her family.

Relics holding cursed objects and confined energies of evil were kept carefully in locked cases. Only the elders of their family could open them, and only then if they were in desperate need. Portraits of the initial seven Warders who survived the punishment of the councils hung proudly on the walls. The portraits of their descendants stretched as far as the eye could see down the endless hall. It was grander than all of the other races' galleries combined.

Dimensional doorways were useful things.

She wandered to the portrait of Alethea. Her own ancestor whose marriage to a dragon produced one of the most creative women in their family. Marissa had created the first of the dimensional gateways that was used to travel to and from Realm. Her grandfather was the creator of the unstable mirror that the elves claimed as their own in the great hall, but hers was the enchantment that made it work. A Warder enchantment.

Her pride swelled as she contemplated the magical advances that had been promoted and created by the women of her family. Although, of course, none of the magical councils would ever admit it. Each and every new spell and object had been carefully documented in grimoires that contained the family histories.

Time flew by as tears tracked down her cheeks. The trauma of the women in those portraits affected her sense of empathy. Most of the brilliant women had found reliable and loving mates, but some had been abandoned by those that they loved when their duties had interfered with their home life.

A few had even been left by their husbands for other women. Women who did not care if they were treated as an equal, only that they were provided for.

The few males that were born to the family chose their wives carefully, knowing what a strain the magic would put upon their marriage.

Sera wiped her eyes and left the gallery, her heart heavy with the burden and joys of life as a Warder. It was why they remained a closely-knit family, even separated by vast distances. Only another family member could understand the stresses that the wards put upon them. A tiny piece of their soul went with every magical field that they generated, and only a close family or mating bond could fill the void.

As soon as she left, the wall sealed completely, leaving no trace for the curator to see. Only another family member would be able to access the cupboard.

The other half of her blood called to her now. She found herself once more in the Vampire gallery. Theirs was a darker history. An offshoot of an elven race, the magic of a vampire was tied closely to its intake of the blood of magical creatures. It was something they hadn't realized until they left Realm and took up residence in the human world. Feeding off humans only extended their lives, it did not give them sufficient power to rejoin the magical races.

They also needed far less blood from magical creatures to maintain themselves. It was a richer substance that would rarely lead to the gorging that had gotten vampires into the public eye of the human world.

It was a noble history, but one with dark overtones of war and conquest.

With that in mind, she found herself in front of the portrait of the warrior once again.

A frown started between her brows. He was wearing a fitted tunic that was far too recent to be right. The vampires had broken with Realm in the early twelfth century. His clothing was from the fourteenth.

She leaned forward to peer more closely at the designs on his clothing and weapons. Her hand touched the frame of the portrait and she felt a surge of power.

"Shit!" She fell to her knees as the power continued to flow out of her. Something was using the puncture wound that she had made to sign the book to suck the power out of her body. She tried to fight it, but the magic was using her blood as a conduit somehow and she began to black out.

The last thing she saw was a figure walking toward her, and funny, he looked just like the man in the portrait.

Chapter Three

"Why the hell am I here?" It was a very existential question being asked by a dark and sexy voice that normally would have had her shivering.

Her own voice was a croak. She felt like she had been screaming, but she knew that only one word had passed her lips earlier. "Because wherever you go, there you are."

Her eyes levered themselves open with difficulty. A scowling vampire was facing her. Here. In Realm. Behind her wards. It was impossible.

"I am not in the mood for jokes, magus. Why did you bring me here?"

She felt him grip her shoulders to shake her. "I didn't."

"Well you are the only one here and your body reeks of magic."

"Reeks? That isn't very flattering." She looked around. They were still in the vampire gallery. He had put her on one of the tables that was left over from the days of humans worshipping the blood-drinkers as gods. It wasn't a very comfortable place to be. Especially as he had shackled her into the sacrificial position. Spread-eagled.

"Flattery is not one of my strong suits. Why have I been brought here?"

Stars, he was persistent. "I don't know. But I do know that something in your portrait over there pulled magic out of me." She paused and took stock. "I need a cup of tea."

"This is no time for the pleasantries. I want to return to my home!" His fist pounded against the table next to her hip. She would have jumped if she hadn't been tied down.

"No, I am not kidding. I need some tea." Her body had begun to hum with hunger. Her body was shaking in the manacles and she refused to meet his eyes. She closed her lids just to make sure he didn't notice anything. She could feel her hunting features taking over and she articulated carefully around her extending fangs. "I have a medical condition that is affected by my use of magic. I need the tea to stabilize myself."

"Well then, I am afraid that you are out of luck as I can't leave the room and there is no way that I am going to release you." His voice hummed against her skin and she could feel his warm breath against her neck. He was leaning over her.

She opened her eyes a crack. She could feel his hunger. It called to her own. That was it. With a snarl she snapped the cuffs and dragged his neck to her mouth. Her teeth dug into the flesh and she groaned as his blood filled her mouth and ran down her chin.

Swallowing rapidly she took in as much as she could before he recovered from his shock and pushed her away.

He stumbled back and clutched at his neck. "What the hell are you?"

Sera unlocked the cuffs on her ankles and stood to face him. "A dhampir. Haven't you ever met one before?" Her fist flew at his face and connected with a sharp snap.

He fell to the floor and she was on him again. Punching, kicking and biting at any exposed skin. Her nails extended and sought purchase on him.

"Son of a bitch!" He wrestled her off him and seemed astonished that it was taking most of his strength to keep her at bay.

With three brutal attempts at keeping her down he finally held her to the floor by the expedience of sitting across her hips and holding her hands beside her head. "What the hell are you?" His own fangs had extended in the heat of the fight and his chest heaved with the effort of subduing her.

"I told you I am a dhampir."

"You can't be. They are always male."

"Surprise."

"How did that happen?" He looked down at her, his eyes carefully tracing every contour of her face, neck and the deep vee of her shirt. His hunting features had emerged in the fight and she was watching red and midnight eyes assess her form.

"Well, first there was this bird, and then a bee was trying to have sex with it…" She trailed off as his features darkened with anger. The grip on her wrists tightened and she flinched with pain. "Fine. My mother is a Warder and my father was supposedly a vampire."

She continued, "Warders tend to have girls. In a twenty to one ratio."

"What is a Warder?"

"Where have you been?" She smirked, "Oh, right. A warder is a magical human with the singular talent of creating a magical barrier to block or allow passage for whatever they wish."

"Fine. I have met some magical creatures, but you still haven't answered my first question. Why am I here?"

"I don't know. As you may have noticed, I passed out when you came through that portrait. Something pulled my power out of me and I have no idea what it was." She squirmed under him and asked, "Since we are talking now, could you get off me?"

"Not just yet. You haven't answered all of the questions that I have." He settled his pelvis more firmly against hers and she felt something firm and heated against her belly.

"Fine, but you have to answer mine as well."

"Fair enough. Where are we?"

"Let me welcome you to the Repository of Magical Objects of Realm."

"Realm? How the hell did I get here?"

"I can only guess that whatever pulled out my power brought you through. I still don't know what it was." She was surprised "You know what Realm is?"

"Yes, my parents told me about it. The mythical land of magic where the sun doesn't burn."

"Well you are there, scooter." She relaxed in his grip and tried to fight the rush of hormones that were waking up at his proximity. Having a man she couldn't damage during sex had always been a fantasy, until now. "Are you married?"

"No. You?"

"No, not a lot of the races will join with a freak like me."

"You seem like a very attractive female to me, what is your name by the way?"

"Serafina Zenecar. My mom got knocked up at a Warder Yule party by a vampire named Zenecar. And here I am."

"Zenecar?" He laughed in surprise. "Zenecar is one of the oldest of those who left Realm with no intention to return. I wonder why he did."

"No idea, he didn't stop to chat."

"Well, he left something behind."

"That he did, and my mother never forgave him for it. Or me some days." The wry tone did little to disguise the hurt of her childhood. *Why did I tell him that?*

"My turn, what is your name?"

"Franc, Francesco Berwick."

"Nice to meet you, Franc. I am assuming you are a born vampire?"

"Yes, both my parents were in the exodus from Realm just before I was born. They tell me stories of the magical blood of the inhabitants, and the strength of their own magic when they were here."

"Were they shocked when the magic left them?"

"They adapted. I have never heard them complain."

"So, they wouldn't want to come back?"

"They might wish to visit. But I don't know about returning to Realm."

"Most of us commute." She gave him another small smile and repeated, "Will you please get off of me now?"

"Fine. But you are very warm and cuddly you know."

She blushed furiously, "Thanks. I'll put it on my resume."

He levered off her, but the manner in which he faced her indicated that he was preparing for another attack. Or perhaps something else. There was a focused intensity to his features that hadn't been there earlier. His cuddly comment came back to her and her gaze fell beneath his belt. She bit her lip and sighed slightly at the bulge that was calling her from beneath the fabric of his trousers.

It would have to wait. It was time to charge the wards.

Chapter Four

SHE LED THE WAY OUT OF THE VAMPIRE GALLERY, TAKING HIS HAND TO GUIDE HIM PAST the ward stone and into the main hall. "So, if you were in fourteenth century clothing in the portrait, why did you come through in slacks and a dress shirt?"

"I have no idea. I was just finishing up a business meeting and then I was here." He paused and she could feel him re-constructing the scene in his mind. "There was a whirl of silver and fire, a sharp tug, and I landed on the floor next to you. You looked up at me, said 'I've been waiting.' and passed out."

"I said 'I've been waiting'? I don't remember that." She was scowling now. They were almost to the centre of the Repository and she just wanted to get the charging over with.

"You passed out."

"Yeah, you said that." She stood quietly and began to gather power.

She could see Franc's reaction to her energy as she started and a moment later, she felt it as he slammed her to the floor.

"What the hell are you doing? Casting another damned spell on me?" His lips were inches from her own, his body pinning hers to the floor.

"The only reason that I am in this building at all is to cast that 'damned spell'." His arousal pressed against her stomach and she fought the urge to rock her hips against him.

She almost moaned as a wave of heat ran through her at every point that their bodies connected. His eyes fluttered closed and she didn't have to wonder if he felt it too.

His voice was soft and husky, his breath warm on her lips as his head drew inexorably closer. "What does that spell do?"

"It protects the Repository from being invaded by spirits and any other beings who would seek to take advantage of All Hallows Eve to cross between worlds." Her neck ached with the effort not to lean up and press her lips against his.

A light, teasing kiss was all he brought to her mouth. Sera almost hissed her frustration until he asked, "Then how did I get here?"

Her face went blank with shock. If her wards had indeed been working, how did he manage to come through to Realm? It was a question that acted on her in the same manner as a bucket of cold water. "I don't know, Franc. Get off of me. I need to charge those wards."

"I like you just where you are." This time, he meant business.

This was no gentle kiss by any stretch of the imagination. His tongue parted her lips and swept past the sharp fangs with delicate precision. Her breath caught and held as she returned his embrace with years of pent-up longing.

Sera's fingers tangled in his dark silky hair and held him to her as the fire in her blood began to burn away all of her hesitation.

Skin. She wanted to feel skin. She moved her hands until she felt buttons under her fingers, then popped them loose one at a time. His skin was hot, she felt power sizzle between them as her nails drew a path down his chest and to the snap at the top of his pants.

"Ah, Serafina." Her name had never sounded as sexy as it did coming between his parted lips. He quickly moved off of her and shed the open shirt and his pants. The pants got stuck on his shoes for a moment, but a wet sound of tearing fabric and pants, shirt and shoes were in a heap.

"Now it's your turn." He tugged her shirt of over her head and groaned at the sight of her breasts encased in scarlet silk. It was her 'special occasion bra' and he obviously appreciated her effort as a drop of liquid formed at the angry head of his cock.

He took her shoes and socks off first. The jeans went without a fight, sliding from her with a hiss. The hiss was echoed by Franc as he took in the matching panties.

She fought the urge to cover herself or to go on the attack. Her body was a study in contrasts, chalk-white skin, blood red silk, waves of chestnut hair, which framed her face and her red eyes. Another pulse of heat went through her as his hand covered one breast and stroked her through the silk. Her teeth came out to bite at her lip as sensations tripped through her and she felt the flesh give way. Stars, she was hungry and her mouth craved the taste of the vampire before her.

She drew a line down his chest with her fingers and encircled his erection with delicate curiosity.

"Not yet, Serafina. First it's your turn."

She was confused when he took her hand away. "My turn for what?" The moisture that was leaking from his cock was slippery and her hand had just been finding its rhythm. She brought her fingers to her mouth and licked them clean.

They tasted like salt and musk.

Words that she couldn't interpret spilled from his mouth and his hunting eyes flared as he watched her tongue delicately remove the traces of his pre-cum from her skin.

He brusquely pushed her knees apart and lowered his mouth to the scarlet triangle of silk at the apex of her thighs. His tongue lapped at her through the barrier and she felt herself getting wet, dampening the fabric even more.

At her body's response she heard a dark chuckle. A long and elegant finger pushed aside the inhibiting fabric and he slowly drew it through the open lips of her sex. She shivered and her hips flexed to capture the torturing digit. It moved in a clever dance that circled the throbbing flesh of her clit then delved back down to dip lightly into her opening.

With each trail she felt a different surge of sensation. A harsh hunger as the finger inserted only an inch of itself within her, and a tense shivering expectation as her clitoris screamed for attention.

Her hips were moving in time to his motions, thrusting and retreating in a reflexive dance that had a sweat coating her in minutes.

Finally a shivering cry broke from her as he paused with his finger inside her, to gently bite down on the centre of her sensation at the top of her sex. A scream soon followed as she shuddered in response to her body's release.

He left her. As her body slumped against the cold stone of the floor, he pulled away from her, licking her juices off of his finger. She squirmed against the stone, her eyes drifting closed with satisfaction, only to have them flare open as her panties slid off of her. Well, were tugged off of her. They were far too damp to slide anywhere.

He settled his thighs between her own and their eyes met and held as he pressed the blunt head of his cock against her in a deliberate invasion of her body.

She watched him carefully and saw the instant he realized she was a virgin. Her legs wrapped around his hips and she pulled him into her, shattering the maiden's barrier with a sharp cry from both of their throats.

At last he was fully seated and his head dropped to her shoulder, sweat dampening his inky hair. "Why didn't you mention it?"

"I figured that you could manage to work it out on your own," She threaded her fingers through his hair and brought his mouth to hers in a ravenous kiss. "And now, I would like it if we did more than discuss my ex-virginity, please."

"Oh, really? Like what?" He shifted his hips, dragging the head of his cock back across the abused tissues, then soothing them with a forward thrust.

"Play a hand of cards?" She tried to hold him within her, but his body mastered hers without any trouble. He had all the leverage.

"I don't really like cards." Another slow thrust had her biting her lower lip to keep from moaning.

"Dice?"

"No, I like my hands free." His motions were increasing in speed and intensity.

"Tic-tac-toe?" It was difficult to keep her part of the conversation up while her body was arching and slamming against his, but she wasn't going to give up quite yet.

"I think wrestling would be more appropriate. But I have already won, as I have you pinned." He took her wrists in his hands and held her hands next to her head. "Do you yield?"

"I do indeed." Her body was clenching frantically around him now. Fighting her control, the sensations ripping through her built until she thought she would burst into flame. Wait! She knew that feeling. Magic. Her magic was trying to recharge the wards!

"Franc! Stop!"

He looked at her as if she had lost her mind. He continued to pound into her, oblivious to her squirming struggles.

She arched her hips in an effort to throw him off and shattered into a thousand pieces under him. Her magic flared out and gripped him tightly, setting off his own orgasm as he shouted and spilled his cum into her in a shuddering torrent.

As he came within her, she felt something else enter her. Something that ate her power and consciousness.

Chapter Five

"Serafina, are you alright?" Arms held the body that she occupied. Strong arms. The smell of sex was still heavy in the air.

She moved the body and found that it responded sluggishly to her commands. Serafina was not letting go of her flesh that easily.

Serafina. I only need you for an hour or so. I need to get a message to Eylonwy and this is the only way. She whispered it into the angry corner of the mind and was not surprised to have Serafina come roaring out at her trying to take back supremacy.

So you high jacked my body for a joy ride? Why not just send her an email? She has her own web group. She stopped and waited for an opening. Whatever had grabbed her was far stronger than she was right now. Of course it was. It had eaten her magic.

Because I have been dead for hundreds of years. It is hard to get anyone to carry the signal.

So, Franc knew what you were planning to do?

He didn't even know I was there. I waited until you had to recharge the wards, then entered through your wound.

Wound? What wound? She had a prick on her finger, but she hadn't felt the presence come through there.

The other prick. A tinkling laugh sounded in Serafina's mind as she remembered everything that she had been involved in when she was taken over.

So, you came out of him, and into me? Why?

I told you. So that I could get a message to Eylonwy.

I can pass it along for you.

No, it has to be me.

Sera thought about it. *How did you even get here? The wards should have kept everyone out.*

Everyone except you.

Well, of course.

Blood called to blood. The signature wound in your finger left blood on the picture frame. It is an Athelan mirror under that picture. You simply opened it, and we fell through.

Did he know about this?

Franc never knew a thing. I crept into him weeks ago, in preparation for this evening. I waited, as I have waited for years.

Well, how could you have gotten through? The magic should have filtered you out.

Blood calls to blood, Serafina. You are my descendant.

The name that sprang to her thoughts was answered by a pleased laugh. *Indeed, Sera. Now you know why it must be my voice that speaks to Eylonwy.*

I do. If she had eyes to weep with, tears would have been running down her face. *I will help you.'*

Wonderful. Now, let's be on our way.

"SERA! ANSWER ME! What happened?" Franc was shaking her, trying to get a response. She seemed to have blacked out.

He had felt pretty smug about it until he realized that she was barely breathing and that all the energy she had been exuding had disappeared. Even her scent had changed.

It was as if it was now a completely different woman in his arms.

Her eyes focused on his for a moment, then her gaze frosted over. The magic that had drained from her earlier now surged to the fore. *Please stand aside, vampire. You have served your purpose.* The mouth was Sera's but the voice was echoing in his mind.

"What the hell?" His arms fell numbly to his sides as a surge of energy went through him and broke his grip. "What have you done to Serafina?"

Nothing that she has not since agreed to, now stand aside. She calmly rose to her feet and after shrugging into his shirt, walked to the great doors, flinging them open in a smooth motion. The crowd waiting for her at the base of the stone steps did not seem to surprise her.

It shocked the hell out of him though.

A large group of males were gathered at the foot of the stairs. He could tell that they were males, even though they were no longer recognizable as human.

Dragons, werewolves and goblins faced her in silence. They did not look pleased.

I wish to speak with Eylonwy Warder. Whatever was now controlling Sera was facing the crowd with passive authority. It clearly was expecting them to bring this person forward.

"You won't get to another Warder unless you can make it through us." A dragon stepped forward, his wings flaring. The other species echoed his motions and prepared for an attack.

It was not long in coming. *So be it.*

The power within her flared to life and Franc stood back in amazement as the power formed a second skin. A suit of armour was being created out of air and magic.

As she completed her transformation she began to advance. Supernatural creatures went flying as they came into contact with Serafina's silver body. She staggered slightly at the ferocity of the attacks and that was when he decided to act.

Regaining the feeling in his hands, he surged forward to protect her. No matter what was within her now, he had an unfathomable urge to keep her safe.

As he fought his way to her side, he shook his head at his own monumental stupidity. Whatever possessed her was far stronger than he was. She flicked the dragons out of her way with small surges of power, the wolves were scattered back with kicks and the goblins seemed to enjoy the burning pains that she ignited on their hides.

He, however, was being bitten clawed and finally was thrown to the ground unceremoniously. Sera had stopped her progress and her bare feet were next to him.

A few of the defenders hauled him to his feet, claws digging in to his arms to hold him fast. He looked over to Serafina and was ruefully unsurprised that she did not seem to have a hair out of place.

Whatever had control of her was truly an impressive power. He shivered with pain and hoped that wherever she was, Sera was alright.

Chapter Six

"You have fought your way to me. Now tell me, why you are inhabiting that body?" The elf was furious.

Sera's occupant smiled at the show of temper. It had been unlike Eylonwy in the old days, she had always been so sedate. It must be her choice of vessels that perturbed her. All of the Warders that had assembled for the Halloween celebrations were around them now, creating a field that would destroy both herself and her host if she weren't careful.

It warmed her heart to see the family that had survived her, and recalled her to the purpose for which she had fought her way to Realm.

Eylonwy, I need your help. The voice issuing from Serafina's lips was delicate and had a silvery chime to it. *She needs your help.*

A sob broke through her. *She's all alone. There isn't anyone to help her.*

"Why did you take over, Serafina?" She was gathering power to expunge the spirit from her relative and only her passive treatment of the guards who tried to stop her stayed the elf's hand.

I needed to ask you for help. She is your grandniece. She needs you!

Eylonwy's elegant face twisted in astonishment, "My grandniece? What the hell are you talking about. Serafina is my grandniece!"

No, not her, the other one. I had two girls, Lonny. One was obviously mine and Leon's family left her to die next to me. The other they took.

"A..Amarante?" Tears were welling in the aqua eyes as she looked on the body of her niece, which was holding the spirit of her dead sister.

Yes, Lonny. Her hand slowly reached out and she left it, palm up for Eylonwy to take. *It's me.*

The crowd was eyeing each other in bemusement. No one had been hurt, with the exception of the djinn and dragons that had landed on their butts as she flung them through the air.

"But how?" She took the hand and the Warder armour receded back to the shoulder. "Is Serafina in any pain?"

No, I explained myself to her and she is willing to help.

"Help with what?"

With telling you to look for my daughter's descendant. She is gaining her power and has become a target to a warlock who is seeking to drain her dry. She needs protection and training before it's too late. The other arm was now free of the armour, it melted away from her body as she relaxed and carried out her task.

"Where is she? Where can we find her, Mara?" The armour covering the dhampir was melting away rapidly now. Whatever control Amarante had was being used up quickly.

She lives in a large city, I don't know where. Track her through blood. That is how I was able to do this. Blood calls to blood. Send Serafina to trace her.

"But why did you wait hundreds of years for this? We could have retrieved your daughter at any time."

I needed one of my blood to shed her own blood on hallowe'en when the spirit world is close. Serafina shed her blood to sign the book and take responsibility for the Repository, that was all that I needed.

Thank you, Amranthe, for not mentioning the fooling around in the Repository.

No problem, Sera. I am sorry that your first experience was on this night.

It's all right. I am sure I will recover.

She straightened and met her sister's concerned gaze. *I am fine. Sera and I were just discussing this evening's events.* She paused to look over to where Arov and Decklyn had the vampire in their grip. *He had nothing to do with this. His body was merely the vessel that I used to transfer my spirit into Realm.*

A FLICK OF Eylonwy's fingers and the men released him. He straightened his shoulders and watched the conversation with interest. This whole evening was beyond the fantastic, even for a vampire.

First, he had been sucked through a painting that he had posed for six hundred years earlier and become the first vampire in Realm in centuries—according to records anyway—then he had met the most riveting woman that he had ever seen, consumed her blood and been consumed himself by lust. Finally, he had just started to make love to this fascinating woman when she had been taken over by the ghost of one of her ancestors.

Getting his butt handed to him by werewolves, dragons and goblins, not to mention the women binding him in magic were just cappers to the weirdest evening in his very long life.

I AM GETTING weaker, dawn is approaching, Lonny. She sighed heavily and looked down at the body that was now only wearing an open shirt that obviously belonged to the vampire.

"Amarante, I just have to ask you one question before you go."

Yes?

"Why did you die?" She wailed her grief and loss to the assembly. "You could have chosen to survive, you could have summoned me. Why did you choose to die?"

She moved forward to hug her sister. *I chose to die because there was nothing to live for. He never loved me, Eylonwy. Not ever. I was a trophy for him and then a freak. He was having three separate affairs and had two other children while we were married. It broke my heart.*

"Then why did you leave your daughters?"

Because the only thing that I felt was betrayal, and I didn't want to teach them that. I knew that you would come for Fianli, and that Morgiani would be taken and raised as human. I saw it. But I did not see myself in their futures. I was always with them, standing by. Offering guidance when I could, however I could. There was no reason to step in until now. Her name is Audrina and she will be dead by Yule if no one saves her. Serafina's body swayed.

It was her own voice that spoke now, "She's gone. She gave me a picture of Audrina and her location. I'll start looking as soon as I recharge." Tears were tracking down her face as the grief and frustration of her ancestor filled her.

She staggered, then tried to make her way back to the Repository where the remains of her clothing lay. A helpful arm came around her and supported her back to the steps. "It's cool, I can take it from here." She looked up and saw Franc, his eyes wide with astonishment as he watched the rising sun of Realm.

The rest of the Warders stood and watched them go, the creatures that had earlier barred their way parting to let them pass.

"Yeah, I know. Fascinating. The sun of Realm doesn't burn vamps, it doesn't hurt, and lets you live a fairly normal life. The vampires left because they didn't want to stop eating the locals. The werewolves left so that they could completely control their own societies. Both races lost a lot of magic in the process."

She was nodding off. Amarante had drained off all of her power and left her limp. She staggered inside and was unsurprised to feel herself falling to the floor. It didn't hurt. She blinked drowsily and realized slowly that she was being held off the floor by two hands gripping her arms.

Those same arms lifted her and cradled her face against his neck while he issued a command. "Bite me." He settled at the desk with her in his lap.

Her fangs had extended and she was practically drooling at the warm source of sustenance just inches from her lips. "I hadn't ever consumed blood before tonight."

"Then this will be another first for you, now drink." His hand came up and pushed her mouth into his neck. Her earlier bite mark had faded to nothing and his neck looked so good.

Daintily, she licked out at his flesh, tasting him. Then she let one hand come up to keep his neck from moving and bit down. Oh, the warmth of his blood filled her mouth, her teeth digging deep to keep the wounds open.

Her head spun, but she felt her strength returning with the warm rush of his blood into her body. She also felt arousal returning and that was the sensation that stopped her from feeding.

"Thank you, Franc." On instinct, she licked the wounds on his neck until they closed. The ridge of his own arousal had firmed under her hip the instant that her lips had touched his skin.

He didn't reply.

She cautiously met his eyes and shuddered with the urge to wrap herself around him and bear him to the floor. No. She wouldn't.

The only reason that he had come to her was that he had been under the influence of a Warder's ghost. It had never been his idea.

Reluctantly, she pushed herself away from him. "Well, I think that we need to get you home. Do you have any large mirrors at your home?"

"Yes. There is a large one over my fireplace, but it will be bathed in sunlight by now. I don't think I should be bursting into flame after all that I have seen today."

Something in his eyes made her smile wearily. "You don't actually burst into flame, do you?"

"Well, the older we are, the less likely it is that we will suffer more than light sunburn. I was hoping that you didn't know that." He gave her a sheepish grin and looked around the room. "I was also hoping for a tour."

She staggered again, "One of my cousins will have to take you around. I just need a nap right now and I am heading out. Now, where did I leave my clothes?"

Leaving Franc bemused and looking at her back she moved as quickly as she could to reclaim most of her clothing. Still wobbling, she finished dressing and reclaimed him from his position behind the information desk.

"Come on. I will find you a guide who can show you the wonders of Realm." Her hand grabbed his and she smiled at the warmth that flowed through him now. He had absorbed a bit of her magic, she only wished she had enough energy to take advantage of that warmth.

A small cluster of her family was waiting at the base of the steps and she smiled at Anryn and Decklyn. Perfect.

"Anryn, Decklyn. Franc here needs a tour of Realm. I think that you two would be just the ones to take him around. You know everyone here, and Decklyn has eaten some of their ancestors." She released his hand with regret, gave him a small wave and headed for the mirror station.

The swirling burst of energy of the transport was like a warm cocoon. Sera stepped into her living room with a sense of melancholy and proceeded to bed. It had been one helluva night, and she was nocturnal after all.

Chapter Seven

"So, you want a tour of Realm, huh?" The woman facing him was green. She appeared to have Mediterranean olive skin from a distance, but up close, she was definitely green. Anryn, Serafina had introduced her as Anryn.

Franc didn't know what to do. He had watched the most riveting creature he had ever met in his long life walk through a mirror and disappear, and now he was facing a group of magical creatures that were staring at him with a combination of amusement and hunger.

It was certainly a change from the normal gazes of lust that he received. A few of the women were looking at him with interest, but nothing along the lines of what he was used to. It was simply curiosity in their gazes.

"No, I…" He met her gaze and was compelled to answer honestly. "Yes. I would like a tour. But I also want to learn more about Serafina. Can that be arranged?"

The dragon that had been identified as Decklyn smiled at him for the first time. "Yes, that can be arranged. They should just be getting up now."

"They?"

"Oh, yeah. They would be the right ones to ask." She laughed at his confused expression and began to lead the way into the field that was decorated for a party. "Come this way."

"What are those buildings over there?"

"All in good time. First, you will learn more about Serafina." She skipped lightly over the grass with what must have been her husband following closely. How a woman that attractive could settle for a dragon was only one of the mysteries he had yet to uncover.

He trailed behind them in a bemused state. They were approaching another large cluster of people. The woman stopped to ask some questions and was directed to a small stand of trees.

"C'mon, Franc. They are having breakfast now. You can ask all the questions you want." She strode forward with a swing in her steps, and he quickly averted his eyes when he noted the scowl on the dragon's face.

His feet moved quickly to keep up, they were disappearing into the wood and he lost sight of them for a moment.

He needn't have worried. They had stopped just inside the trees and another clearing, shaded from the morning sun by the green canopy above them.

Children. At least two dozen were seated and having cereal in cross-legged groups on the ground. The little girls outnumbered the boys by close to ten to one. The groups were loose, the little creatures often talking in giggling tones over four or five heads.

Judging by the pallets and blankets on one side of the clearing, the children had spent the night here while their parents enjoyed the party in the field.

Anryn walked forward and clapped her hands. "Warders! Warders, please!"

The children fell silent and gave her their attention. A spokesperson that appeared to be around fourteen stood up. "Yes, cousin? What do you want?"

"Melia. This is Franc, he's a vampire. Franc, this is Melia. She is the daughter of a merman and my cousin Rowan, who never bothered learning how to swim."

"Pleased to meet you, Melia." He executed a bow in response to hers. The delicate scales tracing her scalp were apparent to him, now that he was looking for them.

"We are here so that Franc can learn about Serafina. Can anyone here tell him about her?"

Hands rose all over the clearing. Anryn let Melia point to each one in turn.

A cute little girl with bluish skin went first. "She's half vampire."

"She likes to play hopscotch."

"She can burp the alphabet!" This from an enthusiastic little boy, the comment drew, "Ewws," from the female contingent.

"She will teach you for hours until you get it."

"Her aura is violet. That means she likes blood."

"She drinks a lot of tea so she doesn't need blood, dummy!" A short scuffle broke out involving tugging pigtails and then they were back to business.

"She likes pralines and cream ice cream."

"Her favourite colour is blue."

"She has a little sister that she loves very much."

"She doesn't like gum in her hair."

"Serafina is ticklish." This caused a spurt of giggles and tickling amongst the kids and he had to smile in reaction.

"Is that enough for a start, Franc?" Anryn was laughing with the lighter voices.

"Yes, thank you." He raised his voice, "You have all been very helpful. Thank you very much."

A chorus of, "Your welcome!" rang out and the children went back to their breakfasts.

Anryn led the way out of the grove and he was surprised to see a field snap into position behind him as soon as he had passed.

"You didn't think we would leave the kids unprotected overnight, did you? We had three of our nocturnal cousins watching over them until dawn. They were relieved at dawn by six dryads that were watching us the entire time we were there."

"When the wards at the Repository blew, anyone with combat experience came running. We are sorry that you ended up used in such a way, but the spirits of the elves don't transport easily."

"So, it was an elf that used me as a mule?"

"Half-elf. All of the Warders are half-breeds. It's a curse." She looked back at her husband, "But it has its benefits." Her smile was full of love and affection.

Decklyn returned her smile with a grin that promised more than just a look of affection at the first opportunity.

"A curse? Like a magic spell kinda curse?"

"Exactly. It ensures that we don't form any kind of militia to take over Realm." She paused for a moment. "I am sure that Serafina will explain the details to you at a later time."

"Really? What makes you think that I will meet up with her again?" He was curious. As far as she knew, he had only been the transport for the spirit.

"Well, the little detail of her having had sex with you in the Repository of Magical Artefacts. That's all."

He was stunned. "How did you know about that?"

"There was blood on her mouth. She never drinks blood. So, it must have been a fit of passion. Which would also explain the blood on the inside of her thigh as she returned to fetch her clothes. Serafina doesn't date much, so if she lost her virginity to you, she must have liked you."

He whistled long and low. "You don't miss much, do you?"

"I try not to. Of course, it was Decklyn who pointed out the blood to me. I don't smell it like he does."

Franc looked to the dragon's impassive face and looked quickly away. He himself had been glaringly aware of blood on Sera, but he had thought that their tryst had been private. "How many others noticed?"

"Six or so. They spread the word. Everyone knows that you and Sera…you know." A flip of her hand filled in the rest.

"Let me guess. She isn't going to be happy about that." He had an image of Sera's face as she left. She was exhausted and humiliated. Crap. That was going to make seeing her again difficult.

"Yep. Sera is one of the most private people I know. This whole thing is going to make your courtship of her awkward."

"Courtship? Who said anything about courtship?"

Anryn laughed at him. "Your face did. Your heart was in your eyes as you watched her go, and there had to be some reason that you were chosen by the spirit."

"So you think that the ghost was matchmaking?"

"Of course! It's what the elders do." She stopped and suddenly turned into a tour guide. "This is the main square of Realm. Each race has a building and each building has a gateway to their cities in the far reaches of this world."

He turned slowly and noted the distinct styles of architecture that denoted each individual species. Franc was drawn to one specific building that looked like it hadn't been used in years.

He crossed the square in a daze, the pull of the architecture irresistible. The symbol of the full moon with a dagger thrusting through it was mounted over the door. The doors themselves were carved onyx with depictions of vampires feeding.

He stood before them in amazement as he realized that this was the equivalent of the vampire consulate, and it had not been touched in hundreds of years. Until now. He placed his hand on the plate of the door, jumping back as a shower of debris came down on him. Slowly, soundlessly, the door swung open.

A great entrance way lined with the same onyx led into a hallway that disappeared around a corner. He looked behind him to see his tour guides at the door, unable to enter.

"Franc, did you want to continue the tour? Or did you want to run through an empty building?"

He called back, "What else is there to see?"

"Nothing really, but in that case, would you please invite us in?"

"Why can't you just walk in?"

"We need an invitation to enter another species centre. Every magical creature does."

He laughed at this reversal of vampire lore. "Please, be welcome. I invite you in."

With audible sighs they entered the great room and swiftly caught up with him as he walked down the halls.

"What was this place used for?"

Decklyn answered, "We don't know what this particular centre was used for, but the Dragon Centre is used for council meetings and formal functions."

"So, no one has been here since the vampires left?" He knew it in his bones, but he needed confirmation.

"No one has been able to get through the doors. They are species specific."

Not another word was said as they passed through the halls, which were lined with portraits of dozens of vampire leaders from eons past.

The main council chamber suddenly opened in front of them, the skylight letting in the full light of the Realm day. The slab in front of the podium made them all pause.

It held cuffs and a head restraint. The dark stains on white granite sent a chill down Franc's spine. It was blood.

With slow and careful steps he approached the slab, using his senses to analyze the scent of blood left in this abandoned building. It smelled of wild magic and was definitely female. He touched it and a scene from the past flooded his mind. "Oh hells. No wonder they left."

"What was it?"

"A dryad. But not for long. This was a Turning table. They were trying to make more vampires. It didn't work, and she died screaming for an end."

The horror of what they were hearing was not lost on them. The vampires had been trying to turn magical creatures to create an invincible army. They could not breed quickly enough on their own, so some of them must have tried to turn the supernatural inhabitants.

With fury at the hubris of generations past, he strode to the white granite slab and put his shoulder to it. It creaked and shifted, but he couldn't get it to flip. Until his efforts were assisted by Decklyn. With both of them straining, it toppled and shattered.

"Let's get out of here. This place reeks of death." His guides didn't say a word, but led the way out of the Vampire Hall as quickly as they could.

The doors sealed shut behind them and Franc gasped for air. "That place should be destroyed. What happened in there should be forgotten."

"As you are the only representative from your species. It can be destroyed after the next Great Meeting."

"Great what?"

"Meeting. All the races have representatives and they get together in the Central Hall. They make any policy changes necessary at that time." She stopped for a moment and smiled slowly at him. "Serafina will be there."

"Why will she be there?"

"Warders have to check in for a scan to make sure that they aren't plotting against the council. Unless they are married. Then their husband is responsible for them." An angelic smile that Decklyn didn't believe for a moment judging by his rolling eyes crossed her face.

"And if I request it, they will destroy the building?"

"Yes, they will. The werewolves asked for their Hall to be destroyed when they left, and the new contingent is going to ask for a new building on a new patch of ground. You can do the same."

"So, the werewolves are recent returns to Realm?" He grimaced at his own alliteration. Well, at least he didn't rhyme.

"Very recent. Four months ago one of the Warder's hand fasted with a werewolf. That was the first contact that they have had with Realm in three hundred years." Decklyn had taken over the tour and was leading them to a raised platform covered with large mirrors.

"This is the mirror station and the last stop on the tour. Anryn and I will see you home."

"Wait. How do I get back here? How do I find Serafina?"

"We will get you her contact information. We promise." The dragon grabbed his shoulder and held on while Anryn charged up the mirror in a way that he couldn't see. She only seemed to touch it, and it was humming with power.

Chapter Eight

Sera was exhausted. She made it home to take a shower and change clothes but that was as far as she had gotten. The blood she had taken from Franc had recharged her temporarily, but she wanted more. Her shaking hands prepped her tea and she sipped it slowly.

It took the edge off, but now that she knew what the blood felt like singing in her veins and throat, she wanted it. But only vampire blood would do.

Her body wanted sleep, but first she needed to write down all pertinent information on her new cousin. Everything that she had been given was carefully recorded on paper. Audrina Williams was her name. The city was somewhere in the northwest, near an island. Her eyes, hair and skin tone were carefully written down as her body slumped into a heavy sleep.

A hand shaking her shoulder woke her some hours later. Her face bore the imprint of the pen she had been using to write her hunting statistics. A groan burst from her and she looked up to see the concerned face of an elf.

"I am sorry to wake you, Sera. I know how much energy she took from you and I came to offer to replace some of it."

"Please, Aunt. I am completely flattened." She held out her hand and sighed heavily as the power began to flow between them. Her brain sighed in relief as the stores of energy were replaced.

"Why are you here so soon? You should be at the Warder's council." They didn't have a building so the Warders met after large holidays to discuss their concerns.

"Sera. That was two days ago. You have forty-six messages on your machine and I don't know how many emails have been sent."

"Two days? Aww…hell." She rubbed gently at the pen-impression on her face and contemplated the last rays of the setting sun outside her window. "Why did you decide to show up in person?"

"It was my idea, actually." A masculine voice startled her into turning around. Francesco Berwick stood there in all his glory. "I got worried when you didn't return my calls. You don't seem the type to pretend nothing happened."

"I'm not." She thought about it for a moment. "Well, I don't think I am. I haven't ever been in that position before."

"Naked on the floor of the Repository?"

She flushed scarlet and looked over at Eylonwy's amused face. "I will leave you two to work this out." The elder bowed and walked back to the mirror and disappeared into the silvered surface.

It was now just the two of them.

"I would have returned your call." She was flustered. "I fell asleep."

He was closer now, she could smell his skin and remember the taste of his blood. "I know. That is why I used the numbers that Anryn and Decklyn left me to ask for help."

"Good Lord. A man who asks for directions." Her quip was whispered, as he was leaning toward her and she was spellbound by the tempting curve of his lips.

"Only when I need to know where I am heading. If I know where I am going, I use the direct approach." His lips gently caressed hers and she sighed into him.

For long moments it was the simple meeting of their lips that had her blood singing in welcome. She placed her shaking hand on his jaw and he traced her lips with his tongue.

Sera opened her mouth in welcome, and tasted him in return. A snarl escaped him and she found herself pressed against him from breast to knee.

Her hands were in his hair, holding his mouth to hers as they devoured each other. She heard a soft whimper and only vaguely realized that it was her voice, begging for more.

His hands gripped her ass and pulled her pelvis into his, the firm rod of his erection heating her blood to boiling. All of her hungers were awakening.

She wanted his body and she wanted his blood.

Her fangs extended and her hunting eyes flared. She grabbed his head to hold him and nicked his lips with her teeth, he snarled and drew back for a moment, then locked his lips to hers once more. The blood pooled between them and her busy tongue lapped it up. More...she wanted more.

Her hips rocked against him, drawing a groan from his chest. He lifted her up and she opened her thighs to wrap her legs around his hips. Her weight was now suspended by her hands on his neck, and her grip on his waist.

Without breaking their ravenous kiss he walked her into her bedroom and laid her back on the bed. His hands firmly unlocked her ankles from behind his back and he stepped away to shed his clothing.

She hadn't had a chance to really look at him before, so she did so now. Propping herself up on her elbows she watched every inch of skin he revealed. Including several interesting inches that drew her attention and caused her mouth to water.

She tried to remove her own clothes, but her hands were shaking. Her fumbling efforts drew his attention.

"Would you like some help with that?"

"Yes, please. If you wouldn't mind."

He walked up to her, his awareness of her interested gaze clear on his face. "So polite. Even now."

She fell mute as his hands drew her shirt open with astonishing ease. Her jeans met with the same end, disappearing from her body in seconds. This time, he discarded her bra first, then slid her panties off.

She watched them go and lay back, waiting.

She didn't wait long. The frenzy of their first fuck was still with them, as neither knew how much had been supplied by the ghost and the loss of her virginity had been an obstacle.

His hands and mouth roamed over her torso, paying special attention to her breasts, which she found to set off an answering response in her clit. Each tug of his mouth on her nipples caused waves of sensation to echo between her thighs.

Her throat gave off an endless selection of moans and sighs as she lay back and let him do all the work. A shivering groan ran through her as his tongue and the scrape of his teeth trailed over her soft belly, dipping into her navel before continuing to lick his way to the weeping mouth of her sex.

She expected a slow exploration, but his tongue began a hard stroke that went from the wet entrance to her pussy up to flick her clit. Over and over he continued this treatment, never changing his speed.

She was whimpering for her orgasm in a matter of moments. The slow strokes were driving her out of her mind. Her hands clutched his hair as her thighs tightened around his head and she twisted against him, seeking the stroke that would finish her.

He stopped and drew back, grinning at her through a mouth covered with her juices. He leaned forward to kiss her, his cock nudging against her belly. Her hips shifted against his erection and she started to squirm slowly against him in a plea for completion.

He obliged. With one hand, he supported himself above her, and with the other he guided himself into her willing body. With one thrust past the resistance to his invasion, he was inside her.

She purred with contentment, and arched against him. Trying to draw him into thrusting deep within her. She called out in a voice not her own for him to fuck her hard.

He merely smiled at her through the sweat tracing his brow and slowly drew out of her only to thrust in once again. He moved within her in a slow and deliberate rhythm that was going to drive her nuts. Each time he withdrew, her hips thrust up against him and each time he drove deep her body rose to meet him.

It was something that had the bed sheets soaked with their sweat, his in an effort not to go off, and hers in an effort to achieve it.

Finally, she used her last resort. As he came forward to kiss her, she swung her head away and bit his neck. His cock was hot and hard inside her, giving her intense pleasure with every motion he had given her.

His response was his own snarl of lust and a hard shove of his hips. That had been what she wanted all along. She began to suckle at his neck, drawing more blood into her as he continued to fuck her, harder with each stroke.

At the first hard slam, she felt a shiver, by the time he had reached the third her orgasm was upon her. She let go of his throat and shrieked her release to him. Her whole body going limp and quivering seconds after the contractions hit.

He howled in frustration and returned the favour, biting her shoulder with savage ferocity that still sent a bolt of pleasure through her. His hips now pounded into her, each thrust driving him faster and rekindling her lust.

Finally, he howled his release into her shoulder and she felt a strong suckling of her blood rush out of her as his semen rushed in. He fell heavily beside her. Gasping for breath in a counterpoint to her chest heaving to get back to a normal rate.

The wounds she had made in his neck were closing already, and she could feel the ones in her neck doing the same. Her body was satisfied, the hunger for blood finally sated. But her hormones were still active as she ran her hand idly down his chest, toying with his nipples on the way.

She wanted more, and based on the limp and shining cock on his thighs, it was going to be slow in coming. Sera sighed and snuggled closer.

"That went much better than the first time." Satisfaction was thick in his husky voice.

"Yep, I didn't get possessed or have all my magic sucked into a ghost. I consider it a step up." ***Sucking, yeah, that might work.***

Her lips began a trail of tiny nips and kisses that began at the bite marks on his throat and continued across his chest and down his belly. Tiny sighs and groans emanated from her victim as she approached her destination.

His penis twitched slightly as she wrapped her hand around the shaft and raised him to her lips. The flared head was warm and soft under her tongue as she lapped her juices off the delicate tissues. The salty musk of pre-cum began leaking from him in only a few seconds and she felt the column under hand swell and harden as she licked and swirled her way around his rapidly hardening cock.

A hand wove through her hair and tugged her head up. "How do you know how to do that?"

She crawled up him, straddling his hips and pressed her lips to his in a kiss that rapidly flared her body to full burn. "I like ice cream."

She drew her head back and waited until he stopped laughing. She was drumming her fingers on his chest when he finally stopped snickering.

He used her hair to bring her lips back in range and just before they met, he said, "Pralines and cream."

Her eyes widened in shock, then crossed as she tried to meet his amused gaze at close range. She finally let them close and just enjoyed the feeling of his hands on her back and his erection pressing against her belly. Her body took up a rhythm of its own sliding against his in a dreamy motion as their tongues met and tangled. She arched her back and moved against his cock until it was nestled between the open lips of her sex and her clit rubbed against him with every stroke.

She felt more than heard him groan into her mouth as she began to pant with her own rising need for completion. Her body was slick with sweat and her arms shook as they took her weight. He lifted her hips and guided his turgid flesh into hers.

Sera groaned and sat up, burying him as deep as she could. She let her head fall back and circled her hips on him, enjoying the feel of that warm cock moving within her. Her eyes were closed as she began to rise and fall on him. Almost letting him slip from her, then dropping down with a gasp.

He kept his hands on her hips, speeding and slowing her pace on him while watching her with eyes that had narrowed with intensity. Her orgasm was sudden and intense, freezing her muscles in a spasm of pleasure. His hands pulled her tightly against him and lifted her to thrust into her again.

She squealed and shook helplessly in the grip of the waves of release washing over her, sweat running down her sides and forehead. One by one her muscles went limp and she slumped onto his chest in repletion.

"Are you done with me so soon?" He toyed with her hair, sifting the long strands and separating the locks into a silken cape.

"Mmmff." Her voice against his neck warmed his skin, but even she didn't know what she said. She turned her head to the side and told him the truth. "I am done for the night, but you can go nuts."

A dark chuckle sounded in her ear. "Indeed. Then I shall."

A moment later and their positions were reversed. He was now cradled between her thighs. A slow thrust into her slick channel had her arching against him. It was this slow and steady pace that he maintained, the beat of her heart controlling his pace. As her blood began to pound in her veins, his beat increased to match her tempo.

Her lethargy was soon forgotten and she was arching against him, her legs locking together behind his back as she urged him on. Her next orgasm was upon her in moments, her breath sighing out of her in a wave as sparks danced behind her eyes. It was then that she felt him slam into her with inhuman force and he bit at her joint between neck and shoulder, draining her blood as his body shook with his own release.

His groan was audible through his bite and she felt the magic that he was taking from her, but it was oddly invigorating. As if his gaining strength was making her stronger as well.

The pain of his bite slowly turned into a warm river of pleasure loosening her muscles and keeping her in his power. That was the warning sign.

In reflex she brought up her left hand and—knowing that she couldn't pry him off—smacked him in the ear.

"Oh, hells, Serafina. I am sorry." He scrambled free of her body's embrace and she shook as she struggled to sit up, all the while glaring at him.

"I am not a 'nice light snack' alright?" She tried to leave her bed, but her legs wouldn't hold her. The 'thud' as her butt hit the floor was audible. Knowing herself unable to walk, she simply sat there, her arms curled around her knees and a lost feeling welling within her.

He picked her up, ignoring her feeble struggles, and sat back on the bed with her on his lap.

She began to sniffle and in seconds tears had begun to flow from her eyes. She simply sat there, the echoes of years of loneliness coursing down in pink-tinged rivulets across her face.

His arms held her close, the smell of their coupling still strong in the air.

He raised one of his arms to his mouth and bit deep. He then held the bleeding flesh to her mouth.

She tried to turn her head away, but he grasped it and held his wrist to her lips. She opened her mouth and reached out with her tongue to taste the offering. As she opened her mouth he pushed his wrist more firmly toward her, and she was soon suckling at his arm, the energy of the blood replacing the loss of magic she felt earlier until a strange balance had been struck.

She could sense her magic swirling within him as she could feel his energy now moving within her.

The balance was unmistakable. They had each shared equal parts of themselves and had possession of the others powers.

She looked him in the eye and saw the same recognition in his face, as there must be in hers. As one they said, "Well hell."

Chapter Nine

IT TOOK A MOMENT UNTIL THEY BOTH BURST OUT LAUGHING. THE EMOTIONAL BOND WAS growing stronger by the second and shortly their hearts would begin to beat in time.

"What the hell is happening to us? I can feel your amusement as if it were my own." He didn't seem too upset about it. In fact, he merely tucked her head beneath his chin and cuddled her against him.

"It's one of the Warder's enchantments. It was designed generations ago to keep what happened to Amarante from happening to others. Your pleasure and pain are now bound to me, as are mine to you."

"Did you cast this spell? If so, I didn't see you do it."

"Nope, my mother cast it the day I was born. My sister got the same treatment. It's tradition."

"So, the first guy you slept with was 'the one'? What if I hadn't been dragged through that portrait?"

She began to laugh. It was too funny. "No, it only works with the person we are destined to be with. In our case, the blood made the process faster. Your energy and my magic are exceedingly compatible. Probably why Amarante picked you."

"She picked me?" He seemed puzzled, and his mind echoed the statement. "Why?"

"As far as I can tell, you were near her burial site at some time in the last few months. She chose you deliberately because of our compatibility. She had the gift of foresight, so she knew I would be at the Repository and not my sister."

"How did I end up pulled through the mirror?"

"Blood called to blood. I marked the logbook with my blood and the wound was still open when I touched your portrait. Nice tights by the way." A hiccupping laugh escaped her.

"They were all the rage when it was painted." He slapped her lightly on the thigh and she jumped and giggled. "I think we need a shower."

She couldn't argue and amidst playful teasing and quasi-serious caresses they managed to tidy themselves into normalcy. Well, as normal as they were ever going to get.

She made a light snack and they wandered into the living room, only to be brought up short by the presence of another vampire on the couch.

She smiled as Franc put himself between her and the intruder who was watching her television with the headset on. There was something familiar about him…

“Hello, pet.” He took the earphones off and looked up at them, taking in the defensive stance that the younger male had taken up. “I trust that you know who I am.”

“I do. But why are you here, Zenecar?”

“To meet you at long last, my one and only offspring.” He stood. Franc didn’t move from his position between them.

“Okay, so we have officially met. I think you may want to leave before hostilities erupt.” She was shaken to the core by meeting her sire. She had thought him long dead, or moved to another country. Some reason for him to never contact her or her mother.

“I am not afraid of this pup.” He eyed Franc carefully, belying his words.

“I meant me. You are not welcome here, so state your true business and go.” Sera stepped to the side and met the eyes of the vamp that were so close to hers in colour.

He addressed Franc directly. “You have gone to Realm? You have seen the Vampire Hall?”

“I have.”

“Then I need you to take me back there. I need to go back to Realm.”

“He can’t take you.” She drew his almost fanatical gaze and shuddered. There was definitely something there that he wanted.

“Why not? He has joined with you and siphoned off half your power. He should be able to manage a single transport.”

“Oh, that one is easy. Franc, will you please approach the mirror?” She stood aside and nodded at him. She knew what she was doing.

He walked over and stood before the mirror as directed. His image reflected easily in the silvered surface.

“Now, touch the frame.”

The instant he touched the frame, his image disappeared. There was no way that he could open a gateway without knowing where he was going. The scene on the other side fluctuated wildly from one scene to another. A bedroom featured obviously as he flicked a warm glance over to her.

"You see, Zenecar, since Franc has only been there once, he doesn't know what the station looks like. And since you also don't know where you are going, you had better explain yourself."

"I need a portrait. It is of a woman with light brown hair and riveting blue eyes." He paused and the gleam of his eyes faded. "She was my wife. One of the first to die in the conversion experiments. She was a mage of good family, and they didn't approve of the vampire connection. So, when we began the experiments, she volunteered to try a Turning. It didn't work and she died soon after." Bloody tears were tracking down his face.

"That was the reason that I enchanted your mother. I needed someone with vampire blood who could get me to Realm. I need that portrait."

"Will it do if I fetch the portrait for you? Will you leave then?" It was a plea forced from a desperate part of her mind.

"Freely and gladly. I will never darken your door, or couch, again."

She grabbed Franc's shoulder and shoved him through the mirror. A guardian met them on the other side.

"Just heading out to the Vampire Hall. We will be back in less than half an hour." The troll on guard nodded and stepped out of their way.

"Shall we speed this up?" With a burst of superhuman energy, she began to run flat out to the Vampire Hall. Eager to see if she could open the doors, and relieved to use her abilities to the fullest.

It was magnificent to just run, the half mile flying by in seconds. This was why she loved Realm. The freedom to just be herself was addictive.

She glanced to her right and saw Franc keeping up with her at an easy lope, and in no time they were at the onyx doors.

They opened easily at her touch, swinging aside to let her pass. She sprinted down the hall and selected the picture that she had plucked from Zenecar's mind. She also flipped the portrait over and removed the charm and necklace that were hidden in the back.

That was no mage enchantment, nor a vampire one, but an elven seduction spell that belonged in the Repository. No wonder he had had this image burning in his mind. It would cause any woman he gave it to, to be in his thrall.

"The picture he will get back via Realm post. The medallion hidden in the picture stays here." She smiled brightly at Franc who had remained silent this entire time.

"He knew. He has been planning the retrieval of this artefact for years. It is why he mated with your mother."

"Yep. And it is why I will not let him get it. He started my life, but he has no right to what I choose to do with it." A strange sense of freedom came over her. All her life she had felt a certain obligation to the memory of a man she had never met. Now that she had met him, she could let him go. "And I choose to only give him the portrait he asked for."

Her hunting eyes flared in anger, changing her surroundings to the sharper focus on all things living. She could feel her teeth extending in irritation. That rarely happened.

"You know, you are stunning when you are furious." He gathered her into his arms and planted a kiss on her lips that quenched her fury quite effectively.

"Umm. Thank you." It was all she could manage when he let her up for air. "We need to take this to the Repository before we drop the portrait off at the mirror station."

"Well then, shall we?" He extended his arm to her and she took it with a small headshake at the courtesy. He was so…well, normal. It was hard for her to remember that he was over six hundred years old.

"Yes. This way."

"I remember the way. In fact, it is unlikely that I will ever forget it, as it brought me to you."

She was blushing furiously and it only seemed to amuse him. Their path was only occasionally crossed by members of the other species of Realm, some of whom stopped them for introductions or waved at Sera as they passed.

Finally they were at the steps of the Repository of Magical Artefacts and she took a deep breath to steady herself before facing Asgoth.

The stone rang under her feet, glowing in response to her magic once again. Had it only been two days since she had last climbed these steps? It seemed as if she had lived a lifetime in Franc's arms.

Asgoth was distant and polite. The vampire glowering at him might have had something to do with his alteration in attitude. He accepted the medallion and logged it carefully into the inventory of the Repository.

It would be studied by elves and members of the Magus and Warlock councils at the first opportunity. Asgoth thanked them for bringing the charm to their attention and bid them good day.

She simply nodded, then led the way out to retrieve the portrait that they had left on the steps of the Repository. The trip to the mirror station was made in silence.

The attendant stepped forward, "Do you need some help with that, Sera?"

"Yes. Yes I do." She took a deep breath and rattled off her instructions. "I need this delivered to Zenecar, a vampire who is in my home, then I need a cleaning crew and a warding done on the entire property. Against vampires not of my blood specifically."

The troll took the information down carefully and nodded to her. "So, you will be staying in Realm until this is done? It could take a day or so."

"No, she will be staying with me. At my home." The last was said as much to Sera as to the attendant.

She merely blinked for a moment, then smiled. "Great. I need somewhere quiet to find the missing Warder that Amarante mentioned."

Franc smiled in relief. He had been afraid of her refusal if his face was any indication.

"Let's go home, Sera. You have had a long day. You need something to eat." His eyes were sparkling with triumph at her easy capitulation.

He touched the mirror and tried to hold the picture of his living room in his mind, but it kept leading to his bedroom. She put her hand on his and he felt her touch his mind. The picture of his living room faded and the bedroom came into sharp focus.

"Are you sure, Sera?" He didn't want to rush her again, but hells, she was sexy.

"Franc." She began to pull him into the mirror. "Bite me."

The Warder's Gryphon

Prologue

"I can't find her. I keep getting stuck on a dead zone." Serafina slammed her head against her hand in frustration. "This sucks!"

"Easy, Sera. Just relax. The vision will come." Strong hands began to massage her shoulders and she leaned back into him.

"And what if it doesn't? How am I supposed to find a woman I have never met in a town I have never been to?" Tears of frustration seeped from her closed lids and she relaxed for a moment with Franc. She was still amazed at his strength and adaptation to her ways.

Within a month of their blood sharing he had developed a complete tolerance to sunlight, his nocturnal habits were now by choice instead of compulsion, and he had moved her into his home, complete with the leather-topped desk that she was currently using to focus her search.

"Blood calls to blood. You have narrowed it down more than you thought you could, and the sketch that Vanir made from your description is enough of a starting place." His warm breath caressed her ear. "Perhaps it is time to call in professional help."

"Help? What kind?" Her head tilted back in the grip of his clever fingers.

His twinkling eyes met her own. "I know this Gryphon…"

Three weeks later…

"Sera! We have a letter. It seems that he has found your cousin."

She darted forward to look at the paper in his hand. "What? Where is she? Is she okay?"

"Read it for yourself, sweetheart."

Hey Franc,

I have found the Warder that you sent me for, and I can tell you that it wasn't easy. She has resisted my efforts to meet her in my human form, so I have had to keep an eye on her by other means. You owe me big time.

I will remain with her until the Magus or Demon that is after her makes his move. I haven't seen him yet, but his presence is all around her. It is amazing that she has survived this long.

She is stronger than I would have imagined and all that power without focus is gonna get her into trouble if she doesn't get some instruction before she does some damage.

As soon as I can get her into Realm, I will. But since she is in a dead zone, it could take some doing.

It's absolutely bizarre. There are no traces of wild power in this whole town. It's like something consumed it.

I will keep you informed.
Timmon Lahey

"See, honey? She's fine. Tim will keep us informed. You don't have anything to worry about." He gave her a reassuring squeeze, his warmth trying to reach out to soothe her.

"What does he mean, he is keeping an eye on her by other means? What other means does he have?"

"Timmon is the master of several shapes. He has a gryphon form, a human one and a few others. He is probably using one of them to keep an eye on her."

Sera wrapped her arms around her husband and hugged him tightly. "Thanks for your help on this. But you know that we will have to go in and bring her to Realm to meet the family eventually."

"I know. And I really hope that she has a strong constitution."

Sera's dark chuckle was lost in his chest and she smiled into the heat of his body. "If you can handle it, sweetie, so can an actual Warder."

Chapter One

It was an entirely different universe. Cubes, orbs and amorphous material slid by harmlessly as she watched. Dutifully, she recorded her findings.

Then she removed the slide, tossed it in the biohazard bin and shut off the microscope. The gloves that she wore to protect herself from the substances she handled were tossed into the contaminated trash bin, and she stood to wash her hands for her next patient. The concept of urinalysis was not pleasant, but the actual work was fascinating. There was an entire universe within the human body that no one ever got to see, except her.

Audrina loved working in the lab. The combination of gruelling labour with the satisfaction of assisting patients and calming them before the invasive procedure of having their blood drawn satisfied both passive and aggressive tendencies within her.

Stepping forward, she reached into the drop slot and took out the first requisition on the pile. "Sara?"

She waited for her patient to rise and begin walking towards her, then asked, "And your year of birth is…?"

"Nineteen-forty-five, dear."

"Well, step right this way to the big chair of fun!" At the acerbic look that Sara shot her, she laughed.

"Hey, it stunned you long enough to get you into my clutches, didn't it?" She swiftly assembled the tubes that she would need.

A rueful laugh answered her. The left arm was extended and the samples swiftly drawn.

"So, Sara? How was that on a scale of one to ten?"

"Well, it was at least an eight. Possibly a nine, but you shifted a little on the seventh vial, so you lost points." Her smug features put Audrina firmly in her place as she held the cotton ball to the small puncture in her arm.

"I'll try and do better next time." She placed the band aid quickly over the sealed wound and touched her patient's arm gently. "See yah next month, Sara."

"You too, Rina. I'll have your scarf ready by then."

A grin that seemed to make her countenance glow crossed her features and her patient basked in her energy for a moment before leaving. "Thanks, Sara. I look forward to it."

THE REST OF her afternoon flew by. She processed over forty patients in the morning and thirty after lunch. She was exhausted. It had not been nearly this busy four months ago.

The centrifuge was whirring, and Dorothy, the other lab tech, was finishing up the processing of the immediate samples, the rest were already packed and ready for transport to the main processing lab. A small wave and a, "See you Monday" and she was on her way.

She dragged herself out of the lab after hanging up her white coat and headed for the coffee shop in the mall.

"Hey, Lincoln."

He began to pour out her regular chai latte. "Hey, Audrina. You look like hell."

"Yeah, the afternoon took a lot out of me."

Steam hissed as foam was generated. "Not too much I hope."

"Well, I hope that there is enough to get me home."

She handed over the money. He was the owner of the shop, yet he didn't let anyone else wait on her. At first she thought the reasons were sexual, but he never made a move. She supposed that he just liked her as a person.

And frankly, she loved the tea.

"Watch out for this one, Audrina. It's extra hot to make it back to your house."

"Thanks, Lincoln. Hey did I tell you? I have a new addition?"

"More staff at the lab?"

"Nope. I got a cat." She laughed ruefully. "Well, he got me. I was out for a walk and he just jumped into my arms."

An expression of distaste crossed Linc's face. "Are you sure that it is healthy to take in a stray?"

"Yeah, I could use the company, and I had a vet give him a thorough once over." She inhaled the steam coming out of the vents in the cup. She smiled at the relaxation that welled over her. "He isn't fixed, but he also seems very tame."

"Are you really going to keep it?"

"Well, I have posted notices around the neighbourhood, but no one has come out to claim him. So he and I are going to share quarters for the time being." She gave him a small wave. "See you next Friday!"

The lab that she worked at had tripled its business in the time she had been working there. It seemed that she only needed to take a patient once and they were loyal customers. The doctors that owned the lab were pleased, but had not bothered to increase their employees' salaries as the business increased. Audrina had simply spread the rumour that she was leaving, and the coffers suddenly opened. It had been enough to buy her a small home in the town where she worked, and she was glad to be here.

The drive home was not arduous by any means. She had moved to this small town over a year ago when the press of the big city became too much for her. Businesses blended into homes, which became more and more sparse as she approached her new house.

The ginger breading on the outside was her favourite feature, a little bit too fancy for most, which is what had made her buy the house. It was in her nature to be slightly contrary.

It was also the main reason that she was no longer living near her family. They simply couldn't stand her. She didn't fit in. She never had.

Chapter Two

"Hey, Timmy! Rina's home!" She didn't have to announce herself. He was waiting for her at the door, just like he had every day since she had taken him home with her.

"Mrrrroww." His head butted against her legs and she almost tripped while carrying her purse and her latte to the kitchen.

As soon as her arms were uncluttered, she scooped him up and scratched him behind his ears, smiling at the rumbling purr that threatened to loosen her fillings.

His tawny fur was sleek and silky beneath her fingers and the insistent head steering her touch around his head made her laugh. The dark tips of his ears, and the kohl circles around his eyes gave him the look of a desert cat.

His body however, was pure Maine Coon. Fourteen-plus pounds of muscle, claws and fur, she would rather have him in her home than any wimpy little toy poodle.

Her energy seemed to return as she held him and she carried him to the table and reached for her latte. Timmy hissed in anger and swatted her hand away from the beverage, then tipped it over with another swipe of his claws.

"Hey! That was a six dollar latte!" She dropped him to the floor and ran for paper towels to mop up the sticky milk spill. As she mopped up the mess her eyes widened at the enormous claw marks that scored the side of the cup. He had torn it so that not one ounce of liquid remained in the paper.

The latte was full of milk as well, and her new cat companion was not making a move toward it. He was, in fact, growling at it from his spot near the puddle.

He kept up his impressive act of hostility until all the residue of the beverage was disposed of.

Then, he sniffed carefully at it and gave the floor a small taste. Only to screw up his face in distaste and shudder hard enough to fluff out his fur.

"You know. Most cats like milk. I don't know why the freak cat shows up at my door." She threw out all of the paper towelling and rinsed her hands.

He made no reply to her freak comment and simply followed her into her bedroom where she stripped off her scrubs, underwear, and socks. She unclipped her hair with a sigh of relief and the heavy chestnut locks fell down her back in a heavy wave.

"Oh, man. That feels good. You have no idea how nice it is to let down my fur when I get home." She smiled down at Timmy, who was watching her intently. "I really hate tying it up in the morning, but I can't have it getting into any samples, now can I?"

She padded softly into the bathroom and warmed the water, then started the shower. Audrina sighed with enjoyment as the water pounded on her sore muscles. She breathed the heavy and steamy air in with an almost carnal enjoyment.

Her body loosened as she soaped and lathered her puff and worked off the day's worth of anxiety. It was as she washed the soap off and let her hands travel that she realized that she was heading into self-gratification territory.

Her fingers pulled and tweaked at her nipples, bringing them erect in a matter of moments. Her right hand slid across her belly and through the trimmed thatch of hair at the juncture of her thighs.

The heat coming from her cunt was astonishing. Her body had been flaring out of her control lately and it was driving her to distraction.

Her clit begged for her touch and it shrieked to attention as she circled it with a finger that was slick with her own juices.

Her hand left her breast to support her against the shower wall as the attentions of her fingers made her knees go weak. She gasped, shuddered, and stopped.

With her body screaming in denial she took her hands away and turned off the water. Her knees were still wobbling as she wrapped a towel around her body and another around her hair.

First things were first. She dragged her brush through her hair and towelled it almost dry, then got out the body lotion as she sat on the edge of her bed.

Ah, to be safely in her own bed, with no fear of falling and breaking something. Her hands spread the smooth and cool lotion over her body and the blaze that had had attacked her in the shower flared to life again.

She loved the slick lack of friction that let her hands glide down her body and across her stomach. The very tips of her fingers trailed across her lower belly and she arched and sighed in response. Low moans took over as she moved her clever fingers between the thighs that spread eagerly, and once again began to flick and circle her clitoris.

As she progressed further and further into sensation her thighs began to lock tight in a rigor that her body had designed to hold a lover close. The tension increased her sensitivity and in seconds she was gasping and moaning as her hips rocked, seeking a cock that wasn't there.

She pulled her fingers away when the sensitivity got to be too much and waited for her breathing to settle.

Filled with energy she bounced up out of bed, washed the cum and lotion from her hands and got dressed.

At Timmy's plaintive meowing she let him out the back door.

Now that was the way to start the weekend.

She got her dinner together out of the assortment of leftovers in her fridge and pondered the food she needed to get the next day at the store.

She was halfway into her meal when there was a thump and a scratch at the backdoor. "I'm coming, Timmy." She put her plate aside and opened the door.

He was soaked to the skin. She sighed and got the towel that she kept near the door for just such an event. "You know, it is most unnatural for you to go swimming in a cold pond, Timmy. Most cats don't even like the water."

He gave her a baleful glare and she kept all further observations to herself. Apparently, his evening swim was her fault.

She snuggled him against her chest as she rubbed him down. In moments, he grudgingly began to purr. She fished out a cooked chicken breast out of the fridge and warmed it for him, dicing it into small pieces, then she reheated her own food and resumed her spot in front of the TV.

She dropped Timmy onto the couch next to her, and placed the dish of chicken on the couch. He curled up next to her and nibbled at the food.

With her purring cat and a sated body she had to admit, her life was good.

Chapter Three

Saturday dawned bright and clear, and Audrina resented the heck out of it. Ever since she had moved to this town, weekend mornings had been draining on her.

It was only when she left her little house that her energy level returned. So, out she went. She let Timmy out and headed off for her errand run.

As she drove her sedan down the street, she noted with pleasant surprise that the house next to hers, a few hundred meters away, was being filled with the contents from a moving van.

Apparently she was getting a new neighbour.

Three hours and seven shops later, she returned home tired and triumphant. The moving van was gone from the front of her neighbour's yard, and she made a batch of cookies for the new arrival.

The baking sheet was cooling with its chocolate payload when she noticed something. Timmy hadn't banged on her door.

She went to the backdoor and opened it, looking for any trace of the feline and was disappointed to see no hint of her pal.

She sighed heavily and waited an hour for him to show up. Perhaps he had gone back to the home that he had come from. He wasn't hers after all.

She put the cookies on a plate and covered them with cling wrap. She left her back door open in case he came back and went over to greet her new neighbour.

She rang the doorbell and waited for the occupant.

When he arrived, she almost fell back in astonishment. She recovered quickly. "Hi! Welcome to the neighbourhood. I just live next door." She was babbling, but she couldn't help herself.

A few weeks earlier, she had 'met' this particular hunk of masculinity at the coffee shop near work. He had begun to speak to her in a friendly manner and she froze. She hadn't been able to put a complete sentence together with those dark golden eyes framed by thick lashes watching her with heated interest.

His skin was a few shades darker than those fascinating eyes, and his hair several darker. His body put the hunks on romance covers to shame. The way his t-shirt hugged the muscled contours of his chest was completely devoted to outlining every detail faithfully. The fit of his jeans should have been illegal.

"Are those for me?"

"You, your wife, whoever is home." *Please not a wife, please not a wife.*

The predatory grin she had noticed at the coffee house was back, "No wife. Would you care to come in? I was just unpacking a few things."

"Sure. Um, that would be great." She stepped forward as he stepped back and then remembered, "Oh, my name is Audrina."

"And mine is Tim. Come on in. The kitchen is in the back." He led the way and her eyes immediately fixated on his tush. You could crack granite on his ass. She might be going crazy, but she would swear that he smelled like cinnamon.

"Tim, huh. My cat's name is Timmy." She smiled at the look he flashed her over his shoulder. "Well, he isn't really my cat. I don't know whom he belongs to. But if you see him, could you let me know?"

He seemed nonplussed. "Uh, okay. What does he look like?"

"Well, kinda like you, if you were a cat. He is gold all over, kinda big for a domestic cat, and has freaky golden eyes."

"So, you think I have freaky golden eyes?" He placed the cookies on the table that he quickly set up with two chairs. He then rummaged in his fridge for milk. "Sorry, I don't have any milk. I don't have anything really. I do believe that I need to get some food this afternoon."

"Oh, well if you would like, I can be on my way." She was a little nervous as he sat down across from her.

"You never answered. You think my eyes are freaky?"

She blushed, her own grey eyes firmly assessing the chip-count on the cookies. "Well, golden eyes are a little unusual, you must admit."

That damned smile was back. "Not in my family. They are quite common, in fact."

"Oh yeah. I can see how they would be." She took a cookie and refuge in the act of chewing. The better to keep herself from saying something else that was asinine.

With that smile still in place, he took a cookie of his own. After the first bite, he chewed thoughtfully, then reached for another. Half a dozen cookies disappeared behind those white teeth until finally she dared to ask, "So, do you like them? The cookies, I mean."

"Why aren't you three hundred pounds? If I could bake like that, I would never stop eating." He looked at the plate. "I can keep these, right? I am not exactly up on the new neighbour etiquette."

"Oh, sure. That is why I brought them. They are all for you. The idea is that when you bring back the plate we will have another nice exchange and chat." Finally back on stable social ground, she smiled, and stood to leave.

"You are leaving so soon?" He rose as well and she noted absently that his shoulder was even with her head. He could park his chin on the top of her head comfortably.

"Yes, well. You have to go and find food, and I need to mow my lawn and look for my cat." She began to back slowly toward the door. Uncomfortable letting him enjoy the view of her backside that she had been assured was pleasant to look at.

He sighed deeply. "You are quite right. But, I would like to invite you over for dinner this evening. I always need a second opinion when I cook on a new stove." He followed her down the hall and she was glad that there was nothing in place in the house yet to block her undignified retreat.

"Um, tonight?" The solid thud against her back let her know that the front door was at hand, that and the doorknob in her spine.

"Do you have plans?"

"No. But I thought you might need some time to move in." The knob was in her hand and she closed her eyes at the image that flashed through her hormonally charged brain.

"I only moved in the basics for the first month or so, table, chairs, TV, couch, clothes, and of course a bed."

The door was open now and she navigated her exit while keeping contact with his freaky golden eyes. A bed, why did that have to be the last piece of furniture that he mentioned, and why the hell were her hormones out of control?

"So, will you come for dinner? I promise that I can cook."

"Yeah. What time?"

"Make it seven. I'll need time to find what I need at the local stores."

"Well, Tim, see you at seven." She stuck out her hand and was as surprised as he. His fingers were warm, calloused and very strong. A woman would be safe in those hands. And at their mercy. What would make her think that he's surprised?

Oh, man. She had to go. "See you tonight, Tim." She spun on her heel and walked slowly and deliberately to her house. She looked back only once when she was opening her door and her hormones rushed to the fore again as he was leaning against the wall on his porch, watching her walk the distance to her home. She could see his grin from there.

Oh lord. Just what she needed. The world's sexiest neighbour. Who had just watched her ass all the way back to her place. Crud.

Chapter Four

HER LAWN WAS MOWED IN RECORD TIME, HER BED MADE AND HOUSE CLEANED. TIMMY still had not resurfaced, but his stuffed gryphon was missing from its spot next to her pillow. It had been there in the morning, but was gone now. He loved to tuck that stuffed gryphon between them and then curl up against her.

It was weird, but since she had moved into this odd little town, she was haunted by nightmares. Dark and sinister shadows stalked her dreams. Until the day that Timmy had come to her doorstep. That day her nightmares stopped.

It was also the day that she first saw Tim in the coffee shop. It was also incidentally the day that her slightly more lascivious dreams began. He had starred quite heavily in her dreams. His golden hands moving across her skin with deliberate intent. And always that sexy smile.

Timmy must have come back while she was at the neighbour's and taken his toy. She smiled in relief.

The thought of his beautiful feline body on a road somewhere had been so untenable that she had refused to let it enter her mind.

If he had his gryphon, he was safe, she was sure of it.

SHE KEPT UP her frenzy of activity until after six. At that point she realized what time it was and, cursing all the way, she took a shower to remove the sweat and dust of the impromptu spring-cleaning.

She was towelling herself dry and wrestling with her underwear drawer when the fleeting thought of skipping her underwear ran through her mind unchecked. She stopped multi-tasking for a moment, and smacked the lustful thoughts of Tim on her white sheets out of her mind. He would glow against the pristine white. She just knew it.

All right, regroup. She stood for a moment, then calmly and deliberately picked out her lime green panties and bra. She put them on, wincing at the damp reaction of her body to contact between her thighs. Her nipples were pebbled in her bra and she looked for a button-down shirt with a crisp enough fabric to camouflage them.

Audrina carefully and deliberately picked out her most flattering pair of jeans, slithering into them before she could change her mind.

Her sandals went on quickly and she was on her way over to his place with slightly damp hair five minutes early. Her hand was raised to knock and the door swung open.

The golden god was wearing an apron, and he smelled *good*.

"Hi! Am I too early?" Oh, God, her voice was high-pitched and perky, even to her own ears.

"Nope, right on time. Come on in." He stepped aside to let her enter and she was amazed at what he could accomplish in a few hours.

The house was immaculate. It looked more lived in than her place, and he had been there less than twenty-four hours.

His shopping expedition had been fruitful as well. Daisies and blue irises filled vases in the house, bringing an unexpected burst of cheer to every room.

Oh hell. Flowers, apron, cooking and an immaculate house. "Tim, are you gay?"

He froze in place. The astonished look on his face was answer enough, and she flushed in embarrassment.

"No, Audrina. I am not gay." The arch of his brow asked for an explanation.

"I am so sorry. Your house is just so neat, and you have already moved in, you can cook and you have the same taste in flowers as I do." Her face was on fire now. If she didn't know better she would swear that her body was actually cooking from the inside out.

"So, if I was a slob, left everything in boxes and had burned dinner, you would think I was straight? Interesting criteria." He was laughing at her.

Her chin almost touched her chest as she mumbled, "I don't get out much." Taking a deep and shaking breath, "Can we start over?"

"Of course. Go ahead." The challenge was obvious, as was his plan to bring this up at a later time, based on the raised eyebrows and the challenge in his gaze.

"Hiya, Tim. Something smells terrific. Am I too early?" She began a slow and steady walk to the kitchen to hide her face from his implacable amusement.

"No, you are right on time. I was just finishing up the mashed potatoes." As he passed her in the hall, he gave her butt a light pat. "We are having pot roast. Do you care for beef?" He ignored the startled jump that she executed in the tight quarters and started to set the table for two.

"Oh, I love pot roast. It's my favourite."

"Let me just put the apple cobbler in the oven."

It was on the tip of her tongue to ask him again if he was gay, but she had a feeling that he might just throw her on the table and cover her body with his if she did. Wow, there was an image.

She sat quickly to stop her buckling knees.

"So, why did you move to this tiny little hamlet?" Ah, there was a nice safe topic.

He straightened and finished prepping the dessert, then loaded the table with more food than she could eat in a week. Apparently, he was not a cheap date.

"I work for an architectural design firm that is assisting on a historical renovation in Melville."

She blinked in surprise. "That's just fifteen miles away."

"I know. The location of this house was ideal, and the price was right."

"So, what do you do?"

It proved to be a deadly question. In the next hour over the juiciest pot roast that she had ever consumed she learned about working modern safety materials into historic homes. It was apparently not an easy task, but with modern fabrication, you could get the look of antique structures, with modern materials.

Before she knew it he had turned the tables and asked her what she did.

"I am a professional mosquito." And she left it at that.

"What?" His hands were busy washing dishes and she had an amazing view of his ass as he cleaned up after his orgy of consumption. Nearly the entire roast had disappeared, and into that very fit body. She wondered how he worked it off. Oh, down girl!

"I work in a lab and draw blood for medical testing. It isn't very exciting work." She remembered the past week. "Well, unless we get a Damsel in Distress."

"A fainting woman?"

"Nope, a fainting man. A woman I can shift around on my own, a three hundred pound man who passes out while standing up, however is quite another story."

"So, what do you do with them?"

"Well, I prop them up, tell my co-worker quietly that I have a damsel, and we move him into a recovery room with a bed, cold water, cold towels and usually something like a sucker if he isn't diabetic. Then we just hope he can start moving around on his own."

"Doesn't it embarrass them to be called Damsels?"

"Uh, well, I usually only call them that when I need help from my co-worker so as not to freak out the people in the waiting room. But, you are right, they are usually mortified."

A hot cup of coffee was put in front of her.

"So, why do they faint?"

"Um, they will correct you to say that they have 'passed out'. But usually it is because they are fasting, are afraid of needles, or the sight of blood. Especially their own. It is actually a healthy response. It is a basic reaction to being injured."

"Yes, that may be, but it isn't very convenient if the predator is going to start eating you." He toasted her with his cup of coffee and smirked.

She burst out laughing. "You are quite correct. Just look at the fainting goats. It isn't exactly an effective defence mechanism."

They shared a laugh at the image of a herd of three-hundred-pound males being startled into a mass fainting spell.

One moment they were laughing, and the next he had gripped her hand and tugged her into his lap.

Chapter Five

SHE DIDN'T SAY ANYTHING. THE SMOULDERING HEAT IN HIS EYES WAS WEAVING A SPELL on her senses that she didn't want to break.

She felt tiny and protected in his embrace. An unusual feeling that she wanted to savour.

Her body slowly relaxed against his and he took that as her silent assent. His lips gently touched her own, and as she remained pliant, he increased his attentions. Yep, cinnamon. It was him, his scent and his taste.

Audrina felt like she had known him for weeks, not less than twelve hours. It was with only a fleeting flicker of guilt that she wrapped one hand around his neck and returned his kiss, with interest.

He growled in response to her, one hand tightening on her hip, the other pulling her thighs firmly against him.

As their kisses deepened and tongues came into play, he suddenly stopped. Her eyes had closed and she blinked with lids heavy with passion to meet his serious face.

"If you don't want this, Audrina, say so now. I will escort you home and we can slow this down." His face was earnest and she knew in that instant that he would do whatever she agreed to.

"So, you would just take me home, leave me at the door, and come home to jerk off?"

He laughed. "Something like that."

The erection under her thighs throbbed gently and she wanted it inside her when it released itself. More to the point she wanted her body wrapped around his while that hard cock was inside her.

She shuddered heavily. This was out of character for her, but it just felt so right. "Can you take me home…later?"

His smile was blinding and the heat was scorching, "I can indeed." In a move that made her head spin he stood with her in his arms.

"I am not a fainting heroine, Tim. You don't have to carry me." She squirmed a bit in discomfort, tacky romance novel covers flashed through her mind.

"Oh, but I want to carry you. That way, you can't get away from my fiendish clutches."

Her bark of laughter caught her by surprise. It was like he had picked up on her thoughts and voiced them. "Oh, but I want to be in your fiendish clutches. At least for today."

"I was hoping that you would say that." He carried her up a set of stairs and into a bedroom that was sparse and tidy. Even here there was a vase with daisies and irises, she giggled softly and kept her mouth shut as he deposited her on the bed.

He watched her carefully for several long moments, his head tilted as he assessed her body from head to toe. With a snarl he pounced on her, rolling her across the covers until she was breathless with laughter. She was firmly tucked under him when he stilled.

As the giddy joy welling up in her faded she stroked the sides of his face. She craned her neck up to help her mouth meet his and giggled when his teeth nipped her lips. He bit and fed at her mouth until she was moaning and her hands were knotted in his hair trying to hold his mouth to hers.

"Audrina, you are overdressed." He leaned back and unfastened the buttons marching down the front of her shirt, kissing and licking at the skin that he exposed as he peeled the fabric away. The lime green bra made him blink, and he smiled, passion pushed to the back burner as he asked, "Do your panties match?"

Her face, neck and chest flared red as her embarrassment took over. She had worn them to give her confidence, with no inkling that they would be seen.

One of her hands covered her eyes as his clever fingers fell to the button of her jeans. The slow drag of the zipper had her biting her lip and the hot breath in the vee of the opened fabric forced her to still hips that wanted to squirm closer.

"Hah! They do match!"

Once again she was laughing, and once again he joined her. With precise movements and a little bit of tickling he tugged her jeans and shirt from her. Instead of distracting her, the playful tone that he set was bringing her lust to a fevered pitch.

He rapidly divested himself of his clothing and stood before her, golden and perfect. The layers of muscle that she had speculated about were more detailed and sculpted than anything she could have imagined. The hard and bronze cock that beckoned her was larger than anything her mind would have supplied as well. A creamy drop of fluid gathered at the tip and she could control herself no longer.

She reached up with a pleading and innocent look in her eyes, begging without words for him to come to her. The instant that he took her hand she yanked hard and he tumbled to the bed beside her.

Crowing with victory, she crawled on top of him and slowly rubbed her body against his. He reached up to stroke her back with long slow touches. As if he were petting a cat.

She arched into his touch and was unsurprised to feel her bra loosen, with an impatient snarl she threw it aside. Her hips rubbed her clit against his erection where it was sandwiched between them and the panties that were still in place became damp from both sides.

Audrina sighed, groaned and purred at the feel of him against her, and minutes of this torture later, he had had enough of her playing and took charge once again.

"My turn." She was flipped to her back and her panties were skinned from her to be flung across the room unceremoniously.

"Grab the headboard and don't let go. Whatever you do," His head leaned down and his tongue lapped roughly at her collarbone, "Don't let go."

She wrapped her fingers around the wrought iron vines that made up the framework of his bed. As the heat of his tongue began to explore her, she hung on.

She knew that her skin was sensitive and that the slightest touch would arouse her. She was very surprised that he had figured it out. Most men she had been with were heavy-handed and fumbled briefly before grabbing at her crotch. She knew that this would not be one of those unsatisfying encounters.

Delicate tracing of his fingers and tongue caught her skin on fire. Each nerve that was called to attention sent a racing impulse through her entire body and in no time she was panting with a fine sheen of sweat across her breasts and belly.

His tongue paid homage to each breast, laving each in turn with a slow and steady stroke. She was arching and hissing in reaction to the wet touch of his mouth on hers and he hadn't even crossed her ribcage yet.

The slow progress of his mouth began, preceded by his hands. The outer surface of her belly was caressed as his mouth worshipped the underside of her breasts. The hands left her belly to stroke her hips, and then further down to her outer thighs.

At that point, they changed direction. His fingers delicately dragged up the inside of her thighs, parting them with gentle insistence. They parted eagerly, her dignity long forgotten in the flares of lust that he was bringing to her with his hands and mouth. "More" was the only gasp that she could manage, entreating him to take her.

Her body was an arch, her grip on the headboard and her heels the points of contact. Oh, he was good.

His head had reached the juncture of her thighs and the heat from his mouth was causing the moisture emanating from her body to flow more freely than she would have imagined. He settled himself between her straining thighs and parted her labia with his thumbs. A long slow swipe of his tongue had her mewling and by the third stroke running from her opening to her clit, she was shrieking and shaking in the grip of her orgasm.

He paused, letting her body drink in the fullness of its release, only flicking at her clit and slipping a finger into her to keep the spasms going.

As she slowly slumped back into the sheets, she met his dark golden eyes as he had his head propped up on her pelvis. The fire was there, but ruthlessly banked.

"You let yourself go, and now I have to start from the bottom and work my way up."

Her hoarse voice could only groan in anticipation as his fingers separated her once again and he slowly thrust two of the digits inside her. She could feel the wet embrace of her body on those fingers and tightened to pull them further and further into herself.

He added a third finger, and began to slowly pull almost out of her and then thrust back in a controlled beat. The noise of the wet suction normally would have mortified her, but those long fingers twisting within her made her crave the heat and thickness of Tim's cock moving into her with savage enthusiasm.

"Tim. I want your cock inside me. Now!" She was really in no position to be making demands, but as a partner in this event, it was exactly what she was supposed to be doing.

With feline grace he slunk up the length of her body, licking, biting and sucking all the way. He seemed obsessed with tasting her, and as his head hung against hers, she tasted herself on his lips. Sweat was dripping from them both, and his dark sheets were damp with their exertions.

The blunt head of his cock was seeking entrance to her and her hips were rising to capture him. "Are you sure you want me, Audrina? It's not too late to change your mind."

A snarling growl was all that she gave him as she hooked a thigh round his hips and moved her opening onto his cock. Once the head was in place, she wrapped her other leg around him and crossed her ankles tightly together, pulling him inside.

His breathless groan, "I will take that as a yes." were the last words spoken as he slid fully into her with closed eyes as he fought to enjoy the moment.

Each time he impaled her on his cock, she squirmed against him, seeking more contact. Her hands were still wrapped around cold iron and she was arching and bucking against him with every slow thrust.

Her blood was roaring in her ears as he began to use a little more force and speed. Her body was being played like a classical instrument and she loved every minute of it. But, if he didn't hurry up and make her cum soon, she was going to pass out from frustration.

Mewling cries like a kitten in distress were coming from her throat, and she could swear that she was begging him to fuck her hard and let her come, but she couldn't be sure.

It must have worked, as suddenly his hands lifted her legs to either of his shoulders and he began to pound into her as if he were trying to pave a path to the pillow.

At the first pounding thrust her body was shocked, by the second it was enjoyment, and on the third she peeled away from reality in a paroxysm of sensation. His reaction was to release her legs, lean far enough forward to kiss her fast and to thrust into her in a frenzy of mating that left her breathless as her own body was limp from its exertions.

His head had fallen to the hollow of her neck and shoulder, and as a snarling groan broke from him as his balls emptied themselves into her, he bit her.

With teeth that felt exceptionally sharp, his teeth dug lightly through her skin until her blood broke into his mouth and at the taste, a harder seizure gripped him his body pumping itself dry within her.

As they gasped for air, the tingling on her shoulder barely noticeable, she thought to herself, that this definitely set the bar for all first dates.

"Did we just…?" Her eyes tried to memorize the pattern on the crown moulding in his bedroom. Geometric, with just a hint of fleur-de-lis.

"We did." The amused voice reverberated in his chest. Her position with her head propped up, using his torso as a pillow, gave her the effect of lying on a speaker.

"And you are sure that you aren't gay?"

The pillow fight that ensued resulted in minimal damage to the wrestlers, the furniture and the bedding. Only one small chair got tipped over in the melee, which they carefully righted.

Chapter Six

Good to his word, Tim escorted her home. He had to. Even after their shower her thighs were incapable of closing to a point that would allow her to walk comfortably. Instead of forcing her to waddle, she was carried piggyback to her front door.

There went dignity out the window again.

He seemed only too cheerful to have reduced her to that state, and the look in his eyes as they had dressed told her that he wanted to do it again. Soon.

"Your keys?"

Oh, right she released the grip of one of her arms and dug in her hip pocket then handed the keys to him. "It's the big one with the short teeth."

"Thanks." He moved into the house and carried her straight into the bedroom, dropping her down onto her own bed. He had looked fantastic against his black cotton sheets, but she bet he would look better in her bed.

"Uh, I am exhausted." She stretched the muscles that were not exactly used to this type of exertion. Wow, what a night.

"Me too." He sat down and began to remove his shoes and clothing.

"So, you're staying here tonight?"

"Well, we did get my sheets all sweaty. I need a nice clean bed to rest in."

She eyed him speculatively, his face was all innocence. "Fine, but just sleep. I don't think my body could handle any more activity tonight."

"Fair enough." Splendidly nude, he crawled between her white sheets under the handmade quilt.

She shed her own clothes and crawled between the same sheets. His hands came to her and held her close, and that was the only way he touched her as he snuggled close. Having a man in her bed was unusual enough for her, but to have one holding her in the darkness was completely new. The rumbling purr that seemed to be coming from him was exceptionally soothing as well.

Within fifteen minutes, she was sound asleep.

The pounding on her door was a rude awakening. She sat up and looked over at Tim, who had flown out of bed, and was crouched next to it, facing the door.

"Uh, I don't think that burglars knock, Tim. It must be someone I know." She grabbed for a robe and tugged it into place.

As the knock repeated, she made her way down the hall to the front door. The face peeking in the window was familiar, but surprising.

"Lincoln!" She drew her robe more closely around her. A flush grew across her cheeks as she realized that the collar of the robe did not completely cover Tim's bites. "What are you doing here?"

"I thought you might not be feeling well."

"I am feeling fine. Why would you think that?"

"There was something going around the mall and we linked it to the lattes."

"Really? Well, thanks for checking on me."

"I was wondering if I could come in?"

"Um, that isn't really convenient, I have a visitor."

Lincoln's dark features suddenly became sinister. "Yes we know. We watched you come home tonight. He didn't leave."

A thump and a groan and she saw two men who must have come through her back door dragging Tim between them.

"What have you done to him?" She turned in a fury and she felt a pulse of energy that she hadn't before. Only a handful of times in her life had she felt like this. Each time, she had almost died.

The power seemed to be coming from within her.

"We? We did nothing." He looked at her with eyes gone black and cold "The shadows however nibbled at his soul." His hand came up and it was full of inky darkness, her first instinct was to recoil and as the icy tendril wrapped around her wrist and started to pull at her consciousness, she screamed and fought back with everything in her.

A bright blast of energy caused Lincoln to stagger out of the doorway and in a trice she was past him and into the yard, heading for the safety of the woods.

They wouldn't be able to find her there.

With her muscles stiff, her body nude and the thin protection of her robe almost no protection at all, she did not feel ready for a jaunt into the forest. But here she went.

The branches moved out of her way, drawing a pathway to her safe spot. In this portion of the woods, there was one spot that she had made her own. She raced on bruised and bleeding feet to that spot near the icy pond where her Timmy was fond of his evening constitutionals.

She clambered up onto the rock, her rock and sat with her knees drawn up. Audrina concentrated in spilling her energy into the stones around her, guarding her and making her feel safe from all that would come.

"We have your boy-toy, Audrina." There was a large group of men, Tim hanging between them.

"He isn't my boy-toy. He's my neighbour." Her voice sounded petulant to her own ears, but if she wasn't mistaken she had just been attacked by shadows, wielded by a barrista.

They let the shadows form tendrils and had them wrap around Tim. She gasped at the pain that flooded Tim's features. What ever they were doing to him, it hurt. "Don't drop the Ward, Audrina. Stay where you are."

"Stay where you are, and your golden boy here dies." A tendril of shadow ran through Tim and he gasped in agony.

"Fine. But before I do…what the hell is going on?"

She gathered her little energy to her and kept it there as shadows began to dance on the perimeter.

"You are a woman of power. In our town, that makes you fair prey."

"Prey for what purpose?"

"For the purpose of increasing our energies." Lincoln was at his most pompous.

"What happens to me after?"

"We drain you of your magic, then we will send you on your way." With sudden insight, Audrina knew exactly what that meant. Her dead.

But if there was a chance that Tim would be let go, she would do it.

"Fine. It's coming down." There was a muffled "No!" from Tim before they hit him in the back of the head, and then nothing.

Slowly and carefully, she retracted her energies. As the power came in, the shadows grew closer, writhing in closer and closer proximity to her. As they came within touching distance, she began to be haunted by memories of pain and loss, fear and agony, and in seconds it overwhelmed her. With a scream of panic her power winked out. Pain and fear waited for her in the dark.

Chapter Seven

HER SHOULDERS WERE SCREAMING. SHE COULD HEAR THE TISSUES PROTESTING THE position that they had her in. Her arms shackled over her head were forcing her shoulders to take most of the weight and they didn't like it.

"As soon as the elders are assembled, I will drain your energy and your magic will become mine." Lincoln was there when she opened her eyes. He was surrounded by wildly flickering light that she had to attribute to the pain that was flooding her.

"Why do you have to wait for the elders? Why can't you just do it yourself?" Her voice was hoarse and she remembered screaming as the darkness overtook her.

The dark and shadowy robes flowed around him. "It is a tradition and a ritual. Each member will taste your power before you die."

"Oh, so it doesn't count if other guys don't see it." She shifted awkwardly, transferring some of her weight onto her feet. "Funny, but you don't seem like the sharing type."

He paced away from her with a snarl.

"Lincoln! What did you do with Tim?"

He turned and smirked at her, "Your boy toy? He's sharing your cell. Just look behind you."

She craned her neck and caught a glimpse of a bare masculine foot in one corner. "What did you do to him?"

"Just knocked him out with shadows while he wasn't looking. After the way you screamed, it was easy to distract him."

She closed her eyes and let a tear fall slowly down one cheek. The mocking laughter of her captor was just the final insult to her senses and she let her consciousness creep back into the darkness.

His footsteps fell away and the warm scent of cinnamon overtook her. Her eyes flew open, and there was Tim standing before her as naked as the day he was born.

"How?" She was at a loss for words. He seemed completely unharmed.

He was scowling at her. "Damn it! I thought I would have more time."

"More time? For what?" Couldn't he get sex off his mind? She looked down at his partial erection. At least for a while? Good lord. Now she was ogling his body. While tied like a sacrificial lamb. She had to be going nuts.

"To explain your talents and family history."

"What do you know about my family? I was adopted after being abandoned."

"Do you believe in the powers that you have displayed? That if they exist they can be controlled?"

She thought about it for a long moment, "Yeah, I guess I do. I have always felt something different about myself compared to others. Okay, my talents are actual provable power. They have to be, or they wouldn't be planning to suck them out of me.

"Fine. I have power. Now what can I do with it?"

Tim leaned forward to give her a quick kiss. "Good girl. Now for the complicated part."

He took a deep breath and started, "You are from a magical family known as the Warders. They have one main talent and that is to create protective barriers for themselves and others. With most, this is instinctual after seeing family members do it. You have been doing bits and pieces without knowing it."

She took a deep breath, "So, how do I put it all together?"

"You trust me. To stop them from doing this to someone else and to yourself, you need to use those powers properly."

She shuddered as she thought about those shadows closing over the faces of friends and innocent women who had the bad luck to be born with power. "Tell me what I need to do."

He sighed heavily and caressed her hair with his fingers. "What you are going to need is a doubled ward, what you have to do is…"

The whispers in the dark continued and it was only after she had confirmed and tried out the described technique that he took up his place as the unconscious 'boy toy.'

Lincoln and a few of his creepy friends were at the doorway to her cage a few minutes later. They loosened her cuffs and she almost blacked out as the blood rushed into her limbs. Her comfort was not one of their main concerns as they dragged her out into a gathering chamber.

Or more to the point, a sacrificial chamber. There was a raised dais with an altar in the centre of the room. She would be surrounded on all sides, and she was still stark naked. It was a full house, and she recognized quite a few faces that she could never forgive for their part in this.

Who builds this kind of thing?

Sparks shot behind her eyes as they fastened her to the altar. Her shoulders would never forgive them for this. But if Tim's plan worked, she wouldn't have to.

Lincoln took the position near her head and placed his hands on her forehead and face. "We gather here to drain this woman of power from those energies which are not rightly hers."

The crowd roared their assent.

"It is up to us to drag her light into the shadow. To absorb it and use it to further the development of our families and town."

The roar of hostility rang around her and she could feel the gathering darkness around her.

Okay, time to implement phase one. She focused on her body and soul. Loose tendrils of energy that would unwrap at the slightest touch became her shield. Her soul she wrapped in a core of flaming plasma.

Of course, they had no idea that she was doing anything. All that they could see was her aura of energy flickering as it would when distressed. She had plenty of reason to react that way.

"Now, my brothers! We feed!" Lincoln began to draw the loose tendrils of energy from her and she drew a few taut just to make him work for it.

Other tugs at her energy began to creep into her consciousness, each man taking from her body the magic that would enhance his own power.

The core that surrounded her soul was rock solid. No cracks or crevasses. She was ready for phase two.

Now if Tim would just show up, she could stop the power tendrils that were trying to get to her soul.

As if summoned by her thoughts, *Audrina! Now do it now!*

Taking a deep and shaking breath, she did what her family had done for centuries, she created wards. One ward for every soul-sucking bastard that was out there. Each and every tendril that they had taken into their own psyches was turned into a razor of energy that released all the stolen energy that had been robbed before.

Masculine screams rent the air as the stolen power flowed freely, and away from its captors. The soul of each woman who had been drained, as they were attempting to do to Audrina, was now released and furious.

The glowing and powered ghosts were attacking those who had dared to claim their talents, and they were angry.

Lincoln's hands had fallen away from her as the power sliced through him for the first time, but now his attention was back. "You, you have done this."

"No, a Warder has done this. And if it wasn't for you, I wouldn't have known that I was one jackass."

"Not for long." With that melodramatic statement, he had wrapped his hands around her throat and was squeezing the life out of her.

If only Tim's lessons had covered this. With her hands shackled she couldn't fight, but with her fading consciousness, she tried to make a ward around Lincoln. A ward that would block his air.

He glowed in the embrace of her power and the light in her eyes faded as her own lack of oxygen took over.

She must have been delirious with lack of air, because nothing else would explain the huge golden gryphon breaking through a doorway and using its vicious claws to make its way through the screaming crowd still dodging ghosts.

Another swipe of the claws took Lincoln off the altar and the sharp snap of the beak severed the head from shoulders. Hot blood sprayed across her and for another moment in her life, she was happy that she didn't have any fear of blood.

Relax, Rina, I am going to set you loose and take you somewhere safe. Four sharp snaps and she was being held in claws against a leonine chest as the enormous wings beat heavily at the air.

We have to travel a bit to get to the portal, so just relax. I won't drop you.

Portal? To where? Thinking the question to him came naturally, and it did help as she was fighting for oxygen to compensate for the speed of the flight.

We are going to Realm. You need healing and an infusion of power. You used far too much in fending off the shadows.

Is that what you call them?

They are soul-suckers in human form. They tend to congregate in groups like this.

Great. How long have you known about them?

Only since I was sent to watch you.

Sent? This was astonishing, and rather embarrassing. *By whom?*

By a group of people who want nothing more than your safety and who are dying to meet you.

Chapter Eight

SHE WAS DANGLING FROM THE CLAWS OF A MYTHOLOGICAL BEAST, FLYING THROUGH THE night sky with not a stitch on, trusting him to take her to people that she had never even conceived of. And if the voice in her mind was any indication, the beast that held her was also the man who had screwed her brains out earlier in the evening.

When had her life gotten so weird?

A swirl of melting silver energy opened up into a gateway in front of them. She would have squealed in panic if she hadn't been wracked with pain and exhaustion. Her first trip to Realm was managed while she was unconscious. Her body had finally had enough.

The air was wild and heavy with energy, and Audrina was comfortable. The sheets that she was snuggled between were softer than anything that she had ever felt.

"Audrina. You can open your eyes now." The voice was gentle and feminine. A soft damp cloth trailed across her forehead and down her cheeks.

Dang. No pretending that she was asleep then to avoid whatever was coming next.

Her bleary eyes opened and she was greeted by a view of several women all grouped around her bed. Only one male was in the room, and he looked distinctly uncomfortable. At least she thought that she read the expression correctly, it was hard to do on blue skin with silver tattoos.

Only one woman stood alone. Rina blinked hard. No, her eyes hadn't deceived her, those were indeed pointy ears.

"Welcome to Realm, Audrina. We are members of the Warder's clan. Your family." The elf moved toward her. "My name is Eylonwy, and you are my great grand-niece. Well actually there are fifteen greats in there, but that would take too long."

She took a seat on the side of Audrina's bed. "What do you know of your family?"

"You mean before I was adopted? I was abandoned as a baby. There were no records of my mother, she just left me in the hospital."

"So, you have no way of tracing your family history? What of your adoptive family?"

She closed her eyes. A small tear trickled down her cheek. "I never did fit. They did try, but it wasn't up to me or them."

"If you are up to trying, we have a family here for you to try on for size."

"What?" She struggled up onto her elbows, tucking the sheet under her arms when she realized that it was all that she was wearing.

Eylonwy took her hand. "I have a story to tell you, and it will let you know how you got here. Will you listen?"

She thought about it for a moment. There were enough freaks in this room to fill a circus. And she was one of them. What could it hurt to listen?

"Tell me the story, and I will tell you what I think."

Audrina was told the story of the great Warder attack, the seven surviving women, the great Curse that was to keep them from building a clan again.

She was told of the inability of the Warder's to reproduce with humans every generation, and that they needed to take a mate of the magical races every other generation at least. Audrina had been the product of one such mating.

Eylonwy explained about her sister, Amarante, the loveless marriage to a human that resulted in her death. She told the tale of the twin nieces that she had had. The one brought to be raised in Realm, and the other stolen by her brother-in-law's family.

The lost girl had had no choice but to take a member of a supernatural race as her lover, it was a compulsion, and so the separation of bloodlines had begun. One girl per generation, one child each. A slender thread in history that lead straight to Audrina. A pale and exotic creature stepped forward. "I am Serafina, and the next chapter in your life was written on my mind."

"What?" This was a little much. Magical races, lost families and elves with twins were running through her mind. It was a great story.

Serafina took the other side of her bed and sat daintily. "On hallowe'en, I was watching the Repository of Magical Artefacts and I was possessed by the ghost of your ancestor, well our ancestor. I am descended from the other twin baby.

"Amarante took over my mind and told Eylonwy about her death, and the children. None of the Warders even knew that there had been a second child. The humans had left the elven child to die.

"She wanted us to look for you because you were in immediate danger. I was given the assignment to find you. Blood called to blood."

"What?"

"Well, we are related, and I have an affinity for blood." She smiled and her fangs exposed. "I am the product of a Warder and vampire mating. My own father knocked up my mother and buggered off. Similar to your situation, but the Warders are a helluva family to be related to.

"Anyway, I managed to narrow it down to a thirty five kilometre radius. After that, it was a complete dead zone. There was no way for me to locate you from a distance, and my husband would not let me go in person.

"He contacted Timmon and sent him to watch you."

"Timmon?" Oh, she had a bad feeling about this.

"Timmon Lahey, the gryphon who brought you to us. He is a tracker in Realm and works for an architectural company in the human world."

"Tim was sent to me? He didn't come willingly?" Tears were threatening again. She was really overwhelmed right now.

"He was asked only to locate you. He volunteered to protect you and stay by you." Serafina spoke quickly to stop any emotional cascade.

"But, he only showed up yesterday? How could he have been watching me?"

"He is a shapeshifter, you might have noticed. His gryphon form is only one of them." She smiled and patted Audrina's hand. "Did you want to get dressed and have a tour? There are really some fantastic places to visit, and at least three that serve a terrific lunch."

"That sounds good." She looked around more carefully. She was in a tent. A powder blue and gauzy tent. It was huge, but the Warders were the only ones in it. "Is Tim here?"

"He and some of the others went off to clean up the rest of the shadows. Apparently the entire population of that little cesspool were soul suckers. They grabbed any passing woman with power and drained her dry."

"How many before me?" The knowledge that she was just the latest in a long line was scary. If she hadn't had a tenuous link to this group of people, no one would have come for her.

"At least two per year for the last fifty years. They had quite the racket. They drew them in with promises of employment, and kept them there with cheap housing until it was time for one of their boys to run the ceremony."

"So, they took turns then? It wasn't always Lincoln."

"No. They each got one turn as primary. Quite creepy really."

Audrina shuddered. "I would like to get up now. I feel fine. You mentioned lunch?"

One of the ladies with snow-white hair turned to the blue skinned man and whispered in his ear. A glowing tunic and trouser set appeared in front of her. The underwear appeared fitted directly to her skin and the blue man left the room.

"Arov hates making clothing for women that belong to someone else. It offends his djinn sensibilities."

She slipped on the tunic and pants then stood. Her feet knocked against a pair of sandals that were jewelled to match her outfit, "Well, I admire his attention to detail."

The women all giggled.

"Can we have introductions?"

"After we all are seated with something to eat. We are not a delicate breed." Serafina's fangs exposed again and she giggled like a teenager.

Audrina supposed that there were worse families out there.

Chapter Nine

The tent that they had had her in was pitched near a marketplace. Folk of every variety were wandering through it. And she did see every variety.

Elves, fairies, goblins, more of the blue djinn, green women who bore a startling resemblance to one of her 'cousins', a dragon landed nearby and changed into the form of a human man and Audrina couldn't help but gawk. Either she was nuts, or this was a magical place.

"Hey! Why don't we head to Denna's? She does an amazing al fresco brunch." The slightly green and pregnant cousin spoke. She looked Mediterranean, but when Audrina got closer, she was definitely green.

"You are just in favour of Denna's because she feeds you for free." The white haired woman elbowed the pregnant woman in the side.

"Yep. Let's go." She set off at a quick clip, and two of the other cousins took Rina's hand and tugged her along.

They passed modern buildings, tents, and antique-style taverns. It was outside one of these taverns that the cousins took a seat, Rina with them.

The green woman spoke again. "Alrighty. Time for introductions. You have already met Serafina. She is hand fasted to a vampire named Francesco and will be married in the spring. She is also going to be an aunty around that time, so she has an intense interest in my pregnancy."

"I am Anryn. My husband is Decklyn. He's a dragon. He has a nasty temper and a great ass." The table burst into giggles.

The very pale woman spoke, "He does actually. He has a tendency to run around naked. You should see my wedding pictures." She stood to take Audrina's hand. "I am Albina Warder Lakin Arov. My husband is Imaran, the blue djinn you saw earlier."

"Okay, Anryn and Decklyn, Albina and Imaran, Serafina and Francesco. So far so good. Uh, do you all have non-human husbands?" She felt a little queasy. This was all coming at her rather fast.

The woman who appeared shy and quiet spoke. "It is a lot to take in. My husband had to get used to it as well, his family didn't even know Realm existed."

"Oh, so he's human?"

She flushed pink, "No, he's a werewolf. But the wers left Realm centuries ago, just like the vampires. Oh, I am Ruana by the way."

"Nice to meet you, Ruana. So, your husband is a werewolf huh? Ooookkkaaayyyy."

Ruana laughed at her, "I know, you can accept the dragons, that Anryn is half dryad and therefore green, that Albina's husband is a djinn, but the little fact that both my father and my mate are werewolves is a little beyond the scope of imagination."

Now it was Albina's turn to blush. "You are right. Sorry."

"It's alright, my mate's name is Aleczander, Zan for short, and he is with the rest of the guys mopping up the shadows that tried to drain you."

"What about the rest of the people in the town?"

"They have been told that there was a chemical spill. Big disaster and everyone has to move. Only those who followed the path of the shadows will be eliminated as casualties." Anryn looked regretful, but firm. "Those who were wounded and didn't die would have engaged in a massive search to replace the power that was lost. They would have killed hundreds, if not thousands."

She buried her face in her hands and was quiet for a moment. "I know. But I haven't ever been in that sort of a situation before. I didn't even know that people or creatures like that existed."

"And now that you do?"

"I want lunch." She smiled at the collection of faces that were all watching her with warmth that she had never seen in a stranger before. She felt like part of a select group. A family.

LUNCH WAS SERVED by a grousing goblin, the Denna of earlier mention. Anryn was delighted as her plate was constantly filled with pancakes, fruit and bacon by a watchful proprietor.

"Why is she watching you like that?" Rina just had to ask.

"Well, Serafina here is about to become the aunt of Denna's first granddaughter and grandson actually." Anryn kept her head down to her plate, and yet managed to enunciate around the forkfuls of food. "The better she treats the Warders, the better chance of her new grandchildren becoming fully trained and welcomed into the family. It is a goblin tradition."

"What is precisely?"

"Well, we have taken a useless male off her hands, although Hiruki is not useless by any means, and she is satisfying family obligation by catering to the matriarchal line. Only a mother is left at the moment of birth after all. It is up to her and her family to protect the child." Serafina finished dissection of a sausage and licked her fingers with precise motions.

"Huh, I never thought of it that way."

"And my dear, if we had known of the existence of your line, you would not have had one moment alone without family." Eylonwy touched her hand and that was all that it took.

With her body recovered, her belly full, and her mind bursting, this last stone in the overflowing dam of emotional strain threw her over the edge. Audrina began to cry. Huge wracking sobs that shook her to her very soul.

A family. A real family that accepted her freak factor for what it was. Tears flowed fast and furiously down her cheeks. She felt arms hold her close and she clung to the comfort they offered with desperation.

Instead of trying to hide her emotional outburst, they let her cry herself out. When she cried herself out, she was slumped against Eylonwy and the others were gathered around her all with a hand on her hand or arm. The strength that she was gaining from the contact was not a figment of her imagination. She was actually drawing strength from them. Literally.

Albina's patience, Anryn's good humour, Ruana's gentleness, Serafina's compassion and Eylonwy's boundless love for those of her line. She looked at them, exhausted, "How am I doing that?"

"Blood calls to blood, Audrina. You call us, and we are there."

A watery smile broke over her, "Call me Rina."

"Rina then. So when are you and Timmon planning to wed?"

"What?!" Her startled jump caused a chain reaction of falling cutlery and water glasses.

Serafina smiled at her, "Well, gryphons choose their mates carefully. They only have one per lifetime, and it is a really long lifetime."

"Gryphons?"

"Yeah, you remember Timmon?"

"Tim, right. Of course." She blinked, "Mates?"

"Well given the way that he wouldn't let you go until we had a healer present and he had personally overseen the power transfer. The way he held your hand until he was sure you had been recharged, and the bite marks on your neck, I figured that he had chosen you. And based on the claw marks on his back, you put up a heckuva struggle." Serafina was smiling and leaning back as Anryn got her fourths served to her. She was too full of food for her normal witty commentary, so the rest of the girls had to fill in.

"But, I only met him the day before I was taken. He just moved in." It was another emotional blow and she could only sit in astonishment as she replayed everything that they had mentioned about gryphons.

Serafina smiled. It wasn't a cruel smile, just an 'I know something you don't know' kind of smile. "Of course. You must be correct."

Ruana looked up from watching Anryn stuff her face with the look of a predator picking up on a wounded animal. Her focus was behind them. "Oh, look. The boys are back."

The entire table turned to look, and Audrina's face flamed bright. There were four men coming towards them, and three of them were naked.

She recognized Tim right off. Heated memories of the one time that they spent together made a tiny smile play at the corners of her mouth.

The other two naked men were quite obviously Ruana and Anryn's mates. The clothed one swept Serafina into his arms.

The nude males claimed their women with passionate embraces, and she squawked in surprise when she was plucked out of her seat to greet the ardent kiss of a nude gryphon.

"Hello, Audrina. I am so happy to see you up and about." The erection that was prodding her through the thin fabric of her new tunic indicated his sincerity.

Albina stood to one side and closed her eyes. Her husband appeared near her and sighed deeply at the public display. With a clap of his hands, the tablecloths disappeared and drawstring trousers replace them.

One pair for each of the naked shifters.

Laughing and joking about human and djinn sensibilities, the men got dressed. Then introductions were issued. Having been in conversation with their wives, the matches were easy to make.

With both of his arms now wrapped around her, he turned to the assemblage, "So, have you filled her in?"

"She has heard all pertinent details. A more in depth discussion of Warder history is in her future though." Eylonwy became the spokesperson as the others stood in the embrace of their spouses.

"Can she rest at my place then? And you can send someone up tomorrow?"

"I suppose that it can be arranged. Don't tire her out. She is still getting used to the idea of magic and it has been one helluva introduction."

"Yes, ma'am."

He turned to Rina with his golden eyes blazing with happiness, "C'mon. I want to show you my place." Timmon smiled slyly at her and dragged her away from her newly found family.

Audrina was a little shocked, and terrified. They had embraced her wholeheartedly on the basis that the ghost of an elf told them to look for her. Unbelievable.

They had sent a guardian to her to protect her from the shadows and bring her into the warmth of their family. It was simply bizarre.

Yet, here she was. Now a gryphon that she had slept with was offering to 'show her his place.'

She shrugged in acceptance, "Sure, what have I got to lose?"

He grinned and waggled his eyebrows as he shifted into the graceful and golden beast that had rescued her from the soul-sucking shadows. He was huge. Ten feet high at least with an eagle's head, a lion's body and eagle's wings sprouting from his back. Fantastic.

His paws clawed the air for a moment before settling onto the ground. He seemed giddy to be showing off for her and the words *'Get on'* rang in her head.

She shifted around, then stepped forward and let him boost her into place in front of his wings. The warmth of his hide was still astonishing, and caused a cascade of memories of his human form pressed against, and within hers.

A flutter deep in her belly caused a blush and she heard a small chuckle in her head as he leapt off the ground and into the air.

Chapter Ten

That is the wood where the elves have their villages, those are the entrances to the dwarf caverns, over there are the spires where the dragon council meets, and the meadows below are often used for Warder functions. Parties, weddings, that sort of thing. Your cousin Ruana will be getting formally married soon, as will Serafina and Franc.

The tour of Realm was being conducted from a few thousand feet in the air, and Rina only opened her eyes to peek every few seconds. *"I know that Tim, they told me all about it."*

Anryn is very pregnant you know. She could blow at any moment. It's why Decklyn insisted that Imaran stayed back. If anything happened in Realm, he could transport to us and back in seconds. He missed a good fight though.

So, you got all the shadows?

Yep, had to sniff out a few that were trying to hide, but we got 'em all.

In a desperate attempt to change the subject, *Do you prefer Tim or Timmon?*

Tim is fine. Her mind warmed with the smile that he injected into his thought. *I have been called worse in my lifetime.*

As for the lifetime thing, how old are you anyway?

I think you have had enough shocks for one day. A dark chuckle broke into her thoughts. He banked left and she squealed and held tightly to the feathers that crowned his head and neck.

I think I just lost one of my shoes, Tim.

His beak let out a squawk of laughter. *Sorry about that. There are clothes for you back at my place.*

Where exactly is your place, Tim? We seem to be climbing awfully high.

Do you see that faint sparkle at the top of that mountain?

Her eyes opened and she looked quickly, ignoring the chuckle from the beast between her thighs. *Yep.*

That is my aerie. My family home.

It's really high.

Yep. Don't worry, I won't let you fall.

The rest of the trip was accomplished in silence. As his heavy wing beats pulled them closer, she opened her eyes for longer moments. It was a crystal palace, glittering and sparkling in the mist at the top of the mountain.

Mindful of his human cargo, he slowly circled into landing in a central courtyard. Central, because the structure surrounded this circular and grassed in yard. Sculptures of mythological beings ringed the yard, the middle was obviously a landing pad of sorts.

"Wow." Now that the air was no longer rushing past her, she could speak normally, well croak actually. It had seemed natural to use telepathy while he was flying, but she didn't know how she had done it.

His shoulders shifted under her thighs as he walked toward an open doorway flanked by a gryphon and a cyclops.

"Um, should I get off of you now?" It felt weird to be riding someone that she knew.

You are lighter while I am in this form then when I took you home.

Oops. Right, he had given her a piggyback ride home because she was too stiff to walk. She was glad that he couldn't see her face.

As that thought finished he stopped and his eagle head swivelled back to look at her with one golden avian eye.

Right, birds could do that. She had forgotten that a bird needed to be able to groom themselves with their heads. Apparently the same held for him.

"Uh, did you want something?" She tried to be aloof, but it was hard to meet that piercing eye while less than two feet away.

Yeah. I do. But not in this form. You might want to dismount now. There was a certain heat to his thoughts, and she swung her leg over his back and slithered down his side on her belly.

His hide was warm under her hands and she quickly stepped back as he shook himself and began to shrink. The wings retreated into his back, the feathered head turned into his familiar features and his clawed paws became his hands and feet as his tail disappeared completely.

"Wow. Cool." She stood back and her surroundings didn't even enter into her consciousness. Not when she had Tim coming toward her with concern in his eyes.

The gentle hug was unexpected given the heat of his earlier thoughts. He held her tightly, but gently. "Are you sure that you are alright? You have been through a lot these last few days."

She returned the hug, with interest, "I'm fine. Yeah, it has been stressful, but also kinda freeing in a way. At least I am not alone anymore."

"No, you are not alone anymore." His fingers tilted her chin up and he took her mouth with his own.

She let her body conform to the planes of his and her hands rose to tangle in his hair.

She kept his mouth glued to hers as long as she could. "Wow. Was your tongue always like that?"

A hint of bronze coloured the tight skin across his cheeks. "Hmm. It is my natural form. I have a few feline characteristics that I relax at home."

"It feels nice." Better than nice. The delicate scraping against her mouth had a suspicious dampness forming between her thighs. "I like it."

The grin that bloomed on his face warmed her to the depths of her soul. Her acceptance of his physical quirks was the final straw to his constraint.

He let out a roar of joy and lifted her high into the air over his head and twirled her around and around until she was dizzy.

Before she had recovered, he had stopped, stripped her out of her clothing and shed his in a few economical movements. The next moment she was sailing through the air heading for she-knew-not-what, and ended up skidding across black sheets. Apparently it was his colour of choice.

Her breath was knocked out of her when she landed, and again when he jumped and landed with his hands and knees to either side of her. "Do you know how long I have been looking for a woman like you?" His lips nuzzled at her neck and a deep purring noise began in his chest.

Her fingers tangled in his mane once again and she exposed as much of her neck as she could to his lips and tongue. "I am guessing, quite a while?"

"Mmm. Lifetimes." The purring was very strong now. It reminded her of Timmy when they would watch movies.

Wait, Tim, Timmon, Timmy? "Tim, were you my cat?" She had to tug hard at his hair to get him to look her in the eyes. "Are you?"

With a sigh, he reached under one of the pillows and drew out the stuffed gryphon. "Yes, I was your cat. It seemed the best way to keep an eye on you in the evenings."

Her mind ran through all of her moments with the cat, the cat in her lap. Watching her shower, and his dips in the cold pond. They always coincided with…oh, God. "So, all those times that you jumped in the pond…"

"It was to keep from shifting shape and taking you right there. You were magnificent in your passions, and I wanted desperately to join you in your bed." His lips skated over her flaming cheeks and he lapped at the pool of flushed skin at the base of her throat.

"So you watched me…" She couldn't find the words, and his hands had now joined the effort to distract her.

"Yes, I watched your clever fingers circling your clit, like this." He set words into action and she shivered at the light touch. Exactly what would drive her high and fast.

"And I watched you take two more fingers and slide them into your passage, like this." She arched back as his thicker fingers teased her more than her own ever had.

With his two hands at work and his purring moving in time to his hands, her own breathless moans and sighs joined the symphony and in moments she was gasping, shivering and thrusting her hips against his hands.

His hands withdrew and he took their place between her thighs, licking up the juice from her orgasm and soothing her clit from the relentless pressure that he had put on it. His long and slow strokes with his sandpaper tongue were quickly rebuilding the flames in her body. Every inch of skin craved his touch and only that one centre was receiving it.

Her fingers fisted in his hair and tugged his head up, "Timmon, if you don't fuck me now, I am going to scream so hard that the roof will collapse."

His dark and lust-filled eyes focused on her and he smiled again. Moving far too slowly for her peace of mind, the blunt head of his cock began to press for entrance. Relaxing the muscles that only wanted to grip him tight took most of her self-control, but she managed it until he was fully imbedded in her wet heat.

Then he stopped. He didn't move one inch. She waited for him to move, to do something.

He didn't.

"Listen, mister, either you get your tight ass in gear, or I am gonna wiggle out of here and find my way down the mountain."

"You said you wanted me inside you." He was smug, but sweat dripped from his brow, the sign of his effort to hold himself still in her tight embrace.

"No, I said I wanted you to fuck me. This is just parking." Her internal muscles fluttered around him, once, twice, and then she settled into a rhythm that had his eyes closing and a lot more sweat pouring off his head and body.

The spasms of sensation that her body were generating were becoming more powerful with every contraction. Her hips were arching against him, grinding and twisting in an effort to gain the pleasure that they craved. Finally, she just hooked both thighs around him and locked her ankles behind his back. Using his body for leverage to drive him into her was the last straw.

He subdued her efforts simply by dropping his entire weight onto her. She was flattened and her grip on his hips loosened. "Why did you stop me? I was having fun."

He didn't answer, but leaned off her, snarled in her face and shoved his hips forward to show her that he was now in the game. He drew back almost to the point of her body releasing his cock, then thrust forward with a groan and another snarl.

His neck was arched back as he pounded into her, his face in a rictus of pain. His mouth opened and she saw his 'at home' teeth, delicately pointed fangs, much like his feline form.

Gathering an idea, she leaned forward and closed her own teeth across his neck. She bit down lightly and growled in her chest.

The response was immediate. He began to pound in and out of her with wild ferocity, snarling and growling at her as soon as she released his neck.

He moved in and out with deliberation and one of his hands reached across to press on her clit, she squealed in her release, and that was his final barrier.

His head dropped to her shoulder and his hips hammered into her with only one purpose, to seek his own release. Her head was tilted to the side and she welcomed the feel of his teeth on her neck when they came. And when he bit down, it was with the same triumphant growl that he had given at her acceptance.

He roared his release into the night, then slowly collapsed on top of her. He moved his limbs carefully so as not to crush her, but she was still a little stifled when he finally came to rest on her.

"So, Timmon. Are you sure you aren't gay?" The whisper in the dark was her last bit of defence against the feelings that she was having for this beautiful golden man.

With one hand on her ass, he rolled so that she was now on top. "Yeah, I am, and when I find the man of my dreams, your fantastic ass is history lady. I may only bother to fuck you twice a day."

Yep. It had to be love. Nothing else would make her feel this serene and giddy and insane all at the same time.

Chapter Eleven

BLACK SHEETS, WARM SKIN, A STUFFED GRYPHON, AND A LARGE CAT LICKING HER forehead.

"Go away, Timmy! I wanna sleep." She rolled away and wrinkled her nose as he followed her, his small and raspy tongue insistently working at her face until she sat up. "Fine. I am up. Are you happy?"

He slowly shifted from feline to human and stretched as he finished his transformation. "Yes. I am happy, how are you this morning?"

She stretched under the sheets and took stock of her body. "A little stiff, a little sticky, and still giddy." Her hand came up and drew him to her by the expedience of grabbing his neck and tugging. Their lips met and clung, smiles making a more serious effort at necking awkward.

"You need to get up. One of your cousins is coming to teach you the basics of warding this morning." He stood, stretched again, and yanked the sheet off of her with no ceremony. "The bathroom is this way."

The bathroom was built along the same Grecian lines as the rest of the house. Pools and waterfalls replaced the whole tub and shower assembly. "I thought cats didn't like water."

"Some do, some don't. Now get into the shower before I can't control myself." His erection led her mind straight into the gutter and she turned back to him with parted lips.

"Don't even think it. The Warder's are open minded, but catching us together screwing is gonna lead to all kinds of fun at family gatherings."

Wow. With all of his charms staring her in the face, she had forgotten about the company that was arriving shortly.

"Fine. But you owe me one." She stepped under a waterfall and was pleasantly surprised to find it warm. She reached for the soap and was unsurprised that he was there to hand it to her. He leaned calmly back against a nearby pillar and watched her soap and lather herself.

His eyes grew especially intent as her hands drew the soap across her breasts, building a lather of bubbles across her nipples. She then coasted the soap down her belly and between her thighs searching out every swollen fold of skin and making sure that it was squeaky clean.

With a smirk over his fixation, she turned her back to him and soaped her back and buttocks.

"Heads up!" She flipped the bar at him and was unsurprised when he caught it handily, though his eyes hadn't left their focus on her ass. Mechanically, not wanting to tease either herself or him anymore, she finished rubbing herself down and rinsed out her hair. The soap left her smelling vaguely of lavender and reminded her of the soap she had at home.

"Tim, do you have a towel?" She was as clean as she was gonna get with an audience watching. She walked toward him, water pooling around her feet with each step. A fluffy towel landed around her shoulders and she turned rapidly to look behind her. Too rapidly. If Tim hadn't been so close she would have hit the marble floor with a thud.

"Good morning, Rina!" Anryn was particularly cheerful as she followed after the couple. Tim was taking her back to the bedroom and finding some clothing for her. "Don't get dressed on my account. I wear clothing as minimally as possible."

She looked out the window at the dragon in the landing area. "Decklyn can't stand it. But, hey, I was raised by a dryad, so what are you going to do? Besides, he runs around naked all the time and I don't complain about it."

"The clothing isn't for your benefit, Anryn. I am just not a fan of Audrina being ogled by your husband." At last he located a fresh tunic and trousers for her. No underwear though.

Tugging her to her feet, he towelled Rina dry and dressed her like a life-sized doll.

"Good morning, Anryn. I'd hug you, but I was wondering if Timmon would like to do that for me as well?"

As he fussed with the line of her tunic he froze and blushed. "Aw, geez. Sorry, Rina. I panicked."

He stood and hugged her to him tightly. "For the first time ever, all I could think of was getting clothes on you."

"Fine. But can I get some breakfast? I haven't eaten anything since lunch yesterday."

"Breakfast will be in the courtyard in ten minutes. Enjoy your lessons."

Anryn was glowing this morning. She also looked like she was going to give birth to a small village. Rina went to her and hesitated.

Anryn closed the distance and hugged her, "Morning cousin. I confess, I thought that I would catch you and Timmon in bed, not the shower."

"He thought you might. Apparently he is very familiar with the Warder family."

"Yeah, he gets invited to all the parties and is pretty aware of our quirky brand of humour."

Across the yard Decklyn was resuming his human form and he appeared to have pants on this time. "Can he transform with or without clothing?"

"Yep. He wore pants so that Timmon wouldn't launch him off the aerie."

The women giggled and made their way to an alcove in the courtyard with a table and a set of chairs.

"So, are you ready to begin basic training?"

"What?"

"To learn to use the talents that you have."

"Oh, the warding thing?"

"That's the one. It is quite useful actually. For example. This entire aerie is warded. Each support post on the outer edge contains a ward. There has not been one successful break in here in over five hundred years."

"So you can use them for more than self defence? Cool."

"Yeah, they can be useful. For example if Timmon ticks you off, you can ward portions of your anatomy from access." She giggled girlishly and Rina knew that this would be one of her best friends in the Warder world.

"Okay, explain the process from the beginning."

"Hmm…setting a ward…" She steepled her fingers together and spoke of anchoring, focusing, draining, expulsion, harnessing, and channelling. By the time she was done, Tim had brought out breakfast, and Rina was stunned.

"So, you mean that there are actually hundreds of uses for this particular talent? Holy crud." Toast and eggs were mechanically piled on her plate as her mind grappled with the enormity of possibilities presented to her. She ate while deep in thought.

It seemed that she had fought her entire life for control and power over her environment, and she had had the power to do it all along.

Distantly she heard Anryn announcing that it was enough for now and that she would be back later, felt a hug and then was alone with Timmon again. The dragon's bulk retreated into the sky.

"I know that it is a lot to take in, Rina. You will get the hang of it in time." Tim's hand covered hers in a comforting grip.

He cleared his throat, "I also have to tell you something else, Rina."

She looked at him, unsure of his tone. "What else could there be?"

He gripped her hand tightly. "You're dead."

Chapter Twelve

That got her attention. "Uh, Tim. That isn't funny."

"Oh shit. I didn't mean it to sound like that." He ran one hand through his hair in frustration. "I mean that the day that the shadows planned to drain you, they burned your house and created an obituary in the local and cross-country papers. According to official records, you died in a house fire that day."

Her house, her stuff, and dear God, her clothing! "Wait, so that means that I have absolutely nothing left of my life?"

"I am afraid not. We couldn't get back in time to save anything." He looked devastated. His handsome features collapsed in dismay.

Suddenly she found herself in the odd position of comforting him. "Hey, you saved my gryphon, or rather Timmy's gryphon, and that was really the only thing that I was worried about.

"Speaking of your sojourn as my cat, when did you decide that you had to meet me in person? Or as a person I suppose I should say."

His smile bloomed across his face in an instant. "The day that you took me in and shared dinner with me instead of cracking open a can of tuna. Any woman who would treat a stray like family had to be worth knowing, and the longer I spent with you, the more I wanted to take advantage of your sense of humour and your hormonal surges."

"Ah that." She was embarrassed, but wasn't sure how much was showing on her face. "Well, my sex drive was never that intense."

He looked at her sceptically.

"No, really. It began to pick up when I picked up a stray." She shrugged. "I guess it was just having a warm body around." Rina looked at him dismissively. He didn't like that. Her face fought a smirk and she held her aura of unconcern.

Snarling at her, he grabbed her by the arms and hauled her to her feet. "It wasn't just any body. It was mine. As you are mine!" This was the first real flash of temper she had seen from him, and its result was that he was pulling her to the bedroom by a grip on one wrist.

Gryphon's are possessive by their very nature, and only select one mate in a very long lifetime. The information rang in her head and she stood still as he stripped her of the clothing that he had tucked her into earlier, his own followed.

Not a word was spoken. He sat her on the edge of the bed, his eyes molten. He knelt before her in silence and their eyes met and held. His hands took hers and stilled.

As I am yours, so you are mine. Mated and bound. The words sprang into her mind.

As you are mine, so I am yours. Mated and bound. He leaned forward to kiss her, and she met him halfway.

Energy swirled around them as he bore her back onto the bed. Their minds twisted together as they used their previous knowledge of the other's body to drive them higher.

Rina shoved him onto his back and rubbed her breasts against the flat planes of his chest. Her hands stroked his warm golden skin over and over as she luxuriated in the feel of his body under her. A soft noise crept out of her throat and she noted with amusement that she was purring in enjoyment at the feel of him. He was purring as well and it drove her on.

The hard and throbbing length of him was nudging between her folds and her hips shifted until his heat was teasing at her slick opening. She paused, savouring the sensations, then squirmed to rub against him.

His hands caressed her ribs, then stroked each breast pinching and flicking lightly at the tip. As her hips rocked back against him, coating his erection with her own slick juices, his hips began to rise and fall to her rhythm.

When she recognized the imminent tightening of her body in orgasm, she lifted herself and impaled her channel on his willing and ready member.

The slow thrust of his cock into her wet and willing cunt was enough. She screamed in release and kept gasping for air as he began to pump into her in earnest. His hands on her hips slammed her down to meet him and kept the waves of her orgasm flowing through her. Sparks of light sparked behind her eyes and she felt faint as he controlled her body.

In the blink of an eye he had withdrawn and flipped her to her stomach. She grunted and pushed back against him as he slid back into her with a groan of his own.

She moaned as his new angle stroked her g-spot. Her body began to shiver and he lay flat across her, using his knees for leverage and holding her hands with his own, anchoring her to the bed completely.

Every nerve was humming as the head of his cock stroked back and forth within her. Her body was held immobile and her focus was on the heat, friction and pleasure that she was experiencing. His body was pummelling more rapidly at hers and she knew he was close to culmination. She shrieked into the pillows as her own nerves lit on fire and flew apart with her second orgasm.

She felt teeth in her shoulder and shrieked again as a second wave of fire ran through her body and shattered her into pieces. His own roar of satisfaction was not long in coming. He arched his back and thrust into her as his cock spewed its payload into her belly. His body shook with the violence of his release and he slowly slumped onto her as he relaxed.

Long minutes ticked by as sweat dried on their bodies. He slid an arm under her and rolled to his side with her attached to him, spooning around her. He still had not slipped from her, and she revelled in the joining, even though it wouldn't last.

A small thought crept into her mind. She giggled. It wouldn't leave, so she giggled again.

"Rina, what is so funny?" The husky voice in her ear sent shivers through her.

"Well, you are obviously not gay."

"Right." He seemed resigned to whatever she would say next.

"And I am technically dead in the normal world?"

"Yep." He could tell where she was heading.

"That makes you a necrophiliac."

The slap on her ass was answer enough, and she settle further into his warm embrace. Her life was actually good.

Now, how to get down the mountain on her own was her next challenge. Anryn could probably help her with that.

About the Author

Viola Grace was born in Manitoba, Canada where she still resides today. She really likes it there. Her hobbies have included cross-stitch, needlepoint, quilting, costuming, cake decorating, baking, cooking, metalwork, beading, sculpting, painting, doll making, henna tattoos, chain maille, and a few others that have been forgotten.

Her writing actively pursues the Happily Ever After that so rarely occurs in nature. A brilliant mind, with a twisted sense of humour.

You can contact Viola at: viola@violagrace.com

Viola's website is located at:

http://www.violagrace.com

Other books by Viola Grace

Available in print:

Champions of Terra
The Halfblood Club

Look for them at www.amazon.com

Available as e-books:

Blood Proxy
An Honoured Wife
Burning Ceres
Dragonlord
Getting Lucky
Gift of Wyora
Wardstone

http://www.extasybooks.com

Preview

Getting Lucky

Book 1 of the

Sisters of Silverwood

By

Viola Grace

Prologue

The glow was back. For the last two weeks the girls of Camp Silverwood had gathered near the lake to watch a flickering glow dance over the water, the almost inaudible murmuring didn't jar them from their reverie. They stood silent and still for hours, simply watching the light show of unknown origin until it dissipated near dawn. Sleepy and disoriented they stumbled back to their cabins to rest.

When they left the Camp at the end of the summer, they would never be the same.

Ten years later…

"So, the secret is out? Someone knows about them?" Artemis Whynot let out a frustrated sigh. All those years of preparation, for nothing.

"Yes. It had to be an inside job. No one else knows about Silverwood, let alone has the list of the girls who were trained." Daniel Rollock ran a hand over his shaved scalp. He had the bearing and haircut of a military man, but there were no ranks at the Society. Well, at least none that mattered. His ears were not pointed as modern folk tales said they should have been, but as one of the Wild Hunt, he had adapted well to the twenty first century.

Artemis had founded the Society to explain the lights of a decade ago. In theory, it was a paranormal research facility, but in reality it was a training ground for the other members of the Hunt. If their opponents were indeed the Lios Alfar, they needed to get the women paired with their guardians before they could spirit them away. The last thing this world needed was for the newly sparked magic to disappear. Fortunately, for them, Artemis was watching. "Are they ready?"

Rolluck blushed to the top of his eyebrows, "Uh, yes. And very eager. It isn't every day that a man can be matched with his perfect woman. How do you do it anyway?"

She tented her fingers in front of her and smiled "We all have our talents, Daniel. Now send them out."

"You trust them to bring the women in? Once they have them, they might not decide to follow the plan."

"I trust that they will try." Her smile grew. "The women are their own masters. We will see what happens and tailor our plan to match."

"Fine. They will go today. I hope you know what you are doing." His last sentence was said in a mutter as he left to head to the men's barracks.

Artemis's smile slowly faded as she hoped that she was right. Her matchmaking was a raw skill, one that had been given to her at the council when it was decided that her Hunt would be the guardians of the new magic. She almost wished that she could compel love, but that was beyond her skills. The matches that she had made for the women were solid. Good elves who had the strength of character to keep the women safe and to bring them home. Back to Silverwood.

ted States
/55-57/P

9 781554 870233